ALSO BY ALEX MORA
Silence In The Basement

FRAGMENTED

ALEX MURA

HANABI PRESS

Hanabi Press
London

www.alexmura.com

This eBook edition 2025
10 9 8 7 6 5 4 3 2 1

Copyright © 2025 Alex Mura

Alex Mura asserts the moral right to
be identified as the author of this work.

ISBN: 978-1-0686575-4-2 (print)
ISBN: 978-1-0686575-2-8 (ebook)

This novel is entirely a work of fiction.
The names, characters, and incidents portrayed in it are
the work of the author's imagination. Any resemblance to
actual persons, living or dead, events or localities is
entirely coincidental.

All rights reserved. No part of this publication may be
reproduced, stored in a retrieval system, or transmitted,
in any form or by any means, electronic, mechanical,
photocopying, recording or otherwise, without the prior
permission of the publishers.

"You are your own devil, you create your own hell."
   – Fyodor Dostoevsky

1

I love my job. Scratch that—I *like* my job. It's all right. Working at one of the fanciest private schools in London should be something to be proud of. At least, that's what people tell me. But pride and passion aren't the same thing. I love history. That's why I teach it. Well, that's the excuse I give myself. Truth is, I'd rather lecture to minds that care, not a room of fourteen-year-olds glued to TikTok...

Don't get me started on the rest. The curriculum? Dusty. Unchanged for years. The salary? Laughable really. The only difference between this term and the last is that I've finally mastered the art of shaving minutes off the tedious parts. The moment the last student slams the door behind them, I crack the window open and let the summer breeze filter out the stale adolescent boredom. Then I dig in, marking half-hearted World War II essays, most of them stitched together from Wikipedia. Usually, this takes an hour. Today, forty flat.

I want out. Out of this place. Out of this stiff suit. Home. But first, a drink. A necessary one. The term's nearly over, after all.

I pack up my briefcase, loosen my tie, and slip out before any colleague can corner me with exam gossip or Lake Como vacation plans.

The school sits slap-bang in the middle of Mayfair, where there's no shortage of upscale bars. I prefer the quiet ones. The rowdier ones might as well be my classroom at happy hour.

There was a bar I used to love—tucked away, low-key, perfect. But that love affair ended when I realised it was a local haunt for parents. Running into them? Less than ideal. Torturous conversations about their kids, veiled attempts to squeeze out extra credit for little Sophie or Harry.

Time for a new watering hole.

I wander, directionless. Let my brogues click down quiet roads, turn corners, restless as a stray.

I'm just about ready to cave and check Google Maps when I hear it. A faint whisper of strings.

I stop. Glance down a narrow alleyway. The music swells with each step—Shostakovich. Classical. Refined. Precise. Beneath the melody, I catch the sound of muted laughter. The clink of glasses. A hush of conversation.

I round the corner, and there it is—a hidden outdoor bar wedged between two buildings like it doesn't want to be found. Seven tables, maybe eight. Small. Intimate. Perfect.

I step inside, sidestepping a broad-shouldered man anchored near the entrance—rolled sleeves, cigar jutting from his teeth. He doesn't move much. Doesn't need to. Looks important, maybe the owner, or perhaps just a man with money to spend and the power to make things happen.

The others at his table are younger, my age. All suited up, ties holding their necks hostage. Each one a near replica of the next. Hair slicked back, posture rigid, laughter polite.

I slump into a chair, close enough to watch, far enough to pretend I'm not. Curious if the story I've already told myself about them holds up.

A few couples and small groups dot the other tables. The vibe is lively but restrained, like everyone here obeys the unspoken rules of a place like this. No shouting. No fuss. Just music, murmurs, and glasses of £20 whisky.

And the music? Bloody spot-on. My fingers tap absently against my thigh, syncing with Shostakovich's precision.

I reach for my phone, about to text Grace—let her know I'll be home late—but before I can type out a message, a waitress materialises at my side.

"Pint of Peroni, please." Anything will do, really—any European pisswater.

She offers an apologetic smile. "Sorry, we don't do pints here. Just bottles, if you'd like?"

No pints? *What kind of pretentious hell is this?*

I mask my disappointment with a nod. "Yeah, a bottle's fine."

Around me, the clink of Aperol spritzes and glasses of Merlot. I'll stick to the Peroni, though it suddenly feels pedestrian.

Across the patio, the cigar man tilts his head back, exhaling smoke towards the sky. His expression—pure satisfaction, an endorphin rush carved into his face—nudges something in me. A craving.

I fish a pack from my jacket, tuck a cigarette between my lips, and light it.

Inhale. Recline. Tilt my head back.

The sky holds the last blush of daylight, but I let my mind darken it. In the self-made night, Shostakovich's concerto swells, dragging me out to sea—adrift between stars and waves.

Exhale.

Smoke ribbons upwards, curling into the honeyed dusk before dissolving. The strings seep into the alley, stretching time like slow-poured syrup. It's peaceful here.

Another drag. My thoughts unspool—knots loosening, edges blurred. The cigarette dwindles to a stub as my beer arrives, condensation fogging the bottle's neck. I nod to the waitress, sip, let the cold bitterness anchor me. For now, the world condenses to this: smoke, Shostakovich, the crisp slide of lager.

I set the bottle down and let myself unwind. Taking in the music and the muffled chatter. It's rare I get to sit like this, alone, without having to *be* anything to anyone. Not a teacher. Not a husband. Just me. *Andy*.

Then my eyes drift back to *him*.

The bloke with the cigar dominates the space without uttering a word. His presence is pure gravity, drawing everyone into his orbit. They lean in, rapt, like he's holding court without even trying. He doesn't glance their way. Doesn't need to. Got that air about him—the sort who gets what he wants before you've finished saying *no*.

I check my phone, mindlessly scrolling through recipe blogs as I take another drag of my fag. A swig of lager follows, crisp and cold, cutting through the smoke clinging to my tongue. Just as I'm tucking the mobile back into my jeans, it vibrates.

Grace.

"Hi, darling," I answer.

"Hey! How was work?"

"Same old," I say, blowing a wispy plume into the air. "Counting down the days till summer break. I swear, I can smell the freedom already."

She chuckles, that warm sound I've missed. "Me too, baby. We should do something special. Go somewhere nice."

"Yeah? Where were you thinking?"

"Well, we've always talked about Southern France, haven't we? Fancy a long weekend? Bit of sun, decent wine..."

I grin, glancing around. "Sounds perfect. But I know you and your work..."

She sighs. There's a pause, just long enough to knot my gut. "I know, I know... I'll work something out. Maybe I can get someone to cover my clients for once."

"Good luck with that," I chuckle. "Anyway, just having a drink. Won't be long. Heading home soon."

"Alright, take your time," she says brightly. "What do you want for dinner? I was thinking Thai."

"Sounds perfect. Usual for me." I take another drag. "I'll be home in an hour or so."

"Great. Love you."

"You too," I mutter, chest tightening as I say it, mobile disappearing into my jacket.

I slump against the chair, letting her voice—all bright and breezy—wash over me. Or try to. Instead, it *sticks*. *Gnaws*. Grace and her bloody job, it's woven into her DNA. I know where I stand in her life. I just wonder how far behind second place is.

The cigarette ash gathers between my fingers. I tap it into the tray, watching it disintegrate.

Another drag. Another sip. Let the quiet linger.

My mind wanders back to *that* lesson. The one I can't seem to forget.

I'd actually *bothered* that day.

Tried to channel my enthusiasm for history into them, make it stick for five bloody minutes. I'd been explaining the ripple effects of the Napoleonic Wars—how they reshaped Europe's borders, economies, and ideologies. Voice going all animated without meaning to. Then Chloe cut through it, that sigh sharp as a dagger:

"Sir, d'you mind if we skip to the exam bits?"

No raised hand. Not even a pretence of courtesy. Just her slouched in that plastic chair, shoes drumming the desk leg like my waffle was giving her actual toothache.

I froze mid-word. My train of thought derailed. "Sorry?"

My voice came out sharper than I'd intended.

Chloe didn't flinch. She never did.

"S'just... d'we need all this? Not like it's on the exam, is it?"

Sniggers. A few giggles, performative but loud. The Year 11 chorus.

Palms flat on the desk now, clamped to stop the tremor. "It's important," I said, that teacher-voice I hate slipping out—stiff as a PowerPoint slide, "because history shapes the present. You can't understand the world you live in without understanding where it came from."

Chloe rolled her eyes. That slow, deliberate teenage contempt.

"Yeah, but I'm not fussed about 'shaping the world'. Just need a C. Is this even *on* the exam?"

Laughter. *Proper* laughter this time, the kind that rattles the gum under the desks.

I felt the flush creeping up my neck. "Do you actually want to be here, Chloe?"

It slipped out before I could stop it.

Silence. Not out of respect. Never that. They were waiting, deciding whether this was worth getting invested in.

Then she grinned. Not a real one—that performative smirk sixth-formers weaponise.

"I mean, not really. But it's not like we get a choice, do we?"

The class erupted. Laughter sharp as snapped rulers.

For a heartbeat, the floor tiles tilted.

I stumbled through the rest of the lesson, my words falling flat, my points landing nowhere. By the time the bell rang, they were already halfway out the door, their chatter and laughter filling the space where my authority should have been.

Afterwards, I slumped into my chair, staring at lesson plans. Limbs heavy, like someone'd swapped my blood for gravy.

A thought crept in, uninvited but insistent: Maybe I should've fought harder to be a historian.

It had been a dream once, back when I believed passion could outweigh practicality. But I eventually talked myself into the mindset that teaching was the "grown-up" choice. Stable. Safe.

Now, years later, I'm not shaping minds—I'm barely keeping control of a room. My voice doesn't command respect, it barely holds attention.

And the worst part? I wasn't sure I blamed Chloe.

I didn't believe in what I was saying any more than she did.

I swig my lager, the bottle slick now with condensation. My eyes drift back to the cigar bloke, his frame spilling over the stool like he owns the air around it. No fidgeting, no apologetic hunch. Just there, collar undone a button too far, smoke curling lazy from his lips—a man who's never once Googled "imposter syndrome".

No cracks. No second-guessing. A man already at ease with himself, like he's figured life out.

I drag on my cigarette as the sunset bleeds orange over the terrace bar. Daylight's nearly gone.

When I glance over again, his entourage's vanished. No fanfare, no fuss. Just him left, sipping whisky like he's been alone all along.

He watches the last straggler leave with the indifference of a bloke watching adverts.

Then—suddenly—he's staring straight at me.

A wave. Not the cheery *mate-in-the-queue* kind. A single raised finger, deliberate as a chess move.

I glance behind, thinking he's waving at some finance bro. But no. Those hooded eyes are locked on mine.

Might he be a parent? Not one I recall.

I hesitate. That little voice (the one that nags about marking and recycling bins) hisses *go home, Andy*. But something sharper—wilder, maybe—pins me in place.

I lift my bottle in a half-arsed salute, all nonchalance.

He crooks a finger. *Come here.*

I eye the exit, then the remnants of my drink. I Could leave now. *Should* leave now. Then, without my feet bothering to consult my brain, I'm stubbing out my cig, grabbing my jacket, and walking over.

The beer and nicotine have already gone to my head. Or maybe it's him, the way he's rooted there, unflappable, like a bloody oak tree in a storm. The others peeled off without a murmur, as if he'd dismissed them with a glance.

As I near, he sizes me up, slowly. His gaze snags on my creased shirt, the unsteady sway of my bottle. The cigar glows between his fingers, pulsing like a heartbeat with each drag.

A nod.

He tilts forward as I sit.

The chair groans beneath me, anchoring, but my pulse still thrums.

"Don't tell me your name," he says, before I can open my mouth.

That voice—gravel wrapped in velvet. Not a request. A decree.

I freeze, wrong-footed. My grip whitens on the bottle. "Pardon?"

"You heard me." He taps ash into a tumbler. Smoke hazes the space between us. "Names are useless here. Besides, I don't need yours."

And just like that, I don't push. Don't ask why.

I shut my mouth.

He studies the ash, then leans back, sprawling till the chair creaks in protest.

"Rough day?"

I nod, taking a slow swig of my beer. "You could say that."

"Aren't they always?" A rumble of laughter, no real effort in it.

I huff a hollow laugh. "Suppose."

Silence. Smoke twists upwards, catching the light overhead. He tracks it, eyes half-lidded.

"Funny old world, isn't it?" he says. "No matter what you do, how many hours you sink in... never quite feels like you're *winning*."

I shrug. "Depends on the job, I suppose."

His stare sharpens—proper headteacher glare. "Does it?"

He lets the silence thicken, watching me squirm. Then, smoke curling from his nostrils:

"Everyone's stuck on the same bloody hamster wheel. Chase the promotion, the pay rise, the pat on the head. Then one day you wake up, and you're just... older. More knackered."

Something lodges in my ribs. *Christ, he's not wrong.*

My job's comfy enough, but comfy's just another word for stagnant. Teach, mark, rinse-repeat. Even the summer holidays feel scripted.

He inhales deeply, the cigar's tip flaring like a warning light. Holds it. Exhales. *"Freedom."*

The word hangs, heavier than the smoke.

The way he says it sticks with me.

Freedom.

Can't remember the last time I tasted it. My days are timetabled down to the minute. Bell rings, bins go out, repeat. But this bloke? Moves like rules don't apply. Like he's already untethered.

"So what do you actually do?" I press, leaning forward.

He smirks, ash tumbling into the tray. "Let's not spoil the mystery with CVs, eh?"

A hollow laugh escapes me. "Fair play."

He studies the street—a Bentley glides past, all tinted windows and private plates. "Ever think about just... dropping it all? Starting fresh?

The words hit harder than they should. I swirl the last remainder of my lager, hoping the glass hides my face doing its impression of a faulty neon sign. "Dunno. It's not that straightforward."

He doesn't blink. "Why not?"

What's holding you back?

I want to say *everything*. The job. The wife. The whole sodding hamster wheel. But the truth curdles in my throat. Thick, sour. I shrug. "Responsibilities, mate."

"Responsibilities." He rolls the word like a rancher appraising livestock. "Responsibilities will kill you quicker than cyanide. Everyone's got 'em. Difference is, some know when to bin 'em off."

His words slosh in my skull. Makes it sound easy. Like you can just... walk. But life's not some Richard Curtis film. There's Grace. The mortgage on the Zone 2 flat. The unspoken rules—Sunday roasts, double dates with her pretentious friends.

You don't get to vanish.

He drags on the cigar, watching me with an unsettling calmness.

"It's written all over you," he says. "That itch."

I stiffen. "You don't know me."

"Don't need to." The cigar bobs as he speaks. "Seen it a million times. You're not unhappy. Not properly miserable either. Just... stuck. Right in the middle. And that's the worst place to be."

I say nothing.

He's not wrong. But that doesn't mean I'll hand him the ammunition.

The alley thrums around us. Glasses clinking, drunk laughter, the distant wail of a siren.

"Married, are you?"

I shift uncomfortably in my seat. "Yeah."

"How's that going, then?"

Shit. I pick at the label on my bottle. "It's alright."

He barks a laugh. "*Alright.* Christ, worse than *fine.*"

"Marriage isn't a picnic," I snap, sharper than intended.

His smirk doesn't waver.

I nod at his ringless hand. "What about you?"

"Me?" He lets out a gravelly chuckle. "Nah. Rather stick my bollocks in a wasps' nest. Life's too short."

He flicks ash, the ember briefly illuminating the disdain in his eyes. "People aren't labradors. We're not built for one master."

I scoff. "What if you met someone... different?"

"Different?" He leans back, stretching. "Maybe. But what happens when things go stale? When the novelty wears off? People aren't meant to live in cages, and even the nicest ones end up feeling like prisons."

My jaw clenches at the words he's spuing. All because he's right. Although me and Grace don't bicker, things have in fact, gone stale. Lately, it feels I'm sinking into clay I can't claw my way out of.

"And trust?" I ask, too casually. "If you knew someone was lying... would you bail? Or try to... you know. Fix it?"

He stares—*proper stares*—like he's peeled back the wallpaper and found my mouldy secrets. I stop breathing.

He lets the silence thicken.

"Depends," he finally drawls. "On what's at stake. If it's just a relationship built on convenience, sure, walk away. But if there's something real underneath all the slog?" He exhales, smoke veiling his smirk. "You'd be surprised what people are willing to forgive."

"What about you?" He stabs the cigar at me. "You strike me as a spreadsheet sort of bloke. Relationship, life, all neatly organised. Am I wrong?"

I snort. "It's just how it shook out. Good job. Nice girl. Beautiful flat. Can't complain."

"But."

"But sometimes it's like... you're watching your own life on telly. And the plot's gone to shit."

He nods, like he's heard it a hundred times before. "Yeah. That's where most people mess up. They stop chasing what they really want. Life beats them down, makes them settle for whatever's in front of them. But there's always more. Always something better, if you're willing to chase it."

His words land like a punch to the gut.

I settled. Became Mr. Giles instead of becoming a historian. Chose safe. Chose small.

I lean in, elbows digging into the wooden table. "And you? What do you want?"

He grins, wide as the M25. *"Everything."*

I force a laugh. "Sounds... ambitious."

He shrugs, like I've just asked why the sky's blue. "Not about ambition. It's about hunger. Proper hunger. The kind that leads you places you didn't even know you needed."

His eyes glint through the smoke. "Hunger's the only honest bit left in most of us."

I want to push—*what's that even mean?*—but my tongue feels thick.

"And women?" I ask, defaulting to blokeish deflection. "Got a type?"

He snorts. "Type? Nah. That's the joy of it. Brunette, redhead, posh bird, East End. Long as they're fit and fuck good, I'm not fussy."

I roll my eyes. "No strings, then."

"Strings strangle." He spreads his hands, a mock crucifixion. "Strings make you soft. Predictable. And predictable men..." He leans in. "They get eaten."

The words settle like a bad kebab.

I stare at my empty bottle. Think of Grace. How we've become experts in the *fine and alright.*

Maybe he's right. Maybe love's just another cage.

"Reckon you've got it all sorted," I say, aiming for sarcasm, landing closer to envy.

He raises his cigar. "Sorted? Nah. But I know what I want. And I'm not afraid to go after it."

A moment of silence. Then he leans closer, his voice dropping a notch.

"Question is... do *you* know what you want?"

I study the bottle's label, peeling at the corner.

Do I?

The silence stretches.

Probably.

Or maybe I'm just too scared to want anything at all.

I fish out a cigarette, nod to the barmaid for another lager, and light up. "What I want's irrelevant. Got responsibilities. You said it."

He studies me. Then, the smirk. That *I've-seen-your-search-history* grin.

"Responsibilities? Bollocks. Just shackles you polish yourself. One proper night out—no lies, no sucking up to bosses, no packed lunch box—and snap. Chains broken."

I snort. "One night? That's your master plan?"

"For some." He scans the terrace, motions for a whisky. "Others need... persuasion. A nudge into the deep end."

I lean in, despite myself. "What are you getting at?"

He mirrors me, voice dipping to a growl. "There's this place. Members' club. Not your Chelsea twats in boat shoes. No hedge fund wankers comparing golf handicaps. Just... *freedom*. Proper, unvarnished."

My mind flashes to overheard mums at sports day—*"We're trying Annabel's next month, but the waitlist is a nightmare!"*—and almost laugh. They'd sell their Labradors for a sniff of this.

"Costs a fortune, I bet?" I already know the answer. I wouldn't even be able to afford the cloakroom tip on my salary.

"No fees. That's the best part." He taps his glass. "But it's picky. Only lets in... hungry sorts."

"What's it called? Might Google it."

He chuckles, like I've just asked for the WiFi password at a murder scene.

"Ralph's."

2

That bloke from the bar's been living rent-free in my head all week.

Whether I'm marking essays or dodging Grace's *"How was your day?"*, his voice slithers in, all gravel and certainty. *Freedom. The club.* Can't scrub it out. Part of me wants to hunt him down, buy him a pint, pry loose more details.

Not that I'm *desperate*. Just... curious.

Right now, though, I need to survive this bloody garden party.

Blackwood Girls' School throws one every June under the guise of "celebrating community". Translation: guilt-tripping parents into bankrolling another astroturf pitch. The wicker "donations basket" by the charcuterie board might as well have *Cash Only* Sharpied on it.

I retreat behind an oak tree, feigning interest in a wood warbler perched on a branch.

Ralph's.

The name itches. I thumb my phone: *Ralph's members club London.*

Nothing. A cafe, random people named Ralph. Zero trace of anything exclusive.

Did I imagine it?

The soft tread of footsteps pulls me back to reality. I quickly close the tab and pocket my phone.

"Ah, Mr. Giles."

I turn. A guy in a light Barbour jacket strides over, hand extended.

"Hello." I shake it, scrambling. Definitely a parent. Which one?

"Been a while!" Overbright, like he's auditioning for a mortgage ad. "Stuart Evans. Met back when you were covering Year 11 with Charles. Amy had you for History."

"Right, Amy!" Lie. I don't have the faintest memory. "I was Charles' TA back then."

"She adored you! Still goes on about your Henry VIII rants!"

"Glad to hear it," I say, as a Year 8 mum side-eyes us, clutching Prosecco like a lifeline.

"It was pretty nerve-wracking, to be honest. I was only twenty-four."

"And now look at you!" He beams like he's claiming credit for my Postgraduate certificate. "Proper teacher!"

"Suppose my obsession with history paid off," I chuckle, the lie sour on my tongue.

Then, a sudden silence. The kind you get in lift rides with estranged in-laws. I'm mid-excuse when a hand yanks his Barbour sleeve.

"Dad. Can we just go? Kiera's being annoying."

His daughter. AirPods in. Early twenties would be my guess. Her eyes skate over me. I sense a vague recognition, but it's swiftly buried. We're just two strangers who once shared a classroom.

"We've been here *twenty minutes*," Stuart hisses. "Go network. Or say hi to some of your old teachers."

She rolls eyes perfected through teen rebellion. For a flash, our gazes catch—does she remember Year 11 Tudor debates? Or me begging her to stop vaping in the loo?

Doesn't matter. We're ghosts to each other now.

Stuart turns back, smile stapled on. "Remember Mr. Giles, Ames?"

"Yeah." she says flatly. "Did that WW1 module with Mr. Bird."

I grasp for common ground. "Guessing you're knee-deep in dissertations now? History?"

Stuart's laugh erupts—a pantomime villain cackle. Heads swivel. He sips his G&T like it's oxygen.

"God, no." Amy smirks. "Law. Dad's idea."

"Ah." I nod, automaton-like. "Maybe I'll have more luck with your sister. The world needs more historians, after all. You dive into the past and realise you've barely scratched the surface."

Stuart wheezes anew. Amy mouths sorry behind his back.

Somewhere, a PTA mum drops a Waitrose canapé. The wood warbler I'd been fake-admiring shits on a bench.

I've never related to a bird more.

My throat's turning into sandpaper. I need a drink. *Now.*

Stuart has already moved on, attention shifting to his phone, thumbs hammering away.

Amy's edging towards the exit, just as eager to slip away as I am.

"Best check on the... raffle," I lie, already retreating.

Stuart grunts. Amy mouths *thank fuck* at the grass.

Freedom.

I dodge through the mingling guests, and beeline my way towards the drinks stand.

G&T. Double.

The barman sloshes it into a plastic cup. I gulp, ice clattering against teeth.

Where's Grace?

She was meant to be here an hour ago. It's Saturday, not like she's got to rush from the office.

I stab her number into my phone.

"Pick up, pick up..." The crowd swells. Old boys in boat shoes, mums clutching prosecco. They glance. Whisper. Look away.

Are they laughing at the state of my tie? My Primark loafers?

"Hiya!" Grace's voice crackles.

"You still on the bus?"

"Rush hour purgatory! Two stops, promise!"

Her autopilot apology grates. "Want a drink waiting?"

"White wine? You're a star!"

"See you in a bit."

I hang up, necking the gin. It burns.

She knows I hate these work dos.

Twenty-eight, surrounded by silver-haired Mayfair locals who treat me like the work experience kid. Even the groundsman drives a nicer car.

I sip my gin, eyeing the crowd. Their laughter's all helium, no substance.

Stuart's still texting. Amy's vanished, probably off to vape behind the cricket pavilion.

Another swallow.

I scan for the least wanky clique to survive the canapés. Then it hits me—no one here gives a toss. Not about the Thirty Years' War. Not Louis XIV's wig budget. Not Peter the Great's sauna habits.

I drift through the lawn, a ghost in M&S chinos, praying for a lifeline.

"Ahoy! Mr. Giles!"

The headmaster's bellow curdles my gin.

Richard.

He strokes his Dumbledore 'tache—yes, we all know you moisturise it, mate—and herds over a family straight out of Made in Chelsea.

"The Lewishams!" he trumpets. "Isabelle joins us in September!"

Robot smile engaged. "Lovely to meet you."

Mrs. Lewisham's handshake could crack walnuts. Mr. Lewisham's Rolex glints like a distress beacon.

I turn to the kid. "Isabelle, history's less dull than maths, promise. We've got Henry VIII's divorce drama."

The adults titter. Isabelle looks like she'd rather French kiss a wasp.

"Mr. Giles is quite the scholar!" Richard says, like he's unveiling a new school minibus.

I sip gin to stop myself snorting.

"Specialty?" Mr. Lewisham puffs up. "I'm something of an expert myself. Predominantly in the ancient civilizations of Central and South America—the Inca, Maya, Aztec, Olmec."

Christ.

He reels off civilizations like he's auditioning for University Challenge, wife gazing up like he's just discovered fire.

"He even chartered a plane last summer for fieldwork," she purrs.

I swig the gin. Better finish this one fast and get another. Blackwood really splashed out with the good stuff.

"Very impressive," I lie, leaning into the flattery. You'd run rings round me. I'm just a curriculum drone. But rest assured—" I nod at Isabelle, who's awkwardly standing there, "—your investment's safe here."

It bloody well should be when they're paying forty grand a year, nearly as much as my salary.

Mr. Lewisham opens his mouth—*Incan soil pH levels?*—when my phone vibrates.

Grace.

I excuse myself, and flee through to the main hall. Over the creaky parquet, past mothballed portraits of dead headmasters.

"I'm here!" she says. "Just walking up."

"Okay, I'll come out front. One sec."

"Oh, you don't have to, I—"

I hang up mid-protest. I'll blame it on a bad connection later. I need to distance myself from the garden party before my head explodes from the mind-numbing chatter.

I pass the reception desk, and push open the heavy front doors.

Grace click-clacks towards me, phone against her ear.

From here, I can't hear her conversation, but the second she spots me, she hangs up, flashing me that wide, practiced smile. The one that could charm the world.

She's immaculate: pencil skirt vacuum-sealed to her hips, blazer sharp enough to slit wrists, hair in a bun so tight it probably counts as a face-lift.

"Darling," she says, kissing my cheek. Her *Chanel No. 5* envelops me. "Traffic was *hell*."

"It's alright." I let her thread her arm through mine. "Glad you made it."

"It's okay," I mutter, feeling a small weight lifted now that she's here. "Glad you made it. I was about ready to hang myself. You know how I can't stand forced conversations."

She squeezes my hand. "Rescue mission activated. But first, *wine*. Had to field three conference calls this morning."

I nod, reminding myself that she makes more in three months than I do in a year.

"Close any deals?" I ask, half out of habit, half to fill the silence.

She nods, her face lit with quiet pride. "My biggest one yet."

Of course.

That's Grace, constantly levelling up. Last time she closed her "biggest deal," she came home with a twenty-grand bonus. Who knows what today's payday will be?

Work hard, play hard. The corporate motto, right?

"You're killing it," I say, too quietly.

"Always." She adjusts her blazer, armour against the world. "Still emails to crush tonight, but *later*."

We march towards the party, her stilettos *tap-tap-tapping* like a metronome set to hustle.

"Fancy that new izakaya in Soho next weekend?" I say, desperate to claw back normalcy. "The swanky one you Instagrammed?"

"Love that ide—" Her phone shrieks. A shrill, corporate ringtone.

She pulls it from her clutch, and I catch a glimpse of the name on the screen.

Tom.

I don't know why, but something about it feels... off.

She freezes. Just for a heartbeat—a micro-wince flitting across her face—before thumbing *decline*.

"Client crisis can sod off," she says, too breezy, lacing her fingers through mine.

We continue walking, but my eyes keep snagging on her handbag.

That name.

Tom.

Not a name from her team. Not a name I've heard.

3

It's Friday, which means Grace is working late—*later* than usual. Perfect excuse to grab a pint and, just maybe, bump into that man again. The one who acts like he's cracked the code to this elusive thing called *freedom*.

The no-names vibe last week had a certain mystique. I leave at the same time as last week, telling myself it's just a quick drink. But we both know better.

He dangled a glimpse of what I *might* be after, and now I want more. A taste of something... unscripted.

Stepping onto the street, the faint strains of Vivaldi drift through the night air, swelling as I near the bar. My shoulders loosen. Anticipation prickles.

Rounding the corner, the terrace buzzes louder tonight. More laughter. More bodies. The haze of cigar smoke hangs thicker.

Heads swivel as I reach the entrance, like I've walked into a wake mid-eulogy.

My feet falter. *Turn back. Now.*

Then—

"Oi! Over here, mate!"

That voice.

My pulse stutters.

It's him.

I force a casual saunter to his table. He's not alone.

Three immaculately dressed women orbit him, all flawless, laughter spilling from their lips like they're in on some secret.

Models? Influencers? Escorts?

The man's dressed like a rejected extra from *Mamma Mia!*—linen trousers, shirt screaming palm fronds. He sprawls like he's on a yacht, not a pavement.

"Fancy a proper drink?" he asks, his grin all mischief.

I hesitate, then nod.

The waiter's already gone, reappearing with a black tray: five shots of murky purple liquid.

I grab mine without a second thought. The world lurches, faces smearing like paint in the rain.

Blink.

Normal service resumes. Just a head rush, probably. Not going to start overthinking 'bout it now.

I knock it back. The sweet liquid slides down like honey.

"So," says the woman with honey-blonde waves and Bambi eyes, leaning in. "What's *your* deal?"

I know I should keep things vague. That's how Mr. Palm Trees over here would want it. And honestly, so do I.

"Not much to tell," I shrug. "Just... figuring it out."

"Figuring it out, huh?" She smirks, swirls her glass. "Anyway, I'm Elisa, and this is Ana and Diana."

The girls share a look, then burst out into a giggle.

"He's just like you. All mysterious!" Ana teases, twisting a hoop earring.

The man leans in. "Most blokes drone on about jobs and money. But you? You're different. I like that."

I fiddle with my empty shot glass. "Same to you, Mr. No-Name."

An awkward silence hangs until the next round arrives. I grab mine, grinning.

"Well? Are we drinking or what?"

He raises his. "To freedom."

We clink glasses. The second shot burns less, warmth buzzing under my skin.

The girls laugh too loud, pressing closer to him as he watches me, sly.

"We should do this weekly," he says, setting his glass down.

I nod. Too fast.

The shots keep coming. Five? Six? The room blurs at the edges. My shoulders slump, the tightness I've carried for months melting away.

The girls chatter about Paris Fashion Week, but I'm locked on him.

He lounges, cigarette dangling, that same knowing look.

Diana gracefully rises from her seat, her black dress clinging to every curve. She drapes her Birkin bag over her arm like an afterthought.

"I'm off to the ladies room," she announces.

I trail her movements. Every step poised like a dancer's.

The other two women follow, heels clicking towards the toilets.

I lean in, voice dipping. "How'd you meet them?"

He offers a half-smile, all teeth and no warmth. "Ran into two at Sexy Fish a few months ago—one of those nights where you go out for a laugh and end up with a story."

He swishes the remnants of his shot, watching the liquid spin.

"Third one tagged along at Cirque Le Soir. VIP booths, magnums, DJs blasting till dawn. You know how it goes."

I want to dig deeper—ask what *exactly* happens on those nights—but bite my tongue. He hasn't asked about Grace, the school, the life I've folded myself into.

I pivot. "You into history?"

"Of Course." He sprawls back, legs invading my space. "Got a library at my mine. Last month it was ancient Chinese warlords. Now?" He taps ash into a scallop shell serving as a makeshift tray. "Early humans. Homo Erectus, Homo Habilis... all the homos."

The grin's pure sixth-form cheek. We both snort. A raw, unguarded sound.

"Imagine if other human species were still kicking about," I say, mostly to the dregs of my bottled lager.

"Neanderthals only died out about 40,000 years ago. Blink of an eye, really."

"We killed them, didn't we?" I already know the answer, but I want to hear his take.

"Better tools. Better organisational skills. Better at playing dirty." He mimics stabbing air. "Humans are brutal when we want to be."

"Someone should make a documentary. David Attenborough voiceover and all."

"Narrated by *me*," he jokes. His hand glides across the sticky table, palm upturned to reveal a tiny baggie of white powder. Our eyes meet. A challenge masked as an invitation.

I turn my hand over, casual as checking the time. The bag drops into my creased palm.

The thrill hits like a double espresso. Sharp, electric, stupid.

"I'll be back in a sec," I say, slipping from the table.

The bar blurs as I weave through clusters of suits and perfume, laughter sloshing over the edges of wine glasses, a Bach concerto battling the clatter of ice cubes. The three girls pass me as I head inside, Ana's grin sharp as a papercut. Her finger flicks her nose. A subtle gesture, but I get it. We all know the code.

I glance back once before ducking into the corridor. The bathroom's quiet, just the drip of a tap and the echo of my own breathing. The stall lock clicks shut.

The bag crinkles as I tap it out. A neat white line on the porcelain. For a brief moment, my mind drifts—line infantry in the 17th century, soldiers in perfect rows, muskets raised. I can almost hear the rhythmic beat of war drums, the shrill cry of flutes.

No overthinking. Just bend, snort, wince.

The burn's instant, but I welcome the familiar sting. It drags me back to uni. Those hazy, untouchable nights when the world felt boundless. Back when I believed I could be someone. Before the reality of adulthood settled in, suffocating that wide-open future I once saw so clearly.

The world sharpens, thoughts clicking into place, moving faster, clearer. The rush creeps in, threading through my veins.

I tuck the crumpled bag back into my pocket, unlock the stall door and step back out.

The girls are hunched over a phone, Diana's acrylics glittering. The man hasn't budged. King of his grubby throne, smoke curling from his lips like a Victorian factory chimney.

I slump into my seat, veins buzzing. Not wrecked, just sanded smooth.

"Suitably refreshed?" he asks with a grin.

I nod, smirking as I slide the baggie back under the table. "Ready for round two?"

The conversation flows smoother now. Banter, stories, laughter filling the gaps between drinks. We talk about travel—places we've been, places we want to go. The girls trade stories of Ibiza parties, rooftop soirées in New York. Their words hang in the air like confetti, weightless.

"Bali's next," Elisa sighs, swirling her drink. "Proper detox. No emails, no Tube strikes, just sun."

"I'd join you in a heartbeat," I say, half-joking, half-serious. "Could use an escape myself."

The man raises his glass. "Escape is good, everyone deserves one."

I hum agreement, gin warming my veins. Letting real life fade, even for tonight, feels stolen. Precious.

I set my glass down. "What do you have planned after this? Going anywhere nice? Ralph's, maybe?"

His shoulders stiffen—just a flicker—before he slouches again. "Can't just wander into Ralph's. Even members need invites. You wait. You hope."

The buzz dulls. *Ralph's*. The word is an itch I can't scratch, an allure tugging at me, even though I have no clue what it actually is.

He leans back, casual. "I could put your name in. No promises though. But if they bite... you'll see it for yourself."

Diana props her chin on her palm. "How exclusive are we talking? I've never even heard of it."

"Yeah, can't be better than Annabel's, surely," Elisa chimes in.

He rubs his chin. "Not better, but... different."

Part of me wants to jump at the chance, but fragments of our conversation from last week creep in. *"One night where you let it all go."* The pull of the unknown is alluring, but another thought pushes through the rest.

Grace. My wife.

I force a laugh, shaking my head. "I don't know, mate... It's tempting, but I'll need to think about it. Wouldn't want you to waste a guest spot when I might not be free."

He holds my gaze a second longer than necessary, then grins, easy as ever.

"No sweat." He leans closer, voice dropping to a conspiratorial rumble. "But if you decide you want to take a little break from reality, let me know."

I offer a non-committal shrug, but the offer sticks.

Satisfied, he lights a cigarette, steering us back to safer ground. Football, Glastonbury line-ups, whether Oasis will ever reunite. The girls laugh and drink, occasionally shooting me seductive looks.

The girls giggle, Ana's foot brushing mine under the table.

But I'm miles off.

ALEX MURA

Ralph's hums in my skull like a trapped wasp. Grace's face flickers. Her *"Don't work too hard"* text still unanswered.

4

The next morning, sunlight spills through the kitchen window as I slap two bacon rashers and three eggs into a sizzling pan. Coffee drips into my mug, its bitter scent mingling with the grease spitting on the hob. I rub my face, still groggy, last night's conversation slipping in and out of memory like a half-remembered dream.

Upstairs, Grace stomps around, drawers opening and shutting. She's working today, even though it's a Saturday. At least it'll be from home.

I sip my coffee, wincing at the burnt aftertaste, when a glint by the door catches my eye.

A letter.

Lying pristine among the takeaway menus and junk mail. Thick cream paper, glossy as fresh paint. My name curls across the front in ink-black cursive. No stamp. No address. Just a blood-red wax seal stamped with a looping *R*.

My pulse skips.

He did say he could put in a word. But I never told him my name. Never mentioned the flat.

Footsteps clatter down the stairs. I shove the letter behind my back as Grace shuffles in. Hair wild, wearing that ratty St Andrews Uni jumper she won't bin.

"Mornin'," she mutters, brushing past me towards the fridge.

"Sleep alright?" I ask, too brightly.

She pours herself a glass of orange juice, yawning. "Video call at nine. Need to shower." A hurried peck on my cheek, then she's gone. *Clip-clop* up the stairs.

The bacon hisses in the pan, spitting oil, but I don't care. Moving quickly, I slip into the downstairs bathroom, locking the door behind me. Perched on the edge of the bath, I slit the seal with trembling thumbs. Inside: a single sheet of paper, thick as cardstock, the same elegant script.

Monsieur,
We are delighted to extend an invitation to you.
The time has come to indulge.
Ralph's
16 St James's Square, London SW1Y 4LH
26th April 2024
7:15 pm till late.
We await your presence.
— Management

No signature. No explanation. Just a creeping sense of inevitability.

I read the letter again, slower this time.

Gut churning.

Part of me wants to tear it up, flush it down the toilet, pretend I never saw it. But my fists crumple the paper tighter, unwilling to let go.

A sharp crackle from the kitchen—the *bacon*.

I sit frozen, mind whirring. The sensible part, the Mr. Giles who marks essays in red pen, says *hoax*. *Prank*. But the other part, the one that stayed up till 3am reading about Cortés, whispers *this is how it starts*.

This isn't a joke. It's an offer. And maybe, just maybe, it's what I've been looking for.

I jam the letter into my pyjama pocket, splashing my face with icy tap water. The date, seven days from now, flashes through my mind like a pulsing neon sign.

I turn the door handle, stepping back into the hallway just as the bacon starts to burn.

"Shit." I lunge for the hob, flipping the rashers too late. They're already crisped at the edges, the eggs solid, overcooked. The smell clings to the walls, to my clothes.

Grimacing, I grab a plate and transfer the food over, but in my hurry, a slick of hot grease spits on my shirt.

I curse under my breath, yanking the fabric away from my skin as the grease spreads. *Great*.

I grab a damp cloth, scrubbing at the stain half-heartedly before lobbing the cloth into the sink. Upstairs, I peel off the ruined shirt and chuck it in the laundry. Another casualty of my luck. Pulling on a fresh one, my mind races.

ALEX MURA

The bedroom mirror mocks me. Another bloody wrinkle. In a city like London, surrounded by so many beautiful people, it's hard not to feel like you could be better.

Grace's phone pings on the bedside table. My eyes flick to it as it lights up, a message flashing across the screen.

I tell myself to look away. It's not my business, but I can't.

Tom: I had a great time.

The words punch through me.

The bathroom door creaks open, steam pouring out. Grace glides out, towel-drying her hair, all calm, like Tom's text isn't burning a hole in my skull.

I watch her dress, the phone buzzing again with potential secrets. I try to convince myself it's nothing. Maybe he's just a colleague or a client, but the excuses taste like sour milk.

Desperate to clear my head, I head downstairs and finish drinking my coffee.

Between the letter and that damn message, I can feel myself spiralling.

I should just ask her, *"Who's Tom? Why's he texting you about having a great time?"*

But my mouth stays shut. *Coward*.

The thought festers like a splinter as I choke down breakfast. The eggs sit there, rubbery, overcooked. I stab a forkful, appetite dead.

Seven days.

Seven days until Ralph's.

I take a slow breath. What harm could it do? Show up, have a drink. Leave whenever I want.

Curiosity digs its claws in, the idea embedding itself deeper. A chill creeps up my spine, excitement stirring something in me. I shake it off.

This isn't me.

I'm not the sort of person who sneaks into shady members' clubs no one's ever heard of. The sort who risks it all for *what*?

But then again, *why not*?

Just once.

I shovel toast into my mouth, dry as cardboard.

I'm going to do it, aren't I?

Grace clatters downstairs, her short brown hair tied back, makeup immaculate, phone welded to her palm. I can't help but wonder if Tom's message is still sitting there, waiting to be answered. Or if she's already replied and deleted it.

"Hey." She snatches her laptop. "Lunch ideas?"

"Uhm, maybe we could hit the brunch spot down the road?" My voice croaks.

She nods, already distracted by her phone. *Another message from Tom?*

"Sounds good! Could you make a reservation? It gets rammed on Saturdays."

I nod, throat tight. She leans in for a kiss, her lips barely brushing mine, and then she's gone, disappearing into the living room, door clicking shut behind her.

The letter's back in my hand. *26th April. 7:15 pm.*

It feels less like an invitation now and more like a summons, pulling me into the unknown.

A line I was always bound to cross.

Just one night.

What could it hurt?

5

Seven days later, I'm outside Ralph's, staring down at the invitation in my hand. The gold lettering shimmers under a streetlamp's glow.

7:15 pm. We await your presence.

I glance up at the building, a Georgian townhouse in St. James's with soot-stained bricks and shuttered windows. The sort of place your eyes skip over unless you're *meant* to see it.

No sign, plaque or buzzer. Just black doors swallowed by wrought-iron railings.

It feels alive. Watching. The windows stare blankly, reflecting only the square's skeletal trees and my own hunched silhouette.

I fed Grace an excuse days ago, telling her I'd be out drinking with the lads. She hummed absently, eyes glued to her laptop.

There was no dress code mentioned, but I've stuck to my usual work attire. A pressed shirt, corduroy trousers, polished black shoes. It's safe. Normal. But standing here, I feel underdressed.

What the hell am I doing here?

Common sense screams *run*. Pretend this never happened. But that other voice, the one that's been itching since the bar, hisses *you'll always wonder*.

One step. Then another. The gate creaks.

Before I touch the knocker, the door swings inward.

A man stands before me. Older, dressed in a perfectly tailored suit, his posture rigid as if carved from marble. Bushy grey eyebrows frame eyes that pierce through me, sharp enough to strip secrets bare.

"Monsieur," he rasps, dipping his head slightly. "Welcome."

I open my mouth to speak, but no words come. The invitation feels flimsy in my clammy grip.

Why do I feel like a trespasser?

"You're expected," he adds, tone leaving no room for doubt. "Please, come inside."

I nod, throat tight, and step past him into a dim hallway. The door shuts with a weighty thud.

The interior matches the exterior's grandeur—high ceilings, plush carpets swallowing footsteps. Candlelight flickers against dark wood panels, shadows stretching like claws across the walls.

I catch my reflection in a gilded mirror. My face is pale but ordinary—eyes wide, pupils dilated. Fear? Anticipation? Both?

A woman materialises silently. Her black uniform is crisp, hair scraped into a severe bun. She smiles, but it doesn't warm her marble-cool demeanour.

"Monsieur, we've been expecting you. Welcome to Ralph's."

The way she says it prickles my skin.

I nod, mouth desert-dry.

"We have a few rules here," she continues, voice smooth. "They're simple, but absolute."

I fall into step behind her, the faint scent of aged wood and lavender in the air. The walls are lined with paintings—abstract, chaotic, violent, like they're screaming to be understood.

"You cannot ask other guests any personal questions, nor reveal your own name," she says mechanically. "Here, you are your mask and your number. That's all."

"What if I already know someone here?" I ask. "What if I recognise them?"

She turns just enough to glance at me, her smile unreadable. "Then you'll pretend you don't. Everyone here is a stranger, even if they aren't."

The casualness of her answer tells me this isn't negotiable. I nod, clamping my mouth shut. *Play along. Watch first.*

We walk in silence for a few steps before she continues. "The second rule is that everything that happens here remains confidential. Nothing leaves Ralph's."

A shiver prickles my neck. "What does that mean, exactly?" My voice cracks, too eager. "What *happens* here?"

She pauses but doesn't stop. "You'll see soon enough."

The vagueness coils in my chest, dragging me deeper into the unknown.

"The third rule," she continues, "is that the dress code is sacrosanct. You will always wear the attire provided for the evening."

I glance down at my work clothes—the pressed shirt, quarter-zip jumper, brown corduroy trousers I'd agonised over. "So... this isn't appropriate?"

She doesn't slow, steering me toward looming double doors. "You'll be dressed accordingly before the celebration begins."

Celebration. The word lodges in my throat.

At the doors, she turns fully, her gaze icy. "The fourth rule: all electronic devices must be surrendered at reception. No phones. No communication with the outside world. Here, you're... *untethered*."

She places it on a velvet-lined tray held by another staff member behind a mahogany desk. The second it leaves my hand, I feel lighter. Emptier.

"And finally," she says, her voice sharpening, "you must attend every monthly celebration. Without exception."

I frown. "Every one? What if I'm busy?"

Her smile stretches, cold as a winter pavement. "Then you forfeit membership."

The words hang—*no, threaten*—in the air. This isn't a club. It's a contract.

I open my mouth to protest, but her stare hardens, turning rules into commandments. Silently, she opens a door and gestures me through.

The room is dim, opulent, cavernous. A gilded full-length mirror dominates the centre, reflecting my hunched shoulders. Garments line the walls—black velvet tailcoats, blood-red silk cravats, brocade waistcoats dripping gold thread.

"You'll be changed now," she says. "Tonight's theme is the 19th century. You'll wear what we provide."

I stare at the costumes. My corduroys and jumper suddenly feel like a child's play clothes. This isn't dressing up. It's erasure.

"Remove your current clothing."

She steps back but doesn't look away. No blush, no apology, just clinical detachment.

My fingers hover at my top button. No. This feels wrong. Violating. I glance at her, desperate for a loophole, but her face is a mask.

"No need for modesty, Monsieur," she says. "Nothing here leaves these walls."

I've barely been here five minutes, and already, I feel like I'm crossing a boundary I don't fully understand.

I draw a shaky breath, forcing my fingers to move.

Grace's face flashes in my mind—her smile, the way she kissed me this morning. A little too formal. A little too detached. *Would she care if she knew where I was?*

And then, unbidden, another name slips into my thoughts.

Tom.

I had a great time.

The words from Grace's phone stab through me again.

The suspicion gnaws at me, pushing me forward, making me stop questioning why I'm here.

My heart pounds as I unbutton my shirt, slipping it off and folding it neatly on the bench. Each layer I shed—the jumper, the belt, the corduroys—feels like surrendering a piece of myself. My fingers fumble over the buckle. "Is this really necessary?"

She doesn't blink. "Yes, Monsieur. Completely necessary."

Her words cut through my hesitation. The decision has been made, with or without my consent.

The knot in my stomach tightens as I strip down further, placing my shoes and trousers beside my shirt. The air feels colder now, or maybe it's just my nerves.

Grace's face comes to mind again—her disappointment if she knew. But then, Tom's name.

A reminder of my doubts.

A reminder that maybe I don't care.

The woman clears her throat—a subtle prompt to continue. My hand lingers on the waistband of my boxers. One last hesitation.

And then I step out of them, folding them neatly with the rest of my clothes.

For a moment, I stand there, exposed, as though that last layer of fabric had been the only thing tethering me to my former life.

The staff member remains impassive, hands folded in front of her. No judgment. No interest. Just professionalism. But for me, this is a line I never imagined crossing.

After a pause, she steps forward, handing me a folded shirt. The fabric is rich silvery linen, smooth against my skin as I slide my arms through. She moves around me, buttoning it herself, leaving the top three undone. The exposure feels unnatural.

She kneels, fitting me with a pair of cotton twill trousers. I raise each foot mechanically, like a child's doll being dressed, my mind floating somewhere far from this room. Once my shirt is tucked in, she adds the finishing touches—an extravagant cravat tied too tightly, a brown tailcoat with gold buttons that catch the dim light.

I catch fractured glimpses of myself in the mirror as she moves around me. The transformation is unsettling.

It's not just the clothes.

It's who I look like. Someone older. Stranger. A Victorian gentleman who'd write angry letters to The Times about the state of the railways.

She slides a pair of polished black boots toward me. My size. How?

I slip them on, the leather stiff and unyielding. The question gnaws again—*how do they know so much about me?*

I stand there, fully dressed, barely recognising the reflection. The man in the mirror is someone else entirely. Not Andy Giles, the overworked teacher. Someone hollowed out and remade.

The staff member places a wooden box on a side table. Engraved on its lid: *13.*

She opens it slowly, almost reverently. Inside lies a mask—the stark, haunting visage of Japanese Noh theatre, all sharp angles and frozen rage.

"This is your mask," she says quietly, running her fingers over its carved, angular features. "Mask 13 is yours now. Hannya."

I step closer. The mask's cold metallic eyes stare back, mocking. Twisted horns curl upward, giving it a sinister, otherworldly edge—something ripped from a fever dream. My throat tightens, but I swallow the questions. I already know she'll offer no answers.

This is it. This is who I am now, at least for tonight.

She hands me the mask. I brush my fingers over its jagged edges, the wood smooth yet unnervingly alive under my touch. No turning back now.

I lift the mask, pressing it to my face. The leather straps bite into my temples as she secures them. The moment it's fixed, I release a breath I hadn't realised I was holding. Strangely, it feels comforting, like armour.

I'm no longer Andy Giles, the history teacher who forgets parents' names at school events.

I'm 13. Hannya.

***

The concierge leads me out of the fitting room and down the main hallway. The plush crimson rug muffles our footsteps, and I tug at the jacket around my waist, shifting uncomfortably. The stiff, confining fabric feels like I'm being stitched into an identity I never chose—some Victorian gentleman's hand-me-downs. The trousers pinch at my thighs, forcing me to walk with my legs slightly apart like an agitated cowboy who's forgotten his horse.

At least the mask fits. The leather straps cradle the back of my head, distributing the weight evenly, and I can breathe easily through the wide nostril holes. The narrow eye slits create a tunnelled view of the world, but oddly, the limited vision dulls the chaos around me, like blinkers on a nervous racehorse. It encases my head completely, moulding over my jaw and chin, but stops just above my lips, leaving only my mouth exposed.

"The celebration awaits, Hannya," the woman says, pushing open a set of heavy wooden doors to reveal a vast, vaulted hall.

Chandeliers smothered in crystal hang from the ceiling, scattering prismatic light across the room. The walls are gilded with intricate, swirling patterns that shimmer under the glow of candlelit sconces, their restless flames casting shadows that writhe like living things. The space is breath-taking, decadent in a way that feels almost obscene.

I step forward, my boots striking the polished wood floor with a confidence I don't recognise. Masked figures drift past, their costumes as absurdly opulent as mine. Men in high-collared tailcoats and boots polished to a military shine. Women in corseted gowns that cinch their waists to waspish proportions, skirts billowing like sails in the candlelit draft.

My palms sweat inside my gloves, nerves humming as I venture deeper into the hall. I glance back, but the staff member who led me here has vanished. Alone. I scan the crowd for the cigar man's palm-print shirt or that lazy smirk, but every face is a stranger—grotesque creature masks, beaked Venetian disguises, porcelain doll smiles frozen in permanent glee.

A waiter materialises beside me, silver tray balanced on his palm.

"Bienvenue, monsieur," he murmurs, bowing slightly.

I nod and take a champagne flute, watching him dissolve into the crowd. I drain the glass in two gulps and grab another from a second passing waiter. Not bad, this free booze.

I drift through the room, an intruder at a dreamlike masquerade, the mask's horns weighing heavier with every step.

The string quartet in the corner plays something bright and intricate. Paganini, I think. The music is sharp, fast, the notes skittering like blades across ice, like the soundtrack to something that could turn violent at any moment.

Then I see *her*.

She's draped across a plush velvet sofa, layers of sheer fabric billowing around her. A cocktail glass dangles from her fingers, half-empty, the other hand propped on the armrest as she surveys the crowd with the bored elegance of a cat. Her mask is a pale, theatrical face. Delicate feminine features, lips painted blood-red, bold black lines framing eyes that glitter behind the slits. Golden hair spills from beneath the mask's edges, catching the chandelier light like molten honey.

She looks my way. Catches me staring.

I glance down into my half-empty glass, considering slipping into the crowd. But before I can move, her voice slices through the chatter and music.

"Hey, devil-boy!"

I freeze.

She crooks a finger, beckoning. At least two dozen masked heads swivel toward me. They can't see my expression, but it feels like their eyes pierce straight through the Hannya mask, into my rattled nerves.

I can't do this.

Pivoting sharply, I march back toward the doors, downing the rest of my champagne in one gulp. *Bad idea. Bad, bad idea.*

In the few minutes since I arrived, the hall has swollen with bodies. Voices and laughter rise into a feverish symphony, the air thick with perfume and sweat. I elbow through the crowd, but it's like wading through tar.

A firm hand lands on my shoulder.

I freeze. Turn. Ready to shove off whoever it is.

"Hannya. You made it."

It's *him*.

And suddenly, part of me doesn't want to leave anymore.

He leans in, his breath warm and whiskey-scented against my ear. "You finally have a name for yourself."

Before I can reply, he notices my empty glass and throws his arms wide, bellowing: "This monsieur's glass is empty! What an atrocity! Fill it up at once!"

His thunderous voice turns heads. In seconds, a fresh glass appears in my hand. He adjusts his own mask. It's far more discreet than mine. A simple cream-coloured face, sculpted like weathered clay, textured curls framing the forehead, a carved beard along the jawline. His gaze meets mine through the narrow slits, sharp and assessing.

"You can call me Brazen."

I hesitate for only a second before echoing it back, testing the weight of the name. "Brazen."

He raises his glass, a mischievous glint in his eyes. We down our drinks together as if sealing some unspoken pact.

Masked faces begin to crowd around, hands outstretched, eager to make introductions. It's an odd sort of welcome, like being mobbed by overly friendly ghosts. But I remind myself: *It's just one night. Play the game.*

"Good evening... Pleasure to meet you... Glad to be here."

I shake one gloved hand after another. No real names. No details. Just a parade of masks—some snarling, some serene—each person projecting a persona while hiding the rest. The energy's oddly familiar, like those nights at Brazen's Mayfair haunt. No pressure to be *Andy Giles*, just the freedom to vanish into a role.

A towering figure looms into view, shoulders straining the frills of his shirt like a rugby prop in a pantomime costume. His mask sports a hooked nose that nearly jabs my eye.

"Finally got a replacement for H, eh?" His voice booms. "Hasn't felt right with just ninety-nine of us, y'know?"

A cold thought slips through: *Who was the previous Hannya? Why'd they leave?*

He crushes my hand in his grip. "Name's Panta. Good to meet ya."

I flex my fingers, wincing. "H as in Hannya?"

Panta chuckles, giving my shoulder a slap that nearly dislocates it. "Yeah. Full name's a mouthful. H's snappier."

"Fair enough. Got a nice ring to it," I say, pulse steadying as I lean into the madness.

Another figure bulldozes through the crowd. His mask mirrors Panta's but is painted in bold shades of blue and red, a stark contrast to Panta's black and gold.

"What's all this, then?" He scans the group before zeroing in on me. "Oh, bloody hell. So Hannya's finally got a replacement! Been two months since... Well, never mind that." He grins, clapping my shoulder hard enough to knock the wind out of me. "Good to have the full hundred back."

I force a smile, nodding like I'm in on the joke. *Replacement?* Doesn't matter. Tonight's for swallowing questions, not asking them.

"Name's Lóne," he announces, extending a hand for another knuckle-crunching shake. When he lets go, I resist the urge to check if my fingers are still attached.

"Panta, Lóne," I mutter, rolling the names around. Then it clicks. "Ah—Pantalóne. Commedia dell'arte?"

They exchange a confused glance, then look back at me, amusement flickering behind their masks.

"Sure, yeah," Panta jeers, his hooked nose quivering with mock seriousness. "Previous guy was switched on too. Proper genius, he was. Guess they picked right this time!"

"Then what're we standing around for?" Lóne roars, raising his glass so violently champagne sloshes onto his sleeve. "Let's get Hannya some proper welcome drinks! *Proper* ones!"

A cheer rises around us, glasses clinking like a wind chime in a hurricane as more guests press in, their masked faces tilting to scrutinise the "new Hannya." Brazen leads me towards a long, plush sofa upholstered in emerald velvet—the kind that begs you to sink into it and never resurface. He gestures for me to sit. A waiter in a black tailcoat hovers nearby, silent as a gargoyle, tray balanced on his fingertips.

I perch on the edge of the cushion, hyperaware of the masked faces forming a semi-circle around us—*vultures at a feast*.

"Alright," Brazen drawls, snapping his fingers at the waiter. "Bring us a bottle of tequila, three reds, and..." His eyes flick to the champagne bottle in the waiter's hands, half-hidden under a linen napkin. "...might as well toss that one in, too. Waste not, eh?"

Before the waiter can respond, Lóne snatches the champagne bottle straight off the tray, then collapses onto the sofa beside me, twisting the cork out with his teeth. Two women settle down next to him, their wide gowns billowing like sails in a storm, forcing the rest of us into a tight, sweat-scented circle.

I glance at Brazen, who's leaning back, feet propped on the low table, scuffing the polished wood with his boots.

"Do you always have people following you around like this?" I ask, masking my genuine curiosity behind a smirk. "You must be some kind of Z-list celebrity."

Brazen lets out a short, barking laugh, his eyes glinting behind the cream-coloured mask. "They're not here for me, mate. They're here for *you*. I'm just a fat old sod along for the ride." He gestures around at the crowded room, his voice dropping to a conspiratorial growl. "Go on, H. Take it all in. You're the main event."

With a casual flick of his wrist, he drops several small bags of coke onto the coffee table as if they're Ferrero Rocher at a diplomatic function. He opens one and lines up a hit with surgical precision, nodding towards me in invitation.

I hesitate. Grace's face flickers. Tom's text burns. But only for a moment. No one bats an eyelid. Here, it seems, anything goes. Leaning forward, I rip open a bag with my teeth and start lining up the powder, my hands moving as if on autopilot.

One line. Two.

Suddenly, the world snaps into sharp focus—the chandeliers blazing like miniature suns, every note of the string quartet crisp as shattered glass. I'm more than present, I'm *alive*, every nerve singing like a live wire.

I lean toward Brazen, words tumbling out like I've rehearsed them in some hidden corner of my skull. "Time is a river of passing events, and strong is its current. And right now, this current's damn good!"

A cheer erupts. Laughter swells, the room a pub choir on last orders.

"This guy's quoting Marcus Aurelius!" someone shouts, glass aloft.

"Next he'll be slagging off Pliny in the loos!" another shouts, sparking more laughs.

I glance right. The golden-haired woman lounges opposite, chatting up a gaggle of other guests. Her glass tilts toward the ceiling, eyes bright as she toasts the chaos.

"Get it down ya, H!" Lóne sloshes champagne into my glass till it threatens to spill.

I nod at his empty hand. "Not joining?"

He grins, hefting the bottle. "I'll drink straight from the bottle, mate."

We clink—glass to bottleneck—and I skull mine, the fizz burning sweet. Lóne chugs, Adam's apple bobbing like a buoy in a storm. I grab the bottle, refill, drain it again. My skull hums.

ALEX MURA

Lóne wallops my back hard enough to cough up a lung.
"Knew you'd fit right in, H!"

I grin, swiping champagne off my chin.

Christ. I might actually fit here.

6

Six shots of tequila. Two oversized glasses of red. At least, I think that's what I've had. I've lost count. The world blurs around me, masked faces smearing into formless shapes that sway like I'm rocking on the deck of a storm-tossed ship.

One moment, my jacket's on. The next, it's gone and my shirt's flapping open. I blink hard. Flashes of skin. Nude bodies writhing like eels on the Persian rug. Brazen's in the thick of it, cackling, his body half-lost in a sea of grasping hands and eager mouths, each limb taken in by a new tide of flesh.

Left, right—bodies everywhere I look. Shagging on mahogany coffee tables, up against marble columns, definitely behind the velvet curtains. Guess this is Brazen's idea of *freedom*.

Fragmented scenes flicker—slender hands kneading my shoulders, nails raking my chest. Blackout. A drinking game. Brazen slams his shot. We follow like lemmings. I'm shitfaced.

I'm teetering on blackout's edge when a soft hand grabs mine. I turn, vision swimming. *Her*. Mask porcelain-pale, golden hair tumbling over bare shoulders.

"Are you... an angel?" I mumble, words sloshing out.

She giggles, and my eyelids judder, refusing to commit to consciousness.

"Suppose I am," she says, voice laced with mischief. "Brazen said you were in a fragile state, so I thought I'd babysit. Although—" She hiccups. " —I'm pretty wasted too. Name's Red."

"N... nice to meet you, Red,"

"Enjoying your first night here?"

"Can't complain about free booze."

"Yeah, the perks here are great. Ralph's has everything the heart desires. Anything else?"

The question hangs. Flashes of hands, lips, sweat. *How far did I—?*

"Relax," she cuts in, reading my panic. "You didn't wet yourself. Just sat there like a coma patient. Had to shoo the vultures off before they pecked you clean."

She lurches up, nearly face-planting the coffee table, then flaps her arms in a drunken pantomime of scaring crows.

I manage a weak chuckle, scrubbing a hand over my face. "That's embarrassing. I shouldn't have drunk so much. Did I... do anything stupid?"

"Not at all. Honestly, I think the best way to see someone's true nature is to get them drunk. Most first-timers here just go wild—snogging everyone they see, showing their worst. But you? You poured drinks for others before yourself. You drank a lot, sure, but never crossed any lines. Respectable really."

She fishes a cigarette out from her cleavage, pressing it between her red-stained lips. She lights it, the flame illuminating her smirk.

"So, how long have you been coming here?" I ask, toeing the line of the "no personal questions" rule.

She inhales deeply, the cigarette's glow painting her mask in hellish shadows. "Seven months. Give or take." Her voice dips, theatrical. "Best. Decision. Ever."

"What made you join?"

"The thrill," she purrs. "An escape from daily life. To be someone else for a bit."

"Same," I admit, locking eyes with her, wondering what she sees in me.

She leans back, exhaling smoke, her voice dipping lower. "It can be overwhelming at first. But you get used to it... once you *let go*."

"So there's more to this place than free drinks and—" I gesture vaguely at the Persian rug debauchery.

"And shagging?" She finishes, arching a brow. "Loads more. But—" Her fingers skate up my arm, leaving goosebumps. "—not my job to spoil it. Come next month. Then you'll see. Just keep an open mind, Hannya."

I nod, half-dreading, half-craving it. "*If* I come."

Her eyes narrow to slits, as though I've just committed a crime. "You better. Can't miss a celebration. Otherwise, you'll be breaking the rules." She leans in, her voice dropping to a stage whisper that tickles my ear. "Plus, I'll be a *very* unhappy bunny. And you don't want that, do you?"

I chuckle, her mock severity sending a reckless thrill through my veins. "Alright, alright! If it's that important to you, I'll come."

Desperate to lighten the mood, I pivot clumsily. "Right, new topic. What's your favourite food?"

She arches a sculpted brow, the mask tilting. "*No personal questions*, mister. Rules are rules."

"Ah, right," I say, feigning innocence before flashing a roguish grin. "How's this, then? Name any food."

"Just... *any* food?" she repeats, sceptical, swirling her wine like she's deciphering a riddle.

"Yeah," I say, leaning back.

She taps a finger against her lips—stained red as her name—before smirking. "Lasagna."

I bark a laugh. "Lasagna? What are you, Garfield?"

We both break into laughter, the kind that's a little too loud, a little too free. Reaching for the half-empty bottle of red wine, our fingers brush. Hers lingers against mine, warm and deliberate, and for a heartbeat, there's a spark. A jolt of static that prickles beneath the Hannya mask.

"Want a top-up?" I ask, hoisting the bottle higher, my voice steadier than my hands.

She leans back against the sofa, her golden hair fanning out like a halo against the emerald velvet. Her eyes, bright behind the pale mask, lock onto mine as I pour. "Sure you haven't hit your limit, H?"

I grin, sloshing wine into her glass with a recklessness I'd never dare sober. "No plans tomorrow. And..." I let the smirk widen. "...I'm having a rather pleasant time."

"Me too," she murmurs, swirling the wine, watching the dark liquid cling to the glass. "Let's make the most of it. Won't see you again till next month's celebration."

An unexpected pang twists in my chest. "Better not forget about me," I say, the words slipping out raw, tinged with a desperation that surprises me.

"How could I forget a handsome face like yours?" she teases, her gaze drifting to the Hannya mask's grotesque curves.

"Oh, you like these horns?" I tease, brushing a thumb over the lacquered ridges, the mask's snarl cold under my touch.

"And the *teeth*," she purrs, reaching up to trace the mask's jagged edge. Her fingertip skims the corner of my lip, the touch featherlight but electric. My breath hitches. "You really are a peculiar boy, H."

"Peculiar how?" I ask, pulse thrumming in my ears, eyes searching hers through the mask's narrow slits.

She studies me, her stare playful yet piercing—a predator toying with prey. "I wonder what you're hiding. Or maybe... what you're ashamed of."

The words hang, sharp as a blade. My throat tightens. "What do you mean?"

But her smirk says she's already cracked me open.

"You're putting on a persona," Red says, eyes glinting. "The quiet, reserved guy. But I don't think that's really you. Out there, maybe. But here..." She pauses, watching me with a knowing smirk. "I think there's more. You need to *let go*."

My laugh comes out shriller than intended. "I *am* letting myself go. I've been drinking all night and... and talking to you." It sounds pathetic, even to me.

"That's not letting go." She leans closer. "Letting go's doing what terrifies you. Like, singing off-key. That sort of thing."

"I want to dance." The words slip out before I can stop them.

She blinks, then a grin breaks across her face. "Dance, huh?" she says, as though testing the idea. "Didn't expect that, but I'm game."

Tiny embers scatter as she flicks her cigarette to the floor and stands, hand extended, her eyes daring me. "Let's see what you've got, H."

I eye her palm—doubt warring with liquid courage—then grab it. She yanks me up and drags me to the hall's heart. The crowd parts. Curious gazes follow our trail.

"Here?" I hiccup.

"Here." She presses close, hips rolling. "You wanted to let go, right?"

The quartet shifts to a slow, romantic number, strings swelling like a heartbeat. I close my eyes, let the music seep into my bones. My movements start stiff, self-consciousness clawing at me, but gradually it melts. Shoulders drop. Steps grow bolder. For the first time in years, I'm *unbound*.

Red spins beside me, skirts whispering against my legs, her voice harmonising with the violins. Around us, masked faces watch—some smirking, others nodding approval, but no one sneers. No one here judges. Her laughter bubbles up, bright and contagious, eroding the last shard of my restraint.

"You know," she says, twirling close until her mask nearly brushes mine, "you're the first person I've seen dance here. People fuck, fight, snort... but never *dance*."

"That's because they don't know what they're missing," I say, the boldness foreign on my tongue.

The music crests. She grabs my hands, steering me into a waltz that feels ours alone. The room blurs, chandeliers smudging into stars, her hair a gold streak in the haze. No rules. No guilt. Just the thrum of the cello and her hip grazing mine.

She pulls me closer, breath hot on my neck, chest flush against me. Her mask rests on my shoulder as we sway. Two figures orbiting the hall's centre. Another couple joins. Then another. Soon, the whole room pulses like a single organism.

For a heartbeat, we're not strangers. Just bodies suspended. No past, no tomorrow. *This* is freedom.

"Kiss me," she whispers, lips grazing my ear, the words dissolving into the music.

A jolt of lightning races through me. This is the abandon I craved, but my body locks, refusing to bridge that final inch. She feels it, arms cinching tighter, fingers mapping the tension in my shoulders.

"She doesn't deserve you," she murmurs, words hushed as a confessional secret.

My eyes fly open. The warmth in my veins chills. *How does she—?*

"Whoever she is," she breathes, lips a hair's breadth from mine, "she doesn't deserve this." Her thumb brushes my jaw. "Let yourself be free, H."

The words unshackle something. The music swells, cellos throbbing low. I surrender, closing the gap—lips meeting, spinning, coiled like ivy. Her mouth is soft, *sweet*, the kiss erasing London, Ralph's, my own name.

Lost, I trip on her skirt's hem, silk snagging under my boot. We crash down in a tangle, her laughter hot against my throat as we sprawl on the floor. For a suspended moment, we just breathe, ribcages synced, giggles spilling between us. The hall whirls on, bodies grinding, masks leering. But here, we're marooned in our own pocket of time.

My hands drift to her waist, savouring the heat of her through the silk. She leans down, and kisses me again. A stolen slice of heaven, ours alone.

Before long, we retreat to the sofa. Red settles close and we each do a line. The powder hits fast, igniting that instant buzz, propelling the night forward.

She nudges me, jerking her chin toward two figures hogging the room's attention. "Look at those knuckleheads," she says, tone dry.

Panta and Lóne are sprawled in the center of the floor, wrestling like jacked schoolboys overdosing on testosterone. A ring of hyena-laughing spectators eggs them on, loving every grunt and graceless slam.

"What's their deal?" I ask, biting back a snort as Panta flips Lóne, only for Lóne to rebound and tackle him, launching them back into a tangle of limbs and grunts.

"Monthly dick-measuring ritual," Red says, rolling her eyes. "Every month, they come up with some ridiculous contest. Panta swears he's clever, Lóne thinks he's stronger. Spoiler: neither of them is exactly a mastermind."

I grin as Lóne finally pins Panta, flexing for cheers. "I don't know... They seem to have everyone else convinced."

Red scoffs, giving me a wry smile. "It's just noise. They'll be doing shots arm-in-arm by midnight. Still, can't say I'd mind seeing them batter each other for real."

My gaze shifts to the tall, graceful figure lingering just beyond the brawl, watching with icy amusement. She shrugs off her gown, revealing a lacy slip that glides around her legs, emphasising each step as she circles the chaos like she's directing the whole show.

"What about her?" I tilt my head. "Part of the monthly circus?"

Red's lips twitch. "That's Columbina. She's not part of it—she orchestrates it. Acts like royalty. Expects everyone to trail after her like Panta and Lóne over there." She nods at Panta and Lóne, now slumped and knackered, while Columbina observes like a bored empress.

I study Columbina's poise against the raucous scene. "So, what's her deal? Is she like royalty?"

"Only in her own head," Red mutters. "She rubs me the wrong way. Always got her nose in the air, acting like she's special. Truth is, she's no different from the rest of us. She just puts on a better show."

I catch the edge in her voice. "Sounds like there's some history there."

Red drains her glass, glare fixed ahead. "She plays the role well, I'll give her that. But it's all a front. No one's *that* flawless—not even here."

Columbina weaves through the crowd like a dark current, bending the room's gravity. Her pearl-crusted mask glints, but it's the raven feathers arching around it that snare the eye, sharp as crown thorns.

She pauses, her eyes sweeping over the room before landing on mine. A faint smile flickers in my direction, pinning me in place a moment too long. The room seems to quieten. Then, when she looks away, the spell shatters. Noise floods back, louder, sharper.

"She's got them eating out of her hand," I murmur, watching the way Panta and Lóne's eyes track her every move like she's the axis they spin around.

"She always does," Red replies, her voice edged with something between disdain and envy. "They're her guard dogs. All drool and devotion. Pathetic, really."

I glance at Red, noting the tension in her jaw. She catches my look and shrugs, her smile thin and knowing. "But you'll see soon enough. The longer you're here, the more you start seeing the cracks in everyone's masks."

"So, everyone's hiding something?"

"Exactly. And once you spot it, you can't unsee it."

Her words linger as I scan the room again. A dizzying mix of decadence and delusion. Couples claw at each other in dimly lit corners. Groups huddle around low tables, laughter slicing through the clink of glasses. A trio debates near a fireplace, while others slump into sofas, bare bodies dissolving into one another. It's a dance of personas, none of them entirely real, all of them beautifully rehearsed.

My eyes land on Brazen, slouched in a velvet armchair, head lolled back, mouth slightly open. He's out cold. A half-finished drink dangles from his fingers, threatening to spill. Nearby, a hushed cluster of guests keeps glancing his way, as if waiting for him to snap awake and reclaim the room. Even unconscious, he radiates a magnetism.

Red huffs a laugh. "Poor Brazen. Been scrambling to keep pace with you all night."

I snort. "Him keeping up with *me*?"

She grins, swirling her wine. "Wanted to set the tone for you. Make sure you... *let loose*. Didn't expect you to outlast him. Brazen's not usually the one face-down."

I glance at his slumped form. "All those rounds he shoved at me. That wasn't just him showing off?"

"Oh, he's a showman for sure," she says, eyes glinting. "But he was also sizing you up. Seeing how much you'd let yourself slip."

It makes sense. The drinks, the chaos, the indulgence. It's all a test to see how far I'd bend.

Red sips, watching me. "You lasted longer than most, though. I'll give you that."

I grin. "And what does that say about me?"

"I don't know yet. But I'd like to find out."

I suddenly don't feel like an outsider anymore.

My gaze roams the room, soaking in the sweat-slicked glamour, the jagged laughter. Everything's softer at the edges, the coke and drinks blurring the lines. Candlelight licks the walls, shadows swaying, shrinking the cavernous room to something almost private.

Red leans in, her arm warm against mine.

"It's strange, isn't it?" I murmur. "All of us here, hiding behind masks, pretending to be someone else, yet feeling somehow... freer."

She studies me. "It's a paradox, really. We come here to escape, to step into a different skin, but in the end, we're revealing things we'd never admit outside these walls. Strange or not, at least it's honest."

I nod. It's a raw honesty, almost uncomfortable, yet a freedom I didn't realise I'd been craving. A chance to leave myself behind, even if just for a night.

A roar of laughter erupts from the card table. Panta and Lóne, still flushed from their wrestling match, slam down their hands with theatrical bravado, treating the game like a bloodsport. Columbina stands nearby, one hand resting on her hip, her feathered mask casting jagged shadows. Guests crowd around, their interest sharpened to the kind of intensity that makes the game seem like a matter of life or death.

"Think we should join them?" I nod toward the commotion.

Red tilts her head, considering, then shakes it. "Nah. Let them have their game. We've got our own little corner here." She leans back into the sofa, legs stretching out. "Besides, I'd rather just talk. Been a shitty week."

There's something grounding about her honesty. We sink into the worn velvet cushions, letting the chaos dull to a distant murmur, replaced by a silence that feels earned.

"So," she says, breaking the quiet. "if you could ask me anything—one thing you're dying to know—what would it be?"

I hesitate. This place thrives on mystery and secrets, yet she's offering a glimpse behind her mask. I'm tempted to ask about the scars on her wrists, but that's a topic for another time.

Finally, I lean closer. "Why do you keep coming back?"

She swirls her wine "Couldn't have answered that yesterday." A slow sip. "But now? Maybe. If you stick around long enough."

She lifts her glass. I clink mine against it.

"By the way, what time is it?" I ask. "I should get going soon."

She shrugs, scanning the room. "No idea—probably around one? No clocks here, so it's anyone's guess. What's the rush? Party's not over until the host says so."

I manage a small laugh, half-amused, half in disbelief. "Sounds like the host runs a tight ship."

"Careful, mister," she teases, tapping my wrist lightly like a playful warning as she takes a slow sip.

The thought *jolts* me, sharp as an ice bath. I should've been home hours ago. Grace is likely pacing by now, texts piling up, calls ignored. The moment I step outside, reality will come crashing back—back to her, to responsibility, to the version of myself I've tried to shed tonight.

I try to stand, but the second I shift, a wave of dizziness slams into me, dragging me back onto the sofa. This place clings like gravity.

Red chuckles, her fingers brushing mine with soft insistence. "Stay," she murmurs. *"Please."*

My face flushes, mind torn between duty and desire, until one wins.

Just a little longer. One more step into this strange, heady world.

"Okay," I whisper in soft surrender.

7

After all that, Grace didn't even ask why I rolled in late. No texts demanding answers, no sidelong glance when I stumbled through the door. Just a single message, timed hours before I'd surfaced: *Heading to bed. Leftovers in the fridge.*

Now, it's business as usual. She paces through the kitchen, phone in one hand, apple in the other, eyes welded to her screen. I watch from the doorway—*bite, chew, fridge door yanked open, milk grabbed*—every movement a cog in her clockwork routine. Efficiency over intimacy.

Finally, she glances up. "Tea?" Flat. A checkbox ticked.

"Sure." I sink into my usual stool at the kitchen island, watching her pour the boiling water, set the teabags, reach for the milk, all without ever putting the phone down. No *Where were you?* No *You alright?* Of course not. In her world, Andy Giles does nothing unexpected. Safe. Predictable. *Dull.*

And maybe she was right. Until last night.

A strange, petty anger simmers. I want to say something—anything—just to break her focus, to see if I can pull her out of autopilot. But I don't even know where to start.

"What's got you so locked in?" I ask, craving *any* flicker I exist beyond her periphery.

"Monday." She sighs, setting the mug down in front of me a little too hard, just enough for the liquid to ripple. Not enough to be obvious. But I notice. "Need to stay ahead."

I cradle the tea, bitterness seeping into my throat. "Working weekends, though?"

She shrugs. "My work doesn't exactly follow a nine-to-five schedule. Besides, you know I enjoy staying busy."

There's something loaded in the way she says it. Grace, always driven, always in motion, her schedule ironclad.

"Whatever you say, darling." I sip my tea, letting the warmth run through me. But Ralph's still lingers in the back of my mind. This kitchen, this Saturday morning routine—it all feels thin. A flimsy layer of plaster masking something deeper, something I could tear right through if I wanted to.

"What about you?" she asks, almost as an afterthought. "Any big plans today?"

I shrug, feeling last night's recklessness settling in like a hangover. "No, just the usual. Might go for a run."

"Good. You look like you could use it." Her smirk's all wifely teasing, but her eyes stay cold. I'm a footnote in her morning checklist.

I open my mouth to speak, but hesitate, the words catching in my throat—*I was at a member's club last night. A place where no one asks questions. Where I have a new name, a new face. Where I danced with a woman to my heart's content.*

I could say it. Crack this façade wide open.

Instead, I sip my tea, letting the pull of routine—of predictability—settle over me again, but it does nothing to fill the hollow space expanding inside. Grace is back on her phone, thumbs tapping at the speed of light. She's miles away, even though I'm right here.

Her work holds more fascination than her husband on a Saturday morning.

I glance out the window. A Eurasian Jay hops along the fence, oblivious to the silence on the other side of the glass. My thoughts drift back to Ralph's. Last night felt real. This morning? *This* feels like a dream.

I can't decide which is worse.

"You're quiet," Grace says abruptly, eyes still glued to her mobile.

The words catch me off guard. "Am I?"

"Mhm." This time, she glances up, brow creased. "I mean, you're usually quiet, but today, even more so."

There's a flicker of curiosity, but it feels clinical, like she's studying me rather than actually caring.

I force a thin smile. "Just tired. Late night."

She arches an eyebrow, lips twitching into a smirk. "*Late?* Didn't realise you had it in you."

The teasing tone doesn't bother me, but the undertone of disbelief does. Like she's already decided who I am, boxed me up neatly as the quiet, dependable husband.

I want to tell her she doesn't know the half of it. That I saw a world last night she couldn't even begin to comprehend. That I danced like a man who had forgotten himself, that I kissed a woman whose name wasn't mine to know.

But the words stick in my throat.

Instead, I offer a sheepish grin. "Maybe I'm full of surprises."

She chuckles, a short, dismissive sound. "Maybe. Thought we were past the surprise stage."

It stings, like what she really means is: *I know exactly who you are. You don't surprise me anymore.*

I clear my throat, nodding at her phone. "When's your next meeting?"

"Ten minutes," she taps the screen, voice flat. "Just a briefing, but it'll probably drag." Then, as if remembering a spousal duty, she adds, "you should go for that run. Clear your head."

There it is again, that sugared, condescending tone she uses when *handling* me. Like I'm a clockwork mechanism needing adjustment, a hinge squeaking out of rhythm. The urge to hurl my mug against the wall flares—*let ceramic shards scatter, force her to see the mess.*

Instead, I choke it down with the last sip of tea.

"Yeah," I say. "Maybe I will."

"Good." She leans in, brushing a ghost of a kiss against my cheek, wifely duty ticked. By the time I inhale, she's already halfway down the hall, feet tapping toward her home office.

The door clicks shut. I'm left in the hollowed-out silence of the kitchen, staring at her vacant chair.

Outside, the jay flits along the fence. No deadlines. No spreadsheets tethering it. Just wings and instinct. I track it until it disappears into the oak's skeletal branches. The jealousy hits then, sudden and vicious, my fist clenching around nothing.

***

The crisp air bites at my lungs as I hammer the pavement, legs burning, thoughts racing. I push harder, faster, trying to outrun the ghost of last night.

But Red lingers—her touch, her laughter, the whisper of her breath against my skin. The thrill of almost. It wasn't just the alcohol or the coke. It was the way she looked at me, like she saw something beneath the mask, something even I wasn't sure of yet.

I press on, picking up speed. Breath saws through my throat, jagged and hot.

Columbina flashes in my mind. The sweep of black feathers, the steel-grey eyes behind the mask, the way she moved through the crowd like she owned it. The memory of her stare ignites a gnawing hunger—to be *seen*, not just scanned.

The path ahead blurs—then snaps into focus.

A figure. Motionless. Watching.

Faceless. *Wrong*.

A jolt—sobriety slams into me.

I had a great time.

I grit my teeth, fists clenched. My pace quickens. Three-quarter sprint. Breath ragged. Muscles screaming. I race past where the figure stood.

But he's ahead again, further down the path.

Waiting.

Grace's voice invades, honeyed and warm—not for me. For him.

Tom.

A name lighting up her screen. A casual message. The kind you send when there's already a familiarity between you.

Does she see him every day? At work, slipping into quiet corners to laugh over inside jokes I'll never understand? Are her meetings really with clients, or is she somewhere else, phone in hand, texting him like he's a priority?

Has she been slipping away while I wasn't looking? Or have I just not wanted to see it?

The thoughts needle deeper, digging under my skin. I push harder. Full sprint now. Legs pumping. Arms swinging. Breath ripping through me in sharp bursts.

The figure materialises again.

A silhouette, ink-black and motionless.

Watching.

That private smile she'd aimed at her mobile this morning.

Not at me.

Not for months.

Tom.

Jealousy curdles in my gut.

I've tried to decode her screen. Surreptitious glances, casual leans over her shoulder. But she's all passcodes and quick swipes. That phone's a vault.

It wasn't always like this.

Once, we'd sprawl on the sofa, her toes tucked under my thigh, laughing at *nothing*.

Once, her eyes didn't glaze over when I spoke.

Once, she didn't flinch when I touched her.

Or did she? Was I just too bloody dense to notice?

My calves scream as I race toward an imaginary finish line. Faster. *Harder*.

But the figure doesn't flinch.

Just stands.

Waiting.

As if time itself bends to him.

His shadow stretches, grotesque and serpentine, lashing me toward truths I've dodged for years.

Memories of Ralph's surge. Masks glinting like lies, bass throbbing in my ribs, the coke-sharp thrill of being no one. There, I wasn't Andy Giles, the failed historian, dutiful husband, hollow man. I was *alive*.

But here—

Here, I'm choking on mortgage payments and marking essays.

Here, I'm the man who buys daffodils from the local supermarket to fill the silence.

Here, I'm sprinting from a name.

Tom.

It whispers in my skull like a splinter of glass I can't dig out. I see it glowing on her screen, drawing her in: *I had a great time.*

I dig deeper, legs hammering into overdrive—each stride a burst of rage, fear, frustration. But no matter how hard I push, he's still there. Just ahead. Just out of reach.

My vision blurs.

ALEX MURA

I crash past trees, strollers, joggers. Past the edge of sanity. But the park sprawls endlessly, and no matter how far I run, he's there. Just ahead. Just out of reach. Taunting.

The knot in my chest cinches tighter. Strides falter. Breath hitches. Muscles revolt. Sweat slicks my back, my face, stinging in the cold air—and still, he waits.

8

The first week since Ralph's passes in the usual blur of routine.

Exam season looms, and my days turn into an endless cycle of handing out revision prep, arranging group work—anything to avoid *actual* teaching. The kids, jittery with summer's approach, tally the days.

So do I.

But not for the same reason.

At first, I tried drowning in work, clawing back the old me, the teacher who once buzzed at sparking curiosity. Back when I gave a shit. I used to devour history books for fun, fall down rabbit holes just because.

I'd even daydream about fieldwork. Dusty ruins, interviews with elders, unearthing stories buried by time. Maybe publish something. *Proper* academia.

But that was before I realised that the longer you stay in a job, the harder it is to leave. Before I told myself it was too late to be anything but Mr. Giles.

So, I stay.

I go through the motions.

Until Ralph's.

The thought worms in: *What's next? More champagne-soaked parties? Will Red be there waiting for me?* I imagine her fingers skating up my arm, that low purr—*You'd better come back.*

A soft throat-clearing yanks me back.

"Andy, please, take a seat."

I blink. Headmaster's office. Oak-panelled walls amber in the afternoon light, the stench of leather polish and varnish violating my nostrils.

For years, I imagined sitting here would feel like a victory lap. Instead, it's more like waiting for a sentence to be handed down.

The headmaster leans forward, hands folded neatly on the polished desk. "I'll get right to the point. Your recent work has been exemplary. The mock exam results are the highest we've seen in years. Your students have excelled, and I'd say that's largely due to your dedication."

I nod, offering a polite, distant smile. The praise feels muffled, like distant applause through a wall.

He continues. "Because of this, we're increasing your salary to the M5 band, effective next month—£44,615."

Then he pauses. A *rehearsed* pause. The kind that tells me there's more.

"We'd also like you to mentor some of the junior teachers. Offer them guidance, share the expertise you've built here."

A raise. A promotion. The acknowledgment I've been chasing for years.

I know the words I'm supposed to say—*Thank you, I'm honoured, this means so much.* But the satisfaction doesn't come.

Instead, something cold and gnawing spreads through my chest.

£44,615.

It's not nothing, but it's not enough. Not in London. Not in our life. Grace earns triple. Her salary pays for our flat, our trips. These are her luxuries, not mine.

This raise? It won't change anything. Chump change.

And even if it did, would it matter.

Grace enters my mind. We've only had sex twice in the last six weeks. And even then, it was routine. A scheduled meeting rather than something we craved. When I have an urge, I take care of it myself. I imagine she does the same.

At Ralph's, there's none of that.

Red's touch still crackles in my memory—electric, alive. The antithesis of Grace's detached efficiency. At Ralph's, I don't perform. I *feel*.

The headmaster smiles, waiting. The mask clicks into place.

"Thank you," I say, smooth as a parent-teacher conference. "I'm grateful."

He drones on about "legacy" and "mentorship," but my mind floats elsewhere: Year 11's glazed eyes as I doled out worksheets like a factory line. The notepad in my desk drawer, its pages crammed with half-formed sketches of Ralph's—velvet booths, chandelier shards, Hannya's leering mask.

There, I'm not just a teacher. Not Grace's afterthought. At Ralph's, I'm *more*.

The headmaster's still talking, offering everything I thought I wanted—respect, stability, a pension bump. But why does it feel like a noose?

The corridor air feels thin as I trudge back to class. Fluorescent lights bleach the walls. My shoes clack too loud on the vinyl flooring. A Year 7 nods. I nod back, hollow.

Slumping at my desk, I stare at the notepad poking from the drawer—*Hannya's snarling features, the gilt-edged horns.*

Was that confidence ever mine? Or just a borrowed skin?

I rake a hand over my stubble. The classroom walls press closer, fluorescents buzzing like wasps. I need air.

When I get home, I realise it's no better. It carries the stench of roasted vegetables from whatever pre-planned meal Grace put together. Her voice carries from the lounge— "We'll finalise Thursday." A dial tone bleats.

I shrug off my coat, hang it by the door, but my focus snags on the kitchen. The suspicion gnawing at me all week hasn't dulled. If anything, it's burrowed deeper, barbed and insistent. My gaze flicks to the cupboard above the fridge. The little baggie hidden there hums like a coiled viper.

I glug a glass of water, but it does fuck-all for the crawling restlessness under my skin. Muscle memory takes over—hand rising, fingertips grazing the shelf's edge, retrieving the bag. Just seeing it sparks a low current in my ribs.

I tap out a line onto the counter, roll a fiver, lean in. One sharp snort, and the world snaps into hyperfocus. Veins alight. Chest constricting. Mind razor-edged.

I wipe the counter, stow the bag, rinse the cloth. My reflection glares back from the window—eyes wild, pupils blown, a greasy sheen already blooming on my forehead.

The buzz carries me to the lounge.

Grace is curled on the sofa, legs tucked, scrolling. The screen's blue wash hollows her face. She spares me a glance, a ghost of a smile.

"Hey."

"Hey," I echo, slouching in the doorway. "Fancy a wine?"

She hesitates, brow arched. "Wine? It's half-ten."

"It's Friday," I counter, grin tight. "One glass won't murder us."

A pause, then a shrug. "Go on, then."

I pour slow, watching the Merlot swirl—a grounding ritual. When I pass her glass, she finally flips her phone facedown.

A tiny victory. Pulse skittering.

"To us," I say, raising my drink.

"To us."

She sips, shoulders softening. We volley small talk—work, weekend, weather—but my focus hones on the phone. *Silent. Dark.*

I lean forward. "Remember the first bottle we shared? That awful red from the corner shop?"

Grace lets out a laugh. "God, that was terrible. How did we finish the whole thing?"

"We didn't have a choice. It was that or tap water."

She shakes her head, smiling. For a second, it feels real. Then the warmth evaporates. Her hand grazes the phone as she sets down her glass.

"Be right back," she says, rising. "Need the loo."

The second she's out of the room, I move.

Heart jackhammering, coke-steady hands flip the phone. The lock screen glows.

I punch in her PIN—our anniversary.

It unlocks.

Breath shallow, I scroll past family group chats. Stop.

Tom.

The name pulses on the screen.

I tap. The thread spills open.

Tom: Can't wait to see you again.
Grace: Me too. Let's make it happen soon.

A leaden nausea pools in my gut. I scroll.

Tom: That joke in the meeting—still cracking me up.
Grace: Told you I'm hilarious.
Tom: Beyond hilarious. You're brilliant.

FRAGMENTED

The coke sharpens it all.

This isn't corporate small talk.

Their rhythm's effortless. Familiar. A cadence we lost years ago.

Tom: Lunch Wednesday? Same place?

Grace: Can't wait. You bringing the charm, or should I?

I stare, dry-eyed.

No pretence. No professionalism.

This isn't innocent.

I should stop. Slide the phone back. Pretend.

But I don't.

Because this—this *rotten* clarity—is the first real thing I've felt in months.

I swipe up, messages blurring into a streak of in-jokes and coffee emojis. Each one a scalpel twist.

Then—a photo.

It's nothing, really, just a coffee cup and a notebook. But the caption chokes me:

Grace: Fuel for my favourite collaborator ;)

My stomach churns. Not because of what's in the photo, but because of what it means. This isn't just flirting, this is intimacy. Tom isn't some random name on her screen. He's part of her world. A world I've been shut out of.

The toilet flushes down the hall.

Shit.

Panic razors through the coke haze. I fumble to lock the screen, fingers slipping, nearly dropping the phone before slapping it facedown as Grace re-enters.

Her brow knots. "What're you doing?"

A choked laugh escapes. "Just waiting." I clutch my wine, knuckles white. "Thought you got lost."

Her eyes stay on me. Then a shrug as she sinks onto the sofa. "In my own flat? Unlikely."

She sips her wine, but the phone stays between us like a landmine.

I gulp my drink, the Merlot doing nothing to dull the adrenaline still thrashing in my veins.

"You're jumpy," she says lightly, eyes narrowing.

"Am I?" I force my face into something neutral, but the coke heightens it all—the way her thumb strokes the stem, the calculating tilt of her chin.

"You are." Her smirk's edged. "Rough day?"

I nod, throat tight. "Knackered, that's all."

She stretches, toes brushing my knee. "Maybe you should join me and Martha for tennis tomorrow. Clear your head."

"I'll think about it." The words come out stiff, forced. "I'll be rusty as hell. Haven't played in ages." *And Martha's a pretentious cow.*

Her phone vibrates—a single, surgical buzz.

I twitch.

She snatches it, angling the screen away. That *flicker* of a smile as she types.

"Work?" I ask, too casual.

"Mhm." Terse. Three taps, then the phone's down again.

I drain my glass, hand trembling. The coke's still humming in my veins, magnifying every tic, every breath. *Shouldn't have railed that line before facing my wife.*

But without it, I wouldn't have dared look.

"Everything okay?" Grace asks, slicing the silence.

"Yeah," I say, too fast, the word brittle as snapped chalk. "Why wouldn't it be?"

Grace's eyebrow lifts, weighing the charge in the air, then she leans back, dismissing the moment. Her focus drifts to the telly.

She looks detached. Distant. Present but elsewhere.

I swig more wine. It's tasteless as tap water now. The telly drones, but the room feels cavernous.

I steal another glance. She's sprawled casual as a stranger, like I'm just another appliance humming in the background.

And it hits me. Cold, sudden:

Have I lost her already?

Or was she never really mine to lose?

9

Another month has passed, and I've realised something. That if I don't step out of myself, even for just one night each month, I'll rot from the inside out.

The irony's almost funny. From the outside, my life's perfect. I *should* feel lucky. Grateful. *Something*. But inside? I'm slowly crumbling. Bit by bit. Day by day. And no one sees it.

Grace is part of it, sure. But it's more than that. It's everything, everyone. The dullness of it all, the slow, creeping erosion of meaning. I used to fight it, pick it apart. But now I've stopped trying. I've given in.

Knowing that today will mark my second visit to Ralph's makes my skin tingle. Leaving Blackwood Girls' School, I shed Andy Giles like a skinsuit. Become someone none of them—not my co-workers, not my friends, not even my wife—would recognise. I trade in my predictable existence and dive headfirst into the hidden side of London. The part of the city most people never see.

I fish out my phone and scroll through emails until I find the invitation. *7:55 p.m.* No earlier, no later.

Weeks back, I tried to look up the history of the building. The grand Georgian townhouse in the heart of St. James's where Ralph's resides. It once belonged to an aristocrat two hundred years ago, but beyond that? Nothing. No records, no public history, no mention of what it became after that. It's as if it doesn't exist.

But I know the truth. It's a sanctuary for people like me. A place where we strip off the suffocating masks we wear day-to-day, and replace them with ones that let us breathe.

My phone vibrates.

James (Running Club): Oi, u alive? Ghosting us now?

I hover over the chat—weeks of missed runs, unanswered texts:

Mate, where've you been?
Everything alright?
Pint this week? My round.

I exit without replying. My inbox brims with ghosts:

You avoiding us or what?

I sit there, staring at the words, feeling nothing. They're reaching out, trying to pull me back. But what would I even say? That I've found something better? That the idea of running in circles or nursing warm pints feels like a distant memory, one I don't miss?

The guilt should sting, but it doesn't.

I pocket my phone. There's nothing to say. They can't bring me back, and they sure as hell can't make me whole.

I exhale, shake the thoughts loose, and lift my gaze.

Ralph's black double doors tower before me.

This is where I belong now.

The doorman greets me in his velvet Parisian drawl. "Good evening, Monsieur."

His eyes scan the road, missing nothing.

"Good evening, Monsieur," I echo. No names here. Just *Monsieur, Madame.* Clean. Simple.

With a nod, the doorman presses the heavy door open with his white-gloved hand, ushering me inside. The hard pavement disappears beneath my feet, replaced by the soft embrace of a deep-red rug stretching down the corridor. The air changes instantly. Quieter, richer, as though I've stepped into another world.

I drift past walls lined with chaotic, abstract paintings. Relaxed now, I take the time to observe them. One catches my eye, its frenzied brushstrokes reflecting the turmoil inside me. Wild, unhinged, a hint of madness lurking just below the surface. I pause, staring at the swirling mess of colour. Does the artist know? Have they felt it too?

A voice pulls me from my thoughts. "Good evening, Monsieur."

I glance up from my Oxfords. The same woman from last month's revelries stands by the inner doors, dressed in a black jacket, pencil skirt, and a crisp white blouse.

"Good evening, Madame," I reply, ease replacing last time's jitter.

She gestures down a side corridor toward the changing rooms.

Four identical chambers. She ushers me into the nearest one, shutting us in.

Now that I'm more at ease, I take in the space with clearer eyes. It reminds me of a Savile Row fitting room. Compact, elegant, no more than two metres squared. A plush chair sits in one corner, a full-length mirror leans against the opposite wall. Not that I frequent bespoke tailors. The last time was for Grace's brother's wedding. She'd insisted I look my best, so, despite my protests, she dressed me in the finest London had to offer.

Funny. She had such opinions on what I wore then. Now, she barely looks at me.

I shrug off my jacket, placing it into the white-gloved hands of Madame. She takes it without a word, hanging it neatly on a rail. I unbutton my crisp white shirt next. No hesitation. No self-consciousness. The ritual of shedding the outer layers is freeing. Here, I don't have to be anyone.

Madame removes each piece of clothing: my shirt, shoes, trousers, and finally, my underwear. Rather than vulnerability, I feel power. Stripped of my everyday identity, I am no longer Andy Giles.

She rifles through the garments on the rail, carefully selecting the one marked with my club ID: *13*. Below it, my new name: *Hannya*.

"Tonight's theme is Olympus," she says, holding up the outfit for me to inspect. It's a simple drape of fabric in an earthy, natural tone, like the tunics wealthy Greeks wore in antiquity.

I stretch my arms out, letting her dress me. She works quickly, fastening the fabric over my left shoulder, letting it drape across my chest, leaving the right side exposed. The material is soft, clinging like a second skin.

She kneels, slipping leather sandals onto my feet.

When I turn towards the mirror, a Greek god stares back.

"Final touch," Madame murmurs, unclasping a large briefcase engraved with 13. The lock snaps open with a soft click, revealing the mask.

The first time I saw it, it unsettled me. The sharp horns, the metallic eyes, the sneering mouth frozen in twisted malice. But now, I welcome it. It's not just something I wear. It's something I am.

I lift it from the case and bring it up to my face. The leather straps slide over my head, snug against my skull, and with a final adjustment, Hannya stares back at me in the mirror.

Then I step forward, through the open doors, crossing the threshold into another world.

The transformation is complete.

The hall has changed.

Towering nude statues rise from the polished floors, their marble bodies bathed in candlelight. Twisting vines creep up the columns, weaving through air thick with the sweet, cloying scent of jasmine incense.

At least fifty guests lounge on plush, low-slung couches, their silk tunics dissolving into the golden glow of the room. They recline like deities, half-shadowed and languid, their masks glinting in the flickering light.

Servants in darker, coarser tunics move silently between them, balancing trays of wine and figs, pomegranates and grapes. Their movements are careful, rehearsed to invisibility. They exist on the edges, not part of this world. Spectral, subservient, meant only to sustain it.

At the far end of the room, acrobats bend and twist in ways that defy anatomy. One performer arches backward until their head emerges between their legs, limbs coiled into a shape both graceful and grotesque. Another balances on a single palm, spine curved like a bowstring.

Beyond them, dancers undulate as fluid as water, their motions equal parts elegance and provocation. Hips sway, arms ripple, and the room seems to pulse with their rhythm. A musician in the corner plucks at a lyre, the notes weaving a spell into the air. Ancient, primal, irresistible.

I close my eyes for a moment, letting the music settle under my skin. The lyre's melody knots with the laughter, the clink of glasses, the low hum of voices.

I should feel like an outsider here, but I don't. Here, I am home.

"Monsieur."

A voice pulls me from my trance. I turn to see a masked staff member bowing his head slightly, his posture deferential but poised.

"Thank you for coming," he says, his French accent polished but faint. "We are happy to see you return and hope you enjoy tonight's entertainment."

"Thank you for inviting me," I reply, matching his formality. "I've been looking forward to it."

He disappears as seamlessly as he arrived, slipping back into the tide of movement. A shadow among shadows.

As I watch him go, a thought stirs at the edge of my mind. Do the staff exist beyond these walls? Do they return to their homes, hang their uniforms in cramped wardrobes, queue for the Central Line at dawn? Or are they ghosts, bound to Ralph's, fading when the night ends?

The rules of the club echo through my mind, crisp and unyielding:

No personal questions.
No names.
Confidentiality absolute.
Attire sacred.
Devices surrendered.
Attendance mandatory.

Straightforward. Brutal in their simplicity. Rules that promise safety and secrecy, the foundation of the masquerade I've willingly stepped into.

With the words still imprinted in my thoughts, I reach for a passing waiter's tray, snatching a glass of chilled white wine. The condensation clings to my fingers as I bring it to my lips. Crisp, citrus-sharp, expensive.

I scan the room.

Many of the guests are familiar now. Not their faces, of course, those remain hidden behind masks of gilt and feathers, porcelain and leather. But their silhouettes, their tells: the tilt of a head as they laugh, the way one woman taps her glass in time with the lyre, the man who gestures broadly when he speaks, his tunic sleeve slipping to reveal a scar. Even anonymised, there are ways to tell people apart.

And just like that, the night begins.

A thought lingers at the edge of my mind, persistent as a splinter. *The club never exceeds or falls below one hundred members.* Absolute precision. What happens when someone fails to show up? How do they vet replacements? Why me? I'm not a CEO. Not some Mayfair trust-fund brat. I don't belong here. And yet, they pulled me in.

Before the spiral tightens, a hand slips into mine.

I turn. *Her.* That familiar mask. Porcelain-pale, bold black liner sharp as a blade's edge, lips stained a deep, theatrical red.

"I've been counting down the days," Red says, releasing my hand only to spin in a playful twirl, the flowing fabric of her Grecian tunic catching the candlelight. She stops abruptly, grinning. "Isn't this *pretty*?"

"I'm truly in awe, Red."

We collapse onto one of the plush circular sofas, its design ensuring every guest is both spectator and spectacle. Lively conversations hum around us. A woman's throaty laugh, a man debating Stoicism with slurred fervour. When I raise my glass, Red plucks a grape from a nearby tray and shoves it into my mouth before I can react.

I half-choke, half-laugh, washing the fruit down with a too-large gulp of wine. "Bloody menace."

She brushes her fingers through her golden hair, a gesture I've come to recognise as her recalibrating. "Let's finish these and get another. Properly celebrate."

I nod, and we clink glasses, downing the wine in unison. The warmth spreads, loosening the knot in my chest.

"Another!" I declare, louder than intended.

A waiter materialises. Silent, efficient, eyes downcast, a tray already extended. We pluck fresh glasses, condensation slick against my palm. I still don't know where they come from, these waiters, or where they vanish to after. Do they slip into hidden passages? Fold into the shadows?

"I can spot troublemakers a mile away."

The voice behind us is dry, amused, tinged with an accent I can't place.

I turn to find a lion mask staring me down. Carved golden mane, eyes slitted and calculating. The woman behind it studies me like a museum curator appraising a dubious artifact.

"Don't get too wasted before the real fun begins," she says, voice raspy with age or cigarettes. "You'll want to remember it."

"Quite the contrary, Madame," Red replies, mischief glinting like a blade. "Drinking makes the night all the more fun."

"Hello, I'm Jumadi."

She extends a hand. Her skin is dark, veined, thin as aged parchment, but her grip is firm.

Before I can utter a greeting, Red vanishes and reappears as if conjured, pressing another glass of wine into Jumadi's hands with a smirk.

"You haven't had enough to drink," Red teases, tilting her head. "That's why you're grumpy."

She raises her glass dramatically, sloshing wine onto the rug. "To the Athenian Empire!"

Jumadi and I exchange glances. Hers weary, mine bemused. Neither of us knows what she means, but we humour her.

"To the Athenian Empire," we echo, glasses raised.

We drink, and laughter erupts around us. The energy pivots. More guests converge on our corner.

"Aren't we popular?" Red whispers, breath hot against my ear.

I suppress a shiver. "We're certainly the loudest."

Jumadi plucks a fig from the table, inspects it like a suspect gemstone, then melts into the crowd with a curt nod.

Red leans closer, voice dropping. "That woman gives me chills."

"Seems harmless. Probably just likes getting under people's skin."

Red hums sceptically, nails drumming her glass.

New guests trickle in, each arrival precisely timed. The invitations must have been staggered to prevent anyone from crossing paths before their mask is on.

Anonymity's the covenant here. The glue holding this circus together, shielding us from the world, each other, our own rot.

The question needles at me: *Who did I replace?*

10

A commanding figure steps forward, clapping once. The room obeys instantly. Conversations dissolve into silence. Every masked face swivels toward him like compass needles finding north.

His Japanese war mask sends a visceral shiver through me. Bold, sharp angles, lacquered black, its surface etched with deep grooves that resemble battle scars. The hollow eyes seem to pierce through the crowd, unblinking.

For a moment, I feel *exposed*. As if he's seeing through the mask, peeling back layers of pretence I've stitched together.

"Thank you all for coming to our monthly celebration of life," he announces, his voice rich. "You all look wonderful tonight. We hope you enjoy this evening's... *entertainment*."

A second clap. The double doors behind him swing open with a theatrical groan.

A line of women enters, moving in perfect, eerie sync. Bare. Silent. Each face hidden behind the same white

Pierrot mask, cheeks rouged, lips frozen in a crescent smile that doesn't reach the hollow eye sockets.

Twenty of them.

They stand motionless, waiting.

Red leans in, her breath warm and wine-sweet against my ear. "Aren't they pretty?"

I swallow, my throat suddenly parched. "Delightful," I manage.

I let my eyes roam down the line. They've catered to every conceivable taste. Some have the soft, rounded curves, others are slender. A few boast full, heavy breasts that draw hungry stares, while others exude a quieter allure. Their stillness renders them statuesque, more like works of art than human.

Then, all at once, the spell breaks.

Guests leap from their seats, dignity abandoned. They grab at the women, pulling them toward plush sofas with frantic urgency.

But Red and I don't move.

We watch, reclining like Roman patricians at the Colosseum, as the frenzy unfolds.

"Patience is the luxury of the well fed," I remark, swirling the dregs of my wine.

Truthfully? I want to be part of it. The idea of grabbing someone by the wrist, yanking them close, indulging in the electric anonymity of it all, sends a primal heat surging through me. And if Red were there too—if her hands joined the chaos, her laughter mingling with mine—that would be the fucking pièce de résistance.

But I'm new here. I don't overstep.

Red's hair brushes my shoulder. A grounding touch, a reminder this is real.

She observes the spectacle. Unbothered. Amused.

"Shall we liven things up?" she asks, draping her arm across my thigh, her fingers tracing idle patterns that skate dangerously close to my knee.

I exhale slowly, steadying my pulse. "Let's."

The room erupts again, conversations resuming in fevered bursts, laughter spilling over the edges. The musicians lean into their strings, the melody accelerating into a frenzied gallop, the heartbeat of the night quickening, pounding, *alive*.

Red whistles.

Not a polite call for attention, but a sharp whistle. A group nearby turns immediately. At Red's gesture, they make their way over.

Effortless.

I envy how she bends the room to her will. Brazen could command a crowd, Columbina could silence one. But Red? She doesn't drag people in, she makes them want to come.

Three figures approach. The Pantalone duo and Columbina.

She doesn't rush or acknowledge anyone, just strides forward as if the space already belongs to her.

She looks even more striking than last month. The fabric skims her chest, barely covering her, each step revealing glimpses of skin before hiding them again.

Even Red watches her now.

"What idiotic game will those two come up with this time?" I mutter, nodding toward the men lumbering over, overconfident, thick-necked.

Red twists a strand of hair. "Last month, it was wrestling in spilled wine, wasn't it?"

"Neither won. Let's suggest arm wrestling. They'll bite, and we'll watch the mess."

"Then we'll enjoy the show." Her tone is dry, amused.

The men arrive, already prodding each other, their egos ripe for manipulation.

Columbina stands between them, relaxed. She doesn't acknowledge them; they're here to entertain her. They know it.

"Red. Hannya. How do you do?" Columbina's voice is velvety, every bit as intoxicating as my wine.

"I'm good. You?" I reply, too casual, straightening despite myself. She has a way of making me feel small.

Red cuts in. "Careful, your nipple's showing."

Columbina glances down at the slipping fabric but doesn't adjust it. "Perhaps I like it this way, dear."

Red scoffs. Panta and Lóne?

They're practically salivating.

Their heads jerk towards her like dogs catching the scent of food. Their eyes lock onto the exposed curve of her breast, bodies rigid, as if awaiting permission to devour her. Lóne's throat bobs. Panta's hand clenches into a fist—either to stop himself from reaching out or to suppress some primal urge to snarl. It's grotesque, the way they stand there, helplessly transfixed, as though Columbina has them tethered by invisible strings.

I glance at Red. Unsurprisingly, she's watching them with open disgust. She despises how easily they fall under Columbina's spell. Maybe she hates that I'm watching, too.

"May we join you?" Columbina asks, already lowering herself onto the cushion beside me.

"Please, take a seat," I say, more out of obligation than welcome. She's already settled, her bare thigh pressing against mine.

Red shifts closer, too.

Their bodies press in from either side—a silent, unspoken contest.

Columbina's dress shifts as she moves, the fabric slipping just enough to reveal a sliver of skin before coyly settling back.

It's deliberate. Every gesture, every breath.

And Red knows it.

She doesn't speak, but I feel the tension hardening her posture, the razor-edged glare she fixes on Columbina.

"Go on, entertain us, you two," Red says, her tone clipped. "How about arm wrestling? We haven't seen that yet."

Columbina doesn't react outwardly, but I catch the faintest flicker of amusement behind her mask.

The two men snap to attention like hounds given a command. Their ridiculous posturing evaporates as they drop to the floor, elbows slamming onto the table with a jarring thud. They're so desperate to perform, so eager to prove themselves, it borders on pathetic.

As they grip hands, Lóne leans in, muttering something too low for the rest of us to hear.

I don't catch the words, but whatever he says strikes a nerve. Panta's jaw tightens, the veins in his neck bulging as his grip on Lóne's hand turns bone-white. He's ready to crush bones over whatever insult was hissed.

Columbina stretches her arms above her head, her dress slipping just enough to bait my gaze. I force my eyes away, but her faint smirk confirms she noticed.

Red noticed, too.

"Come on, give it all you've got!" Columbina encourages, shifting her weight, pressing closer into my side.

"Go on, Lóne, you've got this!" Red calls out, her voice dripping with feigned cheer. She doesn't care who wins. She just wants Panta riled.

And it works.

The table groans under their straining arms, veins corded like rope. It's a brutal stalemate—Lóne gains an inch, Panta claws it back. Neither will fold, not with Columbina watching.

Then, one of the Pierrot-masked women materialises silently beside them.

She's silent, waiting for someone to react.

She stands motionless, waiting.

Lóne's eyes flick up. Just a split second.

Panta slams his arm down, the table rattling.

Lóne howls, clutching his wrist. Panta leaps up, flapping his arms in victory. "Cheers, love," he grins at the Pierrot, swatting her arse.

Lóne's face blackens. He glares at the Pierrot. No lust now, just blame.

She doesn't react. Doesn't even seem aware she's done anything.

"You cheating bastard!" Lóne snarls, lunging. They crash to the floor, fists flying—shoulders, ribs, anywhere but the face.

Columbina sighs like a disappointed mother, but her eyes lock with mine. Amusement glints there.

Then, a *reward*.

She lifts the back of her dress, just enough for a teasing glimpse of her backside, then hops off the sofa to break up the fight. It's a flash of skin, nothing more, but the image sears into my mind.

I don't realise I'm gaping until Red snaps her fingers in my face.

"You good there?"

I cough, staring at my drink. "Good, good wine, this."

Red knocks back her glass, already scanning for the next spectacle. I watch Columbina pry the men apart, effortless as parting curtains.

But Red's focus narrows.

On the Pierrot who derailed the match.

"You. Here. Now."

The girl hesitates, then shuffles closer. She's petite, fragile behind that vacant mask.

"Why'd you interfere?" Red's tone shifts. Flat, icy.

A chill creeps down my spine. This isn't the Red who flirts, who laughs, who flicks hair like it's a game.

This is someone else entirely.

The Pierrot shifts on the balls of her feet, shoulders tense. I should stay out of this. Whatever happens next isn't my concern.

Red sits up straighter and gestures for the girl to kneel. The Pierrot does as she's told. No protest. No resistance.

"You know I'm going to have to punish you now, don't you?" Red's voice is soft, honeyed, almost tender.

Then she glances at me. A wicked grin.

"Fancy joining the fun?"

I shake my head. Not yet. I'm not crossing *that* line, not tonight.

Red's hand trails down the girl's shoulder, fingers skating over the bare skin. "You're gorgeous, you know that?"

The Pierrot shivers beneath her touch.

Without warning, Red yanks her hair.

The girl gasps, biting back a cry as Red drags her onto the sofa, straddling her. Fingers tangle in her hair, nails raking red welts down her back. The girl writhes, trapped.

It's a game. A performance. One where no one knows the line until it's crossed.

I push to my feet. "I'll be right back."

Red stays in my peripheral vision. So does the girl. I refuse to look, refuse to see where this is heading.

The restroom feels like an escape, but my mind is a storm of conflicting thoughts. The old me would have left. Walked out, never returned. But not this time. Not now.

Inside, Panta and Lóne are already there.

Their laughter bounces off the tile walls, their bruises barely forming before they've shrugged off the fight like it was a friendly spar.

"So, have you fucked her yet?" Lóne's voice is casual, as if he's asking about the weather.

I pause at the urinal. "Who?"

"That blonde chick. Red," Lóne says, zipping up his trousers. "You two were together the entire party last month, and today's no different. But I haven't seen you two in action. Actually, I've never seen her fuck anyone. Maybe she's frigid."

He laughs, and Panta joins in.

I keep my face blank, but something in me coils tight.

"You know," Panta adds with a smirk, "I've made it my mission to fuck every girl here. All fifty of them. But some of them play real hard to get. Especially Red."

"Why bother?" I say, turning to wash my hands. "Just go have fun with the Pierrots. Looks like they're down for anything."

Lóne snorts. "That's the problem. They're *whores*. Gets boring. The ones who fight, who play hard to get? That's the thrill. More rewarding if you have to *earn* it."

I exhale slowly through my nose. The casual cruelty of it—*of them*—sits like a stone in my gut.

The old me would've snapped. But here? I can't afford to be the old me.

I nod absently, drying my hands.

Re-entering the hall, the air's shifted. A storm's brewing.

The host has reappeared.

He glides between the columns, inspecting his handiwork. Observing guests like chess pieces moved to his whim.

His presence hooks every gaze. Conversations thin to murmurs. Laughter dies.

Even the most reckless guests temper their movements under his scrutiny. Careful not to smudge his masterpiece.

And for the first time tonight, unease prickles my neck.

11

I tread lightly towards Red's table, tension tight in my chest. Each shuffle of my sandals threatens to shatter the fragile silence left in the host's wake. Even the most inebriated guests obey. Slurring laughter dies mid-syllable, slouched postures stiffen, as if his mere presence compels them to perform respect.

Then, as if he senses my hesitation, he halts. His head turns, and his eyes land directly on me. He doesn't scan the room. Doesn't pause to acknowledge others. His focus narrows, as if I'm the only soul here. The eyes behind his mask burn through the slits, searing into me like brands.

My pace slows to a crawl. I lower my head instinctively, staring at my sandaled feet as if they hold the answers to questions I'm too afraid to ask.

"Hannya."

His voice slices through the room.

When I look up, he motions for me to approach with a flick of his fingers. The closer I step, the clearer his mask becomes: the carved snarl, the jagged teeth frozen in a cruel leer that seems to stretch beyond human proportions.

"Good evening, Monsieur," I say, somehow steadying my voice. My mind races, eyes trying to find reassurance from Brazen, Red, anyone familiar, but they're swallowed by the crowd.

"I'm pleased you've joined us once again," he says, tilting his head slightly. "Delighted to see you enjoying yourself these past two evenings."

"Thank you for inviting me," I reply. It's the only honest thing I can say. Flattery would be wasted on a man like this. He'd see through it instantly. "These parties... They're unlike anything I've ever known. The costumes, the freedom, the guests—"

A subtle tilt of his head stops me mid-sentence. He doesn't need to speak. The command is there, embedded in the space between us. A reminder to choose my words carefully.

"You haven't seen anything yet," he says, and the grin on his mask seems to widen. "Pace yourself with the drinking tonight. At least for the first few hours. I have games planned, and I wouldn't want you to miss them."

I nod, though the motion feels more like a bow, involuntary. "What kind of games?"

He lets a silence stretch just long enough to make me regret asking.

"You'll see." A pause, then, softer: "Just remember, nothing is off limits."

He places a firm hand on my shoulder. My skin prickles beneath his touch, not from fear but from something worse—anticipation. He leans in slightly, his voice dipping just enough to feel conspiratorial.

"I'm glad your name was put forward," he murmurs. "You were just the right person. Hannya always has a way of intriguing me more than most."

Then he's gone, sweeping past like smoke. Conversations stutter back to life, the room exhaling in his wake.

I let out a quiet breath, my fingers flexing at my sides. *Just the right person*. What does that mean? I run the words over in my mind, twisting them, flipping them, searching for some hidden meaning. There's something cryptic in the way he spoke.

A brush against my shoulder makes me flinch.

"Been standing there a while," Jumadi says.

"Oh, yeah. Sorry." I shake myself out of my trance.

She doesn't laugh or tease. Instead, she watches me carefully, then turns towards the host's retreating figure. "Trying to figure him out?"

"I guess so," I admit. "It's the first time I've spoken with him."

Jumadi hums, tilting her head. "Best to blend in."

There's something about the way she says it. I catch a flicker of warning beneath, but she snuffs it before I can pry.

"The first time he speaks to you should be the last," she continues, her voice dropping to a murmur that barely clears the thrum of the lyre. "Otherwise, it usually means he has something... less positive to say."

Unease winds through my ribs. "What do you mean?"

Jumadi sweeps a hand through the air, gesturing at the room. "Just enjoy *this*. All of this. Stick to the rules. Stay out of his line of sight. Then there's no reason he'll need to speak to you again."

I nod as if I understand, though the warning gets to me. What rules have I already bent without knowing?

"See you at the games, Hannya." Her lips quirk slightly before she melts into the crowd, swallowed by a knot of guests laughing too loudly at nothing.

A strange tightness lingers in my chest as I watch her go. I don't know what happened to the previous Hannya. Was there violence? A fall from grace? I don't know why I was chosen. I am nothing but a school history teacher with a mortgage and a marriage quietly crumbling.

I don't know if I want to find out.

But when I glance across the room, my worries fragment.

Columbina.

She's watching me from the edge of a marble column, one shoulder leaned against it like she's posing for a portrait only I can see. I eye the sheer fabric of her dress clinging to every dip and curve, and the long, elegant lines of her legs crossed at the ankle.

My tongue darts over my lips, gone suddenly dry. I let my eyes drag over her, greedy, taking in the way the fabric pools at her hips, the deliberate arch of her spine. Is she sizing me up because she wants me pressed against that column, or because she's measuring the threat of a newcomer?

And yet, as if sensing the heat of my stare, she lifts her hand. Slowly, deliberately, her nails graze the column of her throat—a painter's brushstroke. They slide lower, tracing the hollow of her collarbone, then drift down, down, skimming the swell of her breast. A siren's call carved into flesh.

I turn away before it can pull me under, knuckles white around my empty glass.

Returning to Red feels like slipping back into a well-worn jacket. Familiar, safe. She doesn't look up as I slump into the sofa, but slides a tequila shot across the table, the salt crusting the rim like frost. We throw them back in unison, the burn carving through the fog in my head, smoothing the night's jagged edges. Another. Then another. My body relaxes into the warmth pooling in my veins, limbs liquid, the room tilting gently..

Red traces a thin white line across the coffee table with a fingernail. She rolls up a £20 note, and offers it to me.

"Want a bump?"

I nod, too eager, the coke already whispering promises in my ear.

She hands me the note, and I lean down without hesitation, the glass cool against my forehead as I inhale sharply. The sting hits instantly, a crackle of lightning up the septum, the world snapping into hyperfocus. The lyre's melody weaves through pockets of laughter, sharper now, each note plucked like a nerve. The air thickens with exotic oriental scenes and the musk of bodies pressed too close, the scent intoxicating.

Red watches me. "Better?"

"Better," I lie, because the rush is already forming into something hungrier.

Red prepares another line for herself, but before she moves, something shifts in her expression. Her fingers hesitate over the powder—a pause that feels out of place.

I rest a hand on her knee, instinct more than intent. "You alright?"

She stares down at the table, then, almost to herself, asks, "What do you do when you feel lost?"

The question catches me off guard. I blink, scrambling to recalibrate. "Try to find your way, I guess."

"And if you can't?"

She still doesn't look at me.

The mood shifts. I don't like it. Too close to something I've buried.

"Then you fight like hell," I say. "Or it drags you under."

She nods, not agreement but acknowledgment. As if she already knows.

Her fingers tighten around the rolled-up note. "To not getting swallowed whole."

Red leans in and does her line.

For the first time since meeting her, Red looks tired. Not in her limbs, but somewhere deeper, like something's been gnawing at her for too long. It unsettles me, how it lingers even here, where we're supposed to be untouchable.

I want to ask. I don't. The rules forbid it.

Instead, I grab the bottle and pour us another drink. If we can't talk about it, we'll drown it.

Before we down the shots, a sharp clap fractures the air.

The host stands at the hall's centre.

His voice cuts through the noise, dragging every gaze to him. "For those brave enough to join tonight's first game... something special awaits."

Guests shift, interest sharpening. Red straightens, shoving her weariness aside. One moment, distant. The next, electric.

"Ready?" she grins, mischief resurrected.

I smirk. "Depends. What's the game?"

The host raises a gloved hand. Silence falls.

"Welcome," he says, "to *The Fox Hunt*."

A ripple surges through the room. Whispers, laughter, anticipation. Behind my mask, my grin widens.

"The rules are simple," he continues. "Some of you will be Hunters, tasked with tracking and capturing the Foxes. The Foxes, in turn, have one objective. Escape."

I'm already hooked, foot tapping eagerly.

"There are a few conditions," the host continues, pacing through the gathered crowd. "The Foxes may hide anywhere within the hall but must remain silent. No speaking. No calling for help. No noise of any kind. The Hunters, however, may move freely, may speak, may do whatever it takes to capture their prey."

Guests exchange glances. A few smirk behind their glasses, already relishing the chaos.

"When a Fox is caught," the host adds, "they owe the Hunter a favour of their choosing. A drink, a secret, a dare." His eyes sweep the room, lingering on the most eager faces. *"No limits."*

I glance at Red. She's already watching me, her gaze sharp as a blade—I'm gonna catch you.

The lights dim abruptly, shadows stretching long and jagged across the room.

A servant approaches, pressing a small card into my hand. I glance down: Fox.

A rush surges through me, equal parts dread and thrill. *Prey.*

I scan the room, catching glimpses of others reading their cards. Those marked as Fox vanish instantly, melting into alcoves and behind curtains.

Beside me, the servant hands Red her card. *Hunter.*

Our eyes meet. A flicker of understanding passes between us. No mercy tonight.

The host claps once. Conversations fade to murmurs.

"Foxes, you have sixty seconds to disappear. After that, the hunt begins."

I smirk at Red, my voice teasing. "I'll see you later, Miss Hunter."

Before she can answer, I slip into the dimness. The thrill of the chase courses through my veins as I weave through the hall, searching for the perfect place to disappear. The space is vast, offering endless possibilities—behind the heavy curtains, beneath low tables, in the narrow alcoves lining the walls.

I push through a velvet drape at the far end of the room, pressing my body into the corner, where shadows swallow me whole. Through a sliver in the fabric, I watch the other Foxes scatter like seeds in the wind.

The lights dim further, dipping the hall into a half-lit dreamscape. A slow, building silence settles over everything, thick enough to choke on.

The seconds drag. My pulse beats against my ribs, loud as a drum.

A gong shatters the stillness, startling me.

The hunt begins.

The hall stirs. Hunters prowl, their footsteps light, voices dripping with mock sweetness.

"Come out, little Foxes," one calls, their tone laced with amusement. "You can't hide forever."

I hold my breath. The quiet makes every creak, every shifting shadow, feel dangerously loud.

A silhouette moves closer. The faint rustle of fabric.

Hunter.

I press further into the curtain, the damask wallpaper rough against my cheek as I will myself into the walls. My body is still, my heartbeat frantic.

They pause just inches from me, close enough that I could reach out and touch them.

"You can't hide from me," they whisper.

I squeeze my eyes shut, bracing for discovery. A single movement, a misstep, and I'll be dragged out, caught.

A slow exhale. Then laughter.

They turn away, slipping back into the darkness.

I let out a slow breath. *For now, I'm safe.*

Across the room I hear the muffled sound of a Fox being captured. A playful gasp, followed by muffled words I can't make out. I catch a glimpse of someone darting between the marble columns, quick but not quick enough. A Hunter lunges, catching their prey by the wrist. A brief struggle, a small rebellion, but it's over too quickly.

The Hunter leans in, whispers something. The Fox nods. Then they disappear into the dark together.

My pulse stirs with something dangerous.

Footsteps again. Closer this time. Whoever it is, they stop just inches away.

I hold still.

They don't move. *They know.*

Without warning, the drape is ripped aside.

My breath catches.

Columbina.

Of course, it's her.

Her grip is firm, dragging me from the shadows before I can react. My heart slams against my ribs as I stumble forward, my mind a jumbled mess of fear and exhilaration.

She tilts her head, the faintest smirk playing at the edges of her mouth. I should have known she'd come for me.

"You've been hiding from me all night, Hannya," she purrs, stepping in close. The space between us vanishes, heat rolling off her skin, her breath feathering over my mask.

I move to steady myself, but the shift makes my mask slip. Quickly, I adjust it, the anonymity of Ralph's wrapping around me like armour. *A necessary boundary.*

Columbina's fingers skim down my arm, slowly. "Caught you fair and square," she murmurs. "You know what that means, don't you?"

I swallow. My throat is dry. *Was she hunting me all this time?*

"What's your price?"

She leans in, lips brushing the edge of my mask. "I think you already know."

Her hands glide lower, tracing the lines of my chest. The curtain around us suddenly feels too tight, too small. This is what I came here for, but now that it's happening, I can't shake the unease beneath the thrill.

She presses against me, her bare skin sliding over mine. "You owe me, Hannya," she breathes, hands wrapping around my waist, pulling me against her. "And I always collect what's owed."

Her fingers move higher, brushing against my mask. Instinct kicks in. I grab her wrist, stopping her just before she lifts it.

"The mask stays on."

Columbina smirks, eyes flashing with mischief. "Wouldn't want to break the rules, would we?" she whispers. "That would land us both in a heap of trouble."

She leans in, her body pressing me against the cold surface of the wall. I feel her heat, her scent enveloping me like a drug. Her breath quickens, the fabric of her dress shifting with the rise and fall of her chest.

"I've been watching you all night," she says, her voice slick as honey. "The way you move, the way you look at me when you think no one's watching."

Her fingers trail over my chest, her touch leaving warmth in its wake. "You want this, don't you?"

My heartbeat hammers. She's right—I do want this. The thrill. The secrecy. The risk. It's why I keep coming back to Ralph's. No history here, no strings, no past to tie me down.

Her hands slip lower, tracing the edge of my tunic, tugging just enough to test my restraint. "Let's see how far you're willing to go, Hannya."

Her lips graze my neck, breath hot against my skin. My head tilts instinctively, my body already betraying me. Electricity crackles between us. I press against her, letting her pull me deeper into her gravity.

A sound breaks the spell.

A faint shuffle of footsteps just beyond the curtain.

I freeze, breath hitching. *Someone's there. Watching. Listening.*

"We're not alone," I whisper, every nerve on edge.

Columbina smiles against my ear, her hands never stopping. "That's what makes it fun, don't you think?"

She pushes further, slipping beneath my tunic, dragging me deeper into her game.

I swallow hard. The footsteps grow closer. The risk outweighs the temptation, and just like that, her hold over me fractures.

I push her hands away, not roughly, but firm enough to make my point. "Not here," I say, my breath uneven.

For a moment, Columbina doesn't move. Her dark eyes remain locked on mine, inscrutable behind the mask. Then, slow as a cat stretching in sunlight, her lips curve into a feline smile.

"As you wish," she purrs, stepping back. She smooths the rumpled silk of her dress, and in an instant, the charged air between us dissolves, as if nothing happened at all.

"I'm willing to wait," she says, "but not for long." She says, studying me like a chess move she's already plotted. "Tick-tock, my darling."

And just like that, she's gone, slipping into the crowd like smoke, hips swaying with confidence, leaving only the ghost of her touch and the faint, cloying trace of her perfume.

I stand there, trying to steady my breath, to shed the residual heat of her against my skin. My hands flex at my sides, restless and empty.

It should feel like a near miss. A bullet dodged.

It doesn't.

It feels less like an escape, more like a forfeit.

The night stretches on. And now, I owe her.

12

I want to find Red, to see if she had any luck with the hunt. But I won't mention Columbina. That would only set her off.

The thrill of the chase has faded. Guests have settled into pairs or small groups—some locked in drug-fuelled conversations, others vanishing into the dim-lit corners of the room. As I pass an alcove, I catch a glimpse of two Foxes who weren't as lucky. Their backs are against the cold stone, cornered by their Hunters. One, a tall figure in a carnival mask, trails her hand possessively along a Fox's waist. Her partner tugs at the neckline of the Fox's dress, letting the fabric slip just enough to reveal a sliver of bare skin. The Foxes don't move. They know the rules. They've been caught, and now, they have to play along.

Near the fireplace, a woman straddles another woman's lap. She laughs softly as her hands disappear beneath the other's tunic. Her fingers toy with the edge of the mask, teasing the boundary of what's allowed, threatening to lift it, but stopping just short. It's as if she alone controls whether the illusion stays intact.

Everywhere, the same scene plays out. Foxes and Hunters, tangled together in the aftermath.

At the bar, I spot Brazen holding court. Glad to see a familiar face.

He's surrounded by a small group of women, no surprise there, and their roaring laughter makes the rest of the place sound like a library. His hand rests on the back of a woman wearing a lace mask, fingers tracing slow circles along her dark skin. A quiet claim.

When he notices me, he raises his glass.

"Hannya! Did you enjoy the hunt?"

"I made it interesting."

Brazen's laughter booms. "Interesting is what we live for here!" He gestures to the empty seat across from him. "Come, join us. You look like you need a refill on your drink!"

I hesitate, scanning the room. No sign of Red, nor Columbina. For a moment, I feel unmoored, caught between the two of them in a way I can't quite explain. But then I remind myself where I am. Ralph's isn't a place for waiting or second-guessing.

I sit.

Brazen snaps his fingers, and a waiter appears, hovering at his command. "Bring him the good stuff," Brazen says, his grin widening. "Hannya deserves it."

Moments later, a glass lands in front of me with a soft clink. The liquid inside is deep red, almost black, swirling like ink under the candlelight. I take a cautious sip. Bourbon. Absinthe. A smoky, herbal bite that sears my throat. It's stronger than anything I've had tonight.

Brazen watches, elbow propped lazily on the bar. "That'll loosen you up," he says, tipping his glass toward mine. His ice clinks as he grins. "Trust me. You'll thank me later."

The warmth spreads through my chest immediately, a slow, molten crawl. I tell myself to pace it—*don't lose control*—but the taste is too good. Another sip. Then another.

The room shifts ever so slightly, the marble floor undulating like water. My grip tightens on the bar.

Something's in this drink.

Brazen watches me too closely, his smirk widening. He knows exactly what he's done.

Before I can react, I feel them.

Two women appear at my sides, fluid as smoke. One wears a mask of black lace that clings to her cheekbones like spider silk; the other's is gold filigree, glinting faintly in the dim light. The lace-masked woman props her chin in her palm, studying me. "Brazen's been talking about you," she muses. Her voice carries a Caribbean lilt. Warm, melodic, syllables rolling like waves.

"Has he?" My own voice sounds detached, muffled, as if I'm hearing it through a wall. I glance at Brazen. Mischievous guilt radiates from his shit-eating grin.

The gold-masked woman shifts closer, her knee brushing mine. "You don't seem like the type who needs much convincing," she says, sharp fingernails grazing my forearm. The touch lingers, predatory.

Brazen chuckles, swirling his drink. "Oh, he doesn't. He just needs reminding why he's here."

The lace-masked woman leans in, her breath hot against my ear. "What's on your mind?"

The world softens at the edges, the drink's grip tightening. I set my glass down with unsteady hands, fingers finding her waist. "I think... I've been far too reserved tonight."

She exhales a quiet laugh, pressing her body against mine. The gold-masked woman sinks to her knees, her hands already working at the ties of my tunic.

Brazen watches, satisfied. "That's it."

I close my eyes, surrendering to the haze.

Soft lips meet mine, the scratch of lace against my cheek. A hand slips beneath my waistband, long-nailed fingers wrapping around my cock.

"You've been waiting for this, haven't you?" I mutter, eyes still shut, head swimming.

The one kissing me trails her mouth down my neck, teeth grazing my pulse. "You taste so sweet," she murmurs, her tongue flicking against my skin.

The girl on her knees hesitates, fingers pausing at my hip. "May I?"

I tilt my head back, the room spinning. "Whatever you want."

Not a second later, her mouth is on me, sucking with a hunger that steals my breath. I press my teeth into my lower lip, but a gasp escapes anyway.

Before I know it, I'm on the floor, stripped bare. My eyes flutter open, to see the gold-masked woman straddling me, riding me hard. Above us, the lace-masked woman leans down, her tits swaying inches from my face, nipples pebbled under the sheer fabric.

Out of the corner of my eye, Brazen lifts his glass in salute, his grin feral.

The room melts around me, candlelight bleeding into shadow, laughter dissolving into white noise. The guests blur at the edges of my vision, their forms smudging into the dark like charcoal sketches.

13

The girls' laughter fades into Ralph's hedonism as I lean against a marble column. That drink really did a number on me.

A waiter silently approaches, offering a platter with three small tablets and a glass of water. Without a word, I grab the tablets, swallow them, and return the glass to the platter.

"Thank you, Monsieur," I say. He melts back into the shadows.

My head is swimming, Colours blur, and the murmurs of the crowd blend in as one. I close my eyes, trying to steady myself, but the ground feels like it's shifting beneath my feet. I take a deep breath, willing myself to focus, to come back to my senses.

Gradually, the noise separates into distinct voices, and the haze lifts enough for me to open my eyes. I can feel my heartbeat steadying, the grip of whatever was in that drink loosening its hold. The room comes into sharper focus, each figure and detail emerging from the fog.

As my senses start to return, my eyes scan the crowd and land on Jumadi, her lion mask in place.

She sits alone on the edge of a velvet sofa, one hand draped lazily over the armrest, the other cradling a glass. Her unhurried, relaxed posture reminds me of a cat lounging in the sun. Perfectly still, yet never fully at rest.

I push off the column and move towards her. There's something about her, the way she observes, the way she communicates without revealing too much. If anyone knows the secrets of this place, it's her.

She notices me before I reach her, tilting her head slightly.

"Enjoying yourself?" she asks.

"It's... something," I say with a shrug, sliding into the seat across from her. I hope she didn't see me getting overwhelmed earlier.

She chuckles, sipping her drink slowly. "Something," she repeats, letting the word linger. "That's one way to put it. Many think they're ready for Ralph's, only to be devoured whole."

Her tone is so casual it's hard to tell if it's a warning.

I rest my arm along the back of the sofa, mirroring her ease. "Not me. I like it here."

She watches me for a moment before setting her drink down. "Do you?"

The way she says it feels like a test. I try not to overthink it. "Yeah. It's easy to get lost in it."

Jumadi hums in agreement. "And yet, here you are, talking to me, instead of getting lost."

I lean forward slightly, lowering my voice. "You've been here a while, haven't you? Long enough to know things."

She doesn't confirm or deny it, just stares into my soul.

"What happened to the last Hannya?" I ask, watching her carefully. "Red hasn't told me much."

Jumadi lifts her glass again, taking her time before answering. "He broke a rule."

That's all she gives me. Nothing extra. No elaboration. Just that. "And the host?" I press. "What about him?"

"Now you're really asking the wrong questions."

I wait, but she only swirls her drink, looking at me like she's debating how much to say. "He knows everything about everyone," she says eventually. "So if I were you, I'd stay in line. Keep your head down."

I let out a short laugh, trying to keep it light. "What, is he some kind of puppet master?"

"More like a man who understands what people want. And what they'll do to get it."

I'm not sure if it's the alcohol or something else, but the way she says it doesn't sit right. I roll my glass between my fingers, watching the way the liquid catches the light. "And Ralph?" I ask, glancing at her. "Who is Ralph?"

"Who knows? Maybe it's the host's name, maybe not. What matters is that he runs this place. He decides who stays... and who doesn't."

"So, who has to leave?"

Jumadi studies me for a moment, then finally says, "The ones who break the rules. Or those who think they can leave without consequence. Or talk about things they shouldn't."

"Consequence?" I echo, my frown deepening. "Why would there be consequences? If someone doesn't like it here, they leave. That's the whole point, isn't it? You can't come back, but you can go."

"Just enjoy yourself, Hannya. That's why you're here." She drinks the remainder of whatever's in her glass, then turns away, slipping into the crowd with the grace of someone who's used to disappearing. "Don't overthink it," she calls back over her shoulder.

I stand there, turning her words over in my head. *Consequence.* The way she said it, so calm and unbothered, makes it sound like more than just a warning. Like a fact. A part of me wants to brush it off. Maybe she's just trying to spook me, play into the whole mystique of Ralph's. But then, why does it feel like something real is lurking beneath her words?

I exhale slowly, shaking my head. I'm being ridiculous. It's a club, not some underground cult. If someone doesn't want to be here anymore, they leave. Simple as that.

Still, a faint, nagging whisper lingers at the edge of my mind. What if Jumadi wasn't just being cryptic for the sake of it? What if there's more to Ralph's than I've been willing to see?

The laughter and conversations in the hall grow wilder. I take the last sip of my drink, letting the burn of alcohol press everything else down into the background.

From across the room, I catch Brazen's eye. He raises his glass as if to say, loosen up, H. It's just a game. I nod back, feeling a strange mix of relief and curiosity. Those tablets the waiter gave me really did the trick. I'm almost sober now, and I can't help but wonder where I could get my hands on more of those.

Thinking back on what Jumadi said, she's probably just messing with me, testing how easily I rattle. Or maybe she's drunk, slipping into the role of storyteller to keep things interesting.

Either way, I didn't come here to get lost in paranoia. I came here to forget. To be Hannya.

I turn back towards the bar, rolling my shoulders, shaking off the last remnants of unease. The night is still young, and I'm not done with it yet.

I switch up to a gin & tonic, wanting to ease into my uninhibited self. The ice clinks softly as I take my first sip.

Jumadi's words can wait. Whatever mysteries Ralph's is hiding, I'll uncover them when I'm ready.

For now, I'm exactly who I want to be.

And Hannya doesn't care about the rules, he makes them.

14

I decide it's time to drift through the night and venture into unexplored territory. The endless thoughts of my conversation with Jumadi cling to me like damp cloth, and I want to shake it off, drown it in something light, something reckless.

The hall is alive with its own small worlds. Each corner holds its own energy—some quiet, others electric. A flash of wild laughter draws me in, dark and unhinged, rolling through the air like it's feeding off the madness of the night. I move towards it, weaving through masked figures until I spot them—a tight cluster of guests gathered around a low table, blue flames flickering between them. The fire's glow paints their masks in shifting light, warping the eye holes, stretching the shadows.

Off to the side, leaning against a column, is Brazen. He's not playing, not yet, just watching, like he already knows exactly how this will unfold.

I consider pressing him for answers, circling back to what Jumadi said, but the alcohol swirling through me makes that thought slow and dull, like trying to grasp something just beyond reach. Right now, the fire has my attention. There's something unnatural about its colour, the way it burns too steadily, too controlled. The scent of burning alcohol sharpens in my nostrils as I step closer.

"Showtime!" Brazen bellows, pushing off the column and stumbling forward. "H, mate, you're just in time!"

"What's the game?" I ask.

Brazen's teeth gleam in the firelight. "Simple. Reach in, grab the raisin or the almond, and eat it to kill the flame. Got what it takes?"

A ripple of babble stirs through the group as they shift, their masked faces turning towards me. That's when I see her. Columbina, just beyond the fire's reach, watching. She doesn't speak, but the look she gives me feels like a challenge.

I kneel beside the table, the heat prickling against my skin. *Don't hesitate.*

I reach in. The heat clamps around my fingers, hot but bearable, more like molten wax than an open flame. It dares me to flinch, but I don't. My fingers close around the almond, the fire clinging to it like a living thing as I pull it free.

A chorus of cheers erupts around me. Brazen lets out a victorious shout. "That's it! That's my boy!"

But it's not over. Columbina is still eyeing me. She hasn't moved, hasn't spoken, but I feel her pull like a thread wrapped around my ribs. There's something almost expectant in the way she looks at me.

I hold her stare as I lift the almond to my lips. The fire flares briefly, like it's trying to resist, before I bite down. A bitter taste fills my mouth, the heat searing the back of my tongue before vanishing into nothing.

The crowd erupts again. Brazen claps me on the back so hard I nearly lose balance. "Now that's how it's done!"

The burnt almond's aftertaste lingers. Smoky, bitter.

A moment of victory. A quiet display of control.

The game ends, and the crowd moves on, their attention drifting elsewhere, already looking for the next thrill. But Columbina doesn't move. She stays where she is. Waiting. Watching.

I step around the table, closing the space between us. My fingers brush the curve of her hip. Her breath catches, just for a second, before she steadies herself. Her lips form into a faint smile, her body still, like a cat considering whether or not to pounce.

"You're full of surprises tonight, Hannya," she teases.

I lean in. "You haven't seen anything yet."

"Good. Keep it that way."

I slide my hand to her waist, pulling her closer, and before I can second-guess myself, I kiss her. She doesn't hesitate. Her lips part, meeting mine with a hunger that matches my own. Her fingers slip beneath my tunic, just enough to tease, before she presses herself against me, her body fitting perfectly into mine.

When we break apart, she brushes the back of her hand against the cheek of my mask.

"Don't think I forgot about the forfeit."

"I'll make the wait worth your while, darling. Don't you worry."

I kiss her again, drunk on the softness of her lips, the way her tongue moves like it already knows exactly what I want. I want to keep going, to give in completely, to let her take whatever she wants, but I remind myself: *Hannya makes the rules. He sets the pace.*

My hand slips lower, squeezing the firm curve of her ass. She lets out a soft gasp, a sound I could easily get addicted to. But I pull away before I lose control. A flicker of amusement crosses her face. She understands. She knows I'll come back for more.

Columbina waves me a teasing kiss before slipping away, disappearing into the night.

I know where I'm heading next. The bar, for a well-deserved drink.

Brazen is already there, no surprise. He spots me as I approach, giving me his signature grin.

"Hell of a night, huh?"

The scent of whisky and leather clings to him, his presence effortlessly commanding, as if he's part of the foundation of this place. Despite barely knowing him, being around Brazen makes me feel seen, like I belong.

He claps a firm hand on my shoulder. "You did well, Hannya. Real well."

"It wasn't all that hard once I realised the fire wasn't anything to fear."

"Still. You put on a good show. I'm proud of you."

The words settle somewhere deep, unexpected. *Proud of you.* The kind of thing my father never said. The kind of thing I used to wish for.

"Thanks," I say, rougher than intended.

Brazen leans against the bar, watching me with that easy smirk. "The more you let go, the more fun it becomes. You stop thinking so much about what's right or wrong, what people might think. You just *are*. That's the beauty of this place."

I nod. He says it like a truth he's learned the hard way. Like he's trying to pass something on.

The bartender slides two tumblers across the counter, something dark and potent sloshing inside. Brazen raises his glass. "Drink up. Here's to finding your rhythm."

I eye the drinks, hesitant.

He lets out a laugh. "Didn't do anything funny to this one, don't worry, mate!"

I take the glass from his hand, switching it for mine. Just to be sure.

"To finding rhythm!"

I take a sip, then another. The burn spreads through me, loosening things, making the room feel warmer, softer. I watch Brazen as he calmly scans the hall. He looks like he's always belonged here.

"You've got it in you," he says, as if reading my mind. "I saw it the first time you walked in. You've been holding back, but tonight? You let some of it out."

The words hit deeper than they should. I take another sip, letting the booze drown out the vulnerability rising in my chest.

Brazen's hand lands on my shoulder. My father used to do that. When he wasn't yelling. A firm grip that said, you're alright. But his touch always came with conditions, with expectations. Brazen's feels different.

"This place," Brazen continues, swirling the amber liquid in his glass, "It doesn't just strip away your mask. It strips away all the bullshit people put on you. The expectations, the rules, what everyone else thinks you should be. Here, you can be whoever the hell you want."

I glance towards the crowd, my eyes landing on Red. She's laughing, surrounded by people, completely in her element. Completely free.

Brazen chuckles as he raises his glass. "Red's a good gal. Real good. She doesn't take a liking to most. Means you're special."

I scoff, trying to brush it off, but the warmth in my chest betrays me. "I don't know about that."

Brazen just shakes his head, smirking. "Trust me, kid. You've got something. She sees it. I see it. Hell, everyone here's starting to. You just have to lean into it."

For a moment, I let myself believe him. Maybe I do belong here. Maybe I can thrive here.

I down the rest of my drink.

Brazen claps me on the back. "Come on," he says, signalling for another round. "Let's drink to that mask of yours, H. Here's to becoming exactly who you were meant to be."

I lift my glass. "To becoming."

The drinks keep flowing, and with each refill, the edges of Andy Giles blur further into the background. Brazen claps me on the back, laughing.

"Right, it's Brazen's turn to get some action. Maybe I'll see you on the other side, Hannya." He winks before disappearing into the crowd.

For a moment, I think about going back to Red, about sinking into a couch beside her, talking about something deep, something real. But there's a different pull tonight, something just as intoxicating as the alcohol burning through my veins. *Columbina*. She's somewhere in this hall, waiting, lurking in the shadows, playing the long game.

But I'm not prey anymore. This half of the night, I'm the hunter. And I'm not playing by her rules.

I slip through the hall, scanning the masked faces, my senses sharpening as I move past the clusters of guests entangled in their own private indulgences. Bodies on bodies, in intimate positions I didn't even know were possible.

I push past a curtain, the texture soft and heavy under my fingers. The atmosphere changes immediately. Hidden corridors, separated by thick linen drapes, designed for those who crave privacy.

I brush my fingers along the fabric, pausing at each concealed alcove. The air is thick with anticipation, my pulse quickening. The distant hum of whispers and muffled laughter adds to the mystery. She's here. I know it.

I exhale, letting the thrill settle deeper in my blood.

"Columbina..."

The name rolls off my tongue like an invitation, meant only for her. "I know you're watching. Come out."

For a moment, nothing. Silence.

Then I feel it. A presence at my back.

I turn slowly. She stands framed against the heavy fabric, her feathered-edged mask catching the dim light, her body still, waiting. A smirk curves beneath her disguise.

I step forward, closing the distance. "Been hiding, have you?" My voice is low, teasing.

She doesn't answer. Instead, with one swift motion, she grabs the front of my tunic and pulls me into her, our lips colliding in a fierce, breathless kiss.

She's all teeth and fire, devouring, demanding. Her body presses flush against mine, grinding against my hips. The mask between us only amplifies the hunger, the secrecy of it all sharpening every sensation. My hands find her waist, fingers digging in as I push her back against the column, claiming her, matching her ferocity.

Her nails rake across my chest, finding bare skin where my tunic has loosened. I grip her hips, dragging her closer, feeling the heat of her body through the thin fabric. She arches into me, her breath ragged, her lips moving to my jaw, my throat.

I brush my fingers along the edge of her mask, trailing them down her neck, teasing. She pulls back slightly, just enough for our eyes to meet through the slits of our masks. The candlelight catches in her irises, dark and glinting with something dangerous.

"Thought you could hide from me?" I murmur, unable to suppress a smirk.

Her laugh is low, velvety. "Maybe I wanted to be found."

With a sudden, fluid motion, she wraps her legs around my waist, binding us. My hands grip her thighs, keeping her steady, keeping her *mine*. Her dress slips from her shoulders, pooling at her waist, revealing smooth olive skin.

I pause, drinking her in. The contrast of her dark eyes behind the mask, the way her chest rises and falls, her lips just parted, waiting.

She tilts her head slightly, a silent dare. "You found me," she whispers, her breath warm against my lips. "Now what are you going to do about it?"

A slow grin spreads across my face. I tighten my grip on her, my fingers trailing lower, pressing into the curve of her hips.

"Everything," I growl.

She gasps softly as I pull her back into me, our bodies moulding together. Her fingers tangle in my hair, tugging just enough to send sparks racing down my spine. I trail my lips down her throat, tasting her, savouring the heat of her pulse against my tongue.

Her nails dig into my back, urging me further. "I thought you were the one in control," I whisper, teeth grazing her earlobe.

She laughs breathlessly, tilting her head back. "Maybe I enjoy surrendering it."

Her hands slip under my tunic, pushing it off my shoulders, exposing more of me. I let her strip away the layers, let her see me the way no one else does.

We tumble onto the cushions nearby, the heavy fabric pooling around us like a shroud. Her fingers trace the lines of my shoulders, my ribs, leaving trails of fire.

She shivers under my touch, her body arching, and when I push her onto her back, pinning her beneath me, her masked eyes flash with something primal.

She gasps, her hands gripping my shoulder blades as we become one.

***

The heat between us lingers, but Columbina is already untangling herself from me—not with the lazy ease of exhaustion, but with quiet intent.

She shifts, sitting up, fingers skimming my chest like she's committing it to memory. Not tender. Not absentminded. Just... observing.

I watch her, head tilted, waiting for her to say something.

She doesn't.

Instead, she reaches for my mask, her fingers barely grazing the edge. A test.

I catch her wrist before she can go further. "No one takes off the mask."

She smirks. "Oh, I know. But you like to pretend you're different."

I huff out a breath, releasing her. She leans in then, close enough that her lips nearly brush mine again—but she stops. Holds there. Waiting.

"You think you've figured this place out?" she murmurs.

I smirk, fingers tracing slow circles over the curve of her hip. "Maybe."

She laughs, but there's something hollow in it. Something older.

Her fingers trail over my ribs, slow, deliberate. "You remind me of someone."

A flicker of something uneasy stirs in me. "Who?"

She tilts her head slightly, considering. "Someone who thought he was in control. That he was carving his own path. That he could keep one foot inside Ralph's and the other in the world outside."

My jaw tightens. "And what happened to him?"

Her smirk falters, just for a second. Then she shakes her head, almost amused at herself. "You'll see."

A slow, creeping sensation prickles at my spine. I prop myself up on my elbows, watching her. "You're enjoying this, aren't you?"

She traces a finger down my chest, a featherlight touch. "Maybe." Then, quieter, almost like an afterthought: "Or maybe I've seen this play out too many times before."

A shiver licks up my spine.

She leans closer again, brushing her lips just over my jawline, but her voice isn't teasing anymore—it's almost soft. "You'll wake up one day and realise you aren't making choices anymore. That the mask has decided for you."

I don't like the way she says it.

I don't like how certain she sounds.

I grip her wrist before she can pull away. "And you?"

She doesn't answer right away. Instead, she watches me—really watches me. Then, in the quietest voice I've heard from her yet, she says, "Who says I ever woke up?"

The words lodge in my throat.

My grip tightens on her wrist. "What do you mean?"

She tilts her head, amusement flickering over her features. "You think you're the first Hannya?"

Something sharp and ugly clenches in my chest. "...What?"

She pulls her hand free, stretching like she hasn't just said something that's made my skin go cold. "Names change. Faces change. But Ralph's stays the same."

I stare at her, words failing me. The implication seeps in, slow and heavy. There was another before me. Another man who wore this mask, walked these halls, sank into this world.

"And what happened to him?" I force out.

Columbina meets my gaze. Then, with an exhale, she leans in, lips grazing my ear. "What do you think?"

Then, just like before, she slips away. Gathering the fabric of her dress, adjusting her mask. She doesn't rush, doesn't look back. Like she's done this a hundred times before.

I watch her vanish behind the curtain, a strange, uncomfortable weight settling into my ribs.

And for the first time since stepping into Ralph's, I wonder if I'm already too far gone.

15

I walk across the hall, glancing around to ensure no one saw me slip away. This should be my secret, my fantasy, a night without consequence. The energy peaks around me. People stumble; laughter spills over itself; bodies collapse onto velvet cushions, limbs tangled. One guest crawls on all fours like a monkey, hooting as he pounds his fists against the marble. Another sprawls on the floor, swimming through a puddle of spilled red wine, arms carving slow, exaggerated strokes. None of it feels strange. Maybe it's the coke, the booze, or simply Ralph's, but tonight, it all makes sense.

I consider finding Brazen again but know where that leads. More temptations, more lines crossed. Instead, I head for Red's table, expecting her there, but she's gone. Only the aftermath remains: empty bottles like discarded trophies, half-melted candles dripping wax onto silver platters, coke smudged across the table's glossy surface. The chaos proves she had fun. That's enough.

I sink into the sofa, rolling my shoulders, stretching my legs. The familiar burn of powder clears the fog. The coke hits fast, sharpening the room's edges, dialing up every sensation. My fingers drum my thigh as I settle into the rush, attention narrowing on the scene across the hall.

Red.

She stands with Panta and Lóne, their bodies angled around a Pierrot strapped to the table. Wrists and ankles bound, naked form splayed beneath them. Scattered light dances over her skin, catching the helpless rise of her chest, the writhe of her body under their touch.

I down a tequila shot, wincing. Another Pierrot moves behind me, pressing soft curves against my back, breasts flush to my shoulders. She drapes over me like silk, hands ghosting my chest, slipping under my tunic. Her nails graze my skin. She nuzzles my neck, breathing me in.

I smirk, letting her play, indulging her hips shifting against me. Just a Pierrot. Red won't care.

But my gaze drifts back.

Red circles the table as Panta fists the bound Pierrot's hair, yanking her head back, forcing her mouth open as he thrusts in. The girl takes him easily, lips stretched, body tense. Behind her, Lóne grips her waist, slamming into her, the force rattling the table. She arches, muscles flexing, surrendering completely.

But Red holds the power.

Her fingers trace possessive lines down the girl's skin—the dip of her waist, the curve of her thighs. She palms the Pierrot's breast, squeezing until the girl jolts, then leans in, lips grazing her ear, whispering something private. The Pierrot trembles.

Red looks over at Panta. The next second, his movements snarl faster, breath ragged. They're not seeing the bound girl at all. They're seeing Red. Imagining her beneath them, mouth slack, skin ridged with their fingerprints.

She knows.

The Pierrot behind me senses my tension, the way my body is wired, keyed up from the spectacle. Her hands knead harder, fingers dipping lower, breath scalding my ear. She's trying to hook me into the moment, but she's a shadow of the woman I crave.

I close my eyes, just for a heartbeat, and swap her touch for Red's.

Red's lips skimming my jaw.
Red's hands claiming my chest.

She leans down further, sliding a hand over the bound Pierrot's face, covering her eyes, tilting her head back just enough to press a kiss to her throat. She's toying with her now, guiding the pace, orchestrating the scene with a cruel sort of elegance.

I tip back another shot, pouring gasoline over the fire already burning inside me.

This place is a syringe. A delirium. A rot I'd swallow twice.

Jumadi's warning surfaces, but I douse it. Whatever caution she offered has already already been swallowed whole.

Maybe this is the only paradise that matters.

I sink deeper, letting the Pierrot's hands pummel my shoulders, her fingers sending jagged heat down my spine. Her breasts crush against my back, her heat bleeding into me, her touch unspooling the last threads of my restraint. The coke sharpens everything. Moans become sharper, skin hotter, her body a silk noose. It feels *too* good. *Too* easy.

I grab another shot, tequila blistering my throat, feeding the high. I don't want to leave. Won't leave. The vow lodges in my skull: Andy's a ghost, a name that doesn't belong here.

A presence prickles. Crimson lips in my periphery. Before I turn, Red fists the Pierrot's hair, yanking her down. The girl stumbles, hitting the floor with a thud.

"Fuck off, *please*," Red snaps.

The Pierrot scrambles up, clutching her mask, trembling. There's a brief hesitation, then she vanishes into the crowd. Red takes her place behind me, claiming the space like owed territory. Her hands clamp my shoulders, nails biting, fingers digging in.

She presses in close, breath searing my neck. Her nose brushes my skin as she inhales.

"I can smell her all over you." Her nails puncture my shoulders. "Naughty, naughty boy."

I exhale, biting back a grin. "She just... fulfilled an urge. That's all."

"An urge?"

"Yeah." I tip my head back into her touch, her hands sculpting lazy circles. "Panta and Lóne said you've never fucked anyone here."

She scoffs, but doesn't refute it. Instead, she looks at me like I've missed the plot entirely.

"You did nothing wrong," she says finally, voice softer now, fingers easing their grip. "You did nothing wrong," she says, grip easing. "It's just... Columbina's like a fucked-up sister to me. Brings shit up. Guess I got twitchy, even if it was just a Pierrot. Pathetic, really..."

"Jealous?" I echo, smirking.

She shrugs, cheeks blushing wine-dark. "She's got this... pull. People melt for her. She's... magnetic."

I catch her chin, turning her face to mine. "I'm here with you, aren't I?"

Her eyes lock on mine.

"You are. That's all I need."

She slings her arms around me. My hands skate her waist, sinking into her. When she pulls back, she fishes a crumpled cig pack from her cleavage, flicking it open.

"Want one?"

"Sure."

She lights mine first, sparking the tip, then hers. We slump into the sofa, smoke whirling as Ralph's unravels around us.

She exhales upwards, a grey spire. "Quite the world, eh?"

"Couldn't ask for anything more," I say, watching ember-glow dance on her lips.

"So... how did the Fox Hunt go for you?"

I hesitate. Her smirk deepens.

"Lucky boy," she purrs. "Just wait for some of the host's other *games*. He really cranks the dial."

"More games like the Fox Hunt?" I ask, intrigued.

She leans in, dropping her voice. "That was child's play compared to some of his other theatrics."

I flick ash. "As long as it doesn't turn into The Purge, I'm game."

Red's reaction is subtle, but I catch it. A tiny fracture in the usual confidence she wears so effortlessly. It's gone almost as soon as it appears, but not before I see it. A shadow crossing her expression, her lips parting slightly, as if she's just remembered something she'd rather forget.

Then, just as quickly, she smooths it over, schooling her features back into an easy smirk. She exhales a slow stream of smoke, shaking her head. "Oh, it won't be that kind of game. But trust me, you'll want to be ready for what's coming."

Best not to think too much into it, so I let it pass, letting the pleasant fog of liquor and nicotine take over.

I watch her, the blue eyes hooded behind the mask, the way her blonde hair spills loose over her shoulders.

Then, without another word, she leans in and kisses me.

It's unhurried, her lips pressing against mine through the narrow slits in our masks. It's different from all the others—the drunken kisses, the hungry, reckless ones. Her fingers thread through my hair, nails grazing my scalp, tugging just enough to send a jolt through me.

My cigarette slips from my fingers, forgotten, burning out against the table.

And I let myself get lost in her.

16

When I step into the house, the scent of coffee wraps around me. I hear the clang of a pan, the soft hiss of something frying.

Grace is there, cooking on autopilot. But there's no ease in her expression when she looks up and sees me standing in the doorway. Her gaze lingers a second too long, assessing, before she turns back to the stove.

She doesn't say anything at first. Just watches. Then, casually, too casually, she asks, "Where were you last night?"

I lean against the doorframe, forcing a yawn, stretching as if I haven't noticed the edge in her tone. "Went out for a drink," I say, the lie slipping too easily. "Nothing major."

She quirks an eyebrow. Just slightly. A small tell, but I see it.

"With James?" she asks.

My body stiffens before I can stop it. The smallest hesitation. Barely a second, but she catches it.

I recover quickly, running a hand through my hair. "Yeah. James. We hit the pub for a bit."

She doesn't blink.

"He called the house phone yesterday."

My stomach sinks.

"Said you weren't answering your mobile."

She's watching me now, really watching me, like she's waiting for something to slip.

Fuck, she's into me.

I force a shrug, keeping my expression casual. "I must've missed him. I'll call him back later."

She doesn't reply. Just keeps looking. Then, instead of responding, she turns back to the stove. The clatter of a spatula against the pan is the only sound between us.

I sit down at the table, rubbing my temples, waiting for her to push further.

She doesn't.

And somehow, that's worse.

She assesses me in that quiet, careful way she does when she knows I'm lying but isn't sure if she wants to press the issue. "You've been out late a lot recently. You're not usually like this."

I hesitate, caught in the space between explanation and evasion. My mind scrambles for something believable, something that won't lead to more questions. "Actually, I was out celebrating."

Her eyebrows lift slightly. "Celebrating?"

"Yeah." I force a smile, leaning into the lie as if confidence will make it real. "I got a promotion last week. Pay raise, new title, more responsibilities. We went out for a few drinks after work."

She sets the spatula down, wiping her hands on a tea towel. The shift is subtle, but something about her posture changes. Like she's deciding if she believes me or not.

"A promotion?"

She doesn't sound excited. Not really.

"A promotion's a big deal, Andy. Why didn't you tell me?"

I shrug, glancing down at the table. "I guess it slipped my mind."

A slow exhale. Her fingers tap lightly against the counter, her mind turning something over. I see it in the shift of her posture, the tension in her grip. She doesn't believe me. Not entirely.

She steps closer, momentarily forgetting the pan on the stove. "We should celebrate," she says, carefully. "Maybe we can go out tonight? Or spend the day together. Do something nice."

For a second, I consider it. Maybe that's what we need—a day together, something normal, something real. But then I picture it: the small talk, the forced smiles, the slow realisation that whatever was holding us together has already rotted through.

Still, she's trying. I can see that now. And maybe that's worse.

"What were you thinking?" I ask, my voice cautious.

She tucks a strand of hair behind her ear. "I don't know. An art gallery? A nice dinner? Something different."

There's something uncertain in her voice. Like she's grasping for something already out of reach.

"An art gallery?" I say, scepticism slipping through before I can stop it.

Her expression tightens. "Yes, Andy. A gallery," she says, her tone sharpening. "We'd look at art. Together."

She's watching me closely now, waiting to see if I'll take the bait.

I summon another smile, a weaker one this time. "Maybe. That could be fun."

She studies me, searching my face for something, but whatever flicker of hope had been there just seconds ago dims.

"Or not," she murmurs, turning back to the stove. "Your eggs will be ready in a minute."

The conversation dies, smothered under the sound of sizzling oil.

I retreat to the dining table, glancing at my phone's blank screen, feeling the itch creep up my spine. I'd give anything to be back at Ralph's. No expectations, no awkward silences, no one searching my face for answers I don't have.

Grace places the plate in front of me without another word and sits across from me, fingers wrapped around her coffee cup. For a moment, it feels like we're strangers sharing a table—two people who once knew each other but have since grown unfamiliar, orbiting in the same space but never truly touching.

I eat in silence, aware of her eyes shifting over me. She considers her words before she speaks, like she knows whatever she says next might crack something open.

"You're different lately," she says suddenly, probing. "Not in a bad way, just... different."

The fork pauses halfway to my mouth. I force myself to keep my expression neutral. "What do you mean?"

She shrugs, taking a slow sip of coffee. "I don't know. You've been going out more. Acting distracted. Like you're somewhere else."

The words land closer to home than she probably realises. I swallow, setting the fork down carefully. "Work's been busy," I say smoothly. "Exam period and all. The promotion's a lot to adjust to. But the summer holidays are coming up soon."

She nods, but she's still watching me, her eyes scanning my face for something I won't give her. Her expression softens, but a flicker of doubt lingers just beneath the surface.

And I wonder, what does she see when she looks at me now?

Does she see the cracks?

Because the man sitting across from her doesn't feel like her husband anymore. Even to me.

I'm playing the part, keeping up the façade, but every word, every gesture feels hollow.

As she watches me with that baffled, searching gaze, her fingers tighten slightly around her coffee cup, like she's grounding herself.

Once, that gaze held something different.

Years ago, she looked at me like I was the only person in the world. I remember it so clearly I could step into the memory, back to a warm summer night on the balcony of our old flat. We'd spent hours out there, drinking cheap wine, our feet tangled together under the table. She had been barefoot, legs curled under her, her laugh breaking through the quiet hum of the city below. I don't remember what she said, only the way she said it—like we were invincible, like whatever future we were building was a sure thing.

She had leaned across the table, eyes locked onto mine, grinning. "We should just do it," she had said. "Pack up. Leave London. Go somewhere wild."

"Where?" I had asked, amused, indulging the idea.

She had shrugged. "Does it matter?"

It hadn't, back then. Not when the thought of leaving everything behind with her had felt exciting instead of impossible.

I'd kissed her right then, over the table, knocking over a half-empty glass in the process. We hadn't cared. We had been laughing too hard.

Now, Grace isn't laughing. She isn't leaning forward, reaching for me. She's studying me, not just with curiosity, but with something closer to apprehension.

"Andy?" Her voice cuts through, pulling me back, searching for something that might still be there. "What's really going on? You've been somewhere else all morning."

I clear my throat, forcing myself to focus. "Sorry," I mutter. "Just... lost in thought."

"Well," she says, hesitation creeping into her voice, "maybe an art gallery's not your thing, but we can do something else. We haven't done much together lately, and I miss that."

Her words should stir something in me. A year ago, they might have. Maybe even six months ago. Guilt, nostalgia, regret. But they don't. They feel distant, like an echo from another life. I nod, offering her a weak smile. "Yeah, maybe," I say, trying to sound sincere.

She studies me for a moment and sighs. "Look," she begins, softer now, almost hesitant. "I don't want to push, Andy, but if there's something going on, I'm here."

She means it. Or at least, she wants to.

Is she, though?

My eyes drop to her hand gripping the coffee cup, the way her fingers tighten, like she's bracing for something. Her thumb traces the ceramic rim in slow, absentminded circles.

I wonder if that same hand held her phone last night. If her fingers hovered over a message, hesitated before sending it. If Tom's name lit up her screen while she sat curled up on the couch.

She's good at this. This act of caring. This performance of the dutiful, concerned partner. But I know better. I know about the muted notifications, the quick glances when her phone lights up with a new message.

But she knows me too. And that's the problem.

Does she think I'm blind? Or just too indifferent to notice?

A part of me wants to confront her right now. To slam my hand down on the table and ask outright: Who is he, Grace? What's so fucking funny in those texts?

But I don't.

The confrontation will come later, if it ever comes at all.

Because what would it change? If she lied, I'd only hate her more for it.

And if she told the truth?

I don't know if I want to hear it.

She's waiting for me to speak, searching my face for a glimpse of the man she once knew. And I wonder if she realises she's just as lost as I am.

A flicker of satisfaction stirs in me. She won't find him. That man is gone. Ralph's stripped him away, piece by piece, until there was nothing left but this.

"Thanks," I say, the pause stretching too long, threatening to drag something real out of me. "I know you're here." The words are empty, a place filler, something that sounds right but feels like nothing.

She presses her lips together, like she's biting back a thousand words that won't change anything. She gives me one last glance before turning back to her coffee.

I exhale slowly. An uncomfortable silence presses between us. She thinks I'm just distracted, that I've let stress and work bury me. But she doesn't know the truth. That every night she sleeps beside me, I'm slipping further into something far darker, something I don't want to escape from. And maybe she's doing the same.

While she's sneaking glances at her phone, waiting for another message from Tom, I'm tangled in sheets that aren't ours, under the hands of women who don't ask questions.

And it's justified.

How can she stand there pretending to care while she's sneaking around behind my back?

I'm not just pulling away. I'm becoming someone she won't recognise. And the further I go, the harder it'll be to come back. Maybe I don't want to.

The thought tightens something in my chest. Impulsively, I close the space between us, pressing my lips to hers.

Grace stiffens, her hand pausing mid-motion as she stirs the eggs. For a second, her whole body goes still. But I don't pull back. I deepen the kiss, my hands sliding over her waist.

Slowly, I feel her hesitance crack. Her fingers twitch, then loosen, her body softening against mine.

"Andy," she mutters against my lips, her voice hesitant.

"The eggs can wait."

My voice is low, insistent, my hands already slipping beneath the hem of her blouse. Her skin is warm under my touch, a familiarity I haven't felt in a long time. She exhales sharply as my fingers glide up her spine, her back arching instinctively.

She hesitates again, her hands pressing lightly against my chest. Not a push, not yet, but a moment's resistance. Her gaze locks onto mine, searching, questioning. I see something there.

Doubt.

She exhales, shaky and unsure, but she doesn't stop me when I lift her blouse, sliding it up and over her head. It pools onto the floor in a careless heap. Her chest rises and falls unevenly, breath quickened, lips parted. Her grip tightens on the counter behind her, like she needs something solid to hold onto.

The curtains are only half-drawn. The morning light spills into the room, pale and soft. Outside, the street is quiet. But if someone walked past, if they turned their head at the right moment, they'd see. See the way I press against her, my hands trailing over her bare skin, the way I unfasten the button of her jeans.

Grace's eyes dart towards the window, her breath catching slightly. I bet the same thought crosses her mind, her lips parting like she wants to say something.

I grip her waist, dragging her forward until her legs bracket mine, pressing her back into the counter. My fingers slide to the button of her jeans, undoing it with ease. She watches me, silent, her breath shallow as I lower the zip and push the denim down, my hands following its path along her hips, her thighs, until they pool at her ankles.

She steps out of them, her body tense but not resisting.

Then she reaches for me. Her hands slip under my shirt, pushing it up, her palms skating over my stomach, my ribs, as she tugs it over my head and lets it drop.

I step back just enough to unfasten my own jeans, letting them slide to the floor. Grace's eyes flicker downwards, then back up. I wonder what's going through her mind. Hesitation? Curiosity? Maybe even longing.

I don't give her time to second-guess.

I grip her hips and lift her onto the counter, stepping between her legs, letting her feel me against her. She gasps softly, her fingers reaching into my shoulders, nails biting into my skin.

Her lips find mine again, rougher now. The scent of coffee swells in the air, mixing with the salt of her skin and the faint, smoky smell of the forgotten eggs on the stove.

She pulls me closer, her body pressing into mine. And I let her.

Because in this moment, it isn't love, or comfort, or even lust.

It's possession.

And I need to take something back.

"Andy," she whispers, softer now, uncertain.

I pause, searching her face for a hint of hesitation, an indicator of the distance that's grown between us. But then she exhales, her lips parting as she pulls me back in, clinging to the moment. Her hands grasp at my shoulders, dragging me closer, and I take it like I'm starving.

The eggs sizzle in the pan, filling the kitchen with the scent of butter and salt, but it's background noise, fading under the sharp gasp she lets out when I move deeper inside her.

She's tight, her body yielding and resisting all at once, and I feel the tension in her, like she's holding back, waiting for something. My fingers dig into the softness of her thighs, my grip possessive as I pull her closer, pressing her back against the countertop. The marble is cold beneath her, but the heat between us burns away the chill.

Her breath hitches. For a moment, our eyes lock. I see something there, something unguarded, a flicker of the woman I once knew. It hits me all at once, an unbearable ache, a craving I can't name.

I take her harder, my body demanding more, my grip tightening, needing to shatter whatever hesitation still persists between us. Her nails bite into my shoulders, trailing red-hot lines down my back, a silent reprimand I ignore.

The awful scent of burnt eggs fills the air.

A shrill, ear-piercing BEEP erupts from the smoke alarm.

Grace jolts, her entire body stiffening beneath me, the moment cracking open like glass splitting under pressure.

"Shit," she gasps, her hands flying to my chest, pressing against me now. Not in pleasure, but in protest.

But I don't stop.

I clamp my hands on her hips, forcing her to stay open for me, refusing to let the moment slip away just yet.

"Andy," she hisses, her breath coming fast, panicked now, but I'm too far gone.

My fingers dig in harder, my thrusts turning desperate, chasing the inevitable. My jaw clenches, my breath ragged as I bury myself inside her one last time, letting the sharp pleasure of release tear through me.

The alarm wails.

The eggs burn.

Grace is barely moving now, her body tense, her hands limp against my shoulders as if she's given up on fighting me off, just waiting for it to be over.

And then it is.

The moment collapses in on itself.

I pull back, reality crashing over me like cold water.

Grace shoves at my chest properly this time, her legs dropping from around me as she scrambles off the counter, yanking her jeans back up with stiff, hurried motions. The alarm is still screaming above us, an unbearable, high-pitched shriek that makes the whole kitchen feel suffocating.

She grabs a dishcloth and waves it under the detector, her hand shaking slightly. The noise cuts out, leaving only the thick scent of smoke and the silence between us.

I turn to the stove, dumping the blackened eggs into the sink. The water hisses as it hits the charred food, breaking it apart into murky chunks that swirl down the drain.

Grace is already busying herself, wiping the counter, straightening things, retreating. Her back is to me, her shoulders stiff, her movements brisk.

"I'll make some toast instead," she says finally, her voice flat.

I lean against the counter, watching her. She's slipping back into the version of herself that fits neatly into this life, the one I don't belong in anymore.

She brushes her hair back, finally glancing at me. There's something different in her eyes. Something fragile, like a line has been drawn, but neither of us are willing to acknowledge it.

"You should get dressed," she says lightly, but there's a firmness to it, a finality that sticks.

FRAGMENTED

I push away from the counter and head towards the bedroom. As I pull on my clothes, I can't shake the feeling that I've left something behind in that kitchen. Something we'll both pretend wasn't missing in the first place.

17

The classroom stinks of sweat and disinfectant, the kind of smell that settles into the walls no matter how many times the caretaker cleans.

I sit at my desk, red pen hovering over an essay on America's entry into World War Two. I've read the same paragraph three times, but the words slide past me, refusing to stick. I blink hard, try again. Nothing. My grip tightens around the pen.

The students are barely pretending to work. I hear them whispering, laughing under their breath, making plans for summer. Beaches, festivals, expensive trips abroad. Their voices needle at me, pushing into the space behind my eyes. They assume I don't notice. Maybe I don't care enough to.

"Mr Giles?"

Emma Walker stands in front of my desk, gripping a crumpled essay. She looks like she's already regretting approaching me.

"What is it, Emma?" I don't bother hiding the impatience in my voice.

She hesitates. "I don't get what you mean by developing the argument." She picks at the edge of her paper. "You said it has to flow, but I don't know how to make it."

I shut my eyes for half a second. *We've been over this.*

"You take the main idea in your introduction and build on it," I say. "Each paragraph has to lead into the next. Otherwise, it's just disconnected points."

Emma blinks. "Yeah, but I did make it connected."

I grip the pen tighter. "Connected means related, Emma. If you're writing about America's economic motives, you can't suddenly jump to Hitler without explaining why it matters. Do you see?"

She frowns. "I thought I did. This is... this is *stupid*."

That word.

It lands like a slap.

My jaw locks. My fingers curl under the desk.

Stupid.

"It's not stupid," I snap before I can stop myself. "It's critical thinking. Something you're going to need if you have any hope of passing this exam."

Emma stiffens, shoulders caving in. "I... I didn't mean—"

"Didn't mean what?" I push my chair back sharply, the legs scraping against the floor. Heads swivel toward us. The low murmur of conversation vanishes. "Didn't mean to waste my time? Because that's exactly what you're doing right now."

Her hands tighten around the edges of her essay, knuckles going white.

"I'm trying," she murmurs.

A humourless laugh pushes past my teeth. "Trying?" My voice is too loud now, filling the space. "Trying looks like effort, Emma. It looks like doing the work, asking the right questions, engaging with the material." I flick my fingers at the paper in her hands. "This? This is not trying. It's laziness."

Her face goes blank. Too blank.

For a moment, I expect her to argue, to fight back, but she doesn't. She just stands there, silent, absorbing it.

Something twists in my stomach.

"Go sit down," I say, voice flat. "You've got two days to figure it out."

Emma nods stiffly, turning without a word. She walks back to her desk, shoulders hunched, head low, staring at nothing.

The silence in the room is deafening.

I sit down, pressing my hands against the desk, trying to steady them. My eyes flick to the clock.

Fifteen minutes.

Just fifteen more minutes.

The students pretend to focus, heads bowed over their books, but I can feel the shift. The stiffness in their shoulders, the way they avoid looking at me for too long.

Good. Let them be afraid. Maybe then they'll stop wasting my time.

The thought rings hollow. There's no satisfaction in it. No sense of control or power. Just the lingering image of Emma's face. Flushed, humiliated, eyes downcast as she retreated to her seat. It plays over in my mind like a stuck reel, each flicker bringing fresh discomfort.

I grip my pen, turning my attention back to the pile of essays on my desk. The words swim. The clock ticks. Ten minutes left. I just need to last ten more minutes.

When the bell finally rings, the tension in the room shatters. Chairs scrape against the floor, bags swing over shoulders, and students shuffle towards the door. They keep their voices low, their usual energy dampened. A few glance at me as they pass, quick and wary, like they expect me to lash out again.

I barely register them.

Emma moves slower than the rest, her essay still crushed in her grip. She doesn't look at me as she collects her things. Just walks straight out into the corridor, swallowed by the crowd.

Say something.

The words lodge in my throat, thick and immovable. I watch her disappear, the guilt tightening its grip.

And the room feels suffocatingly empty.

I slump back into my chair, rubbing a hand over my face. My skin is clammy, my pulse still elevated, the adrenaline turning sour in my veins.

What the hell is wrong with me?

I glance at the essays stacked neatly in front of me, their orderly pile mocking me. The red pen feels like a dead weight between my fingers. I set it down, exhaling sharply.

The door creaks open.

For a split second, my stomach lurches. Emma? No—Lisa.

She steps inside, nursing a chipped coffee mug, old cardigan slipping off one shoulder. Her slow movements scream exhaustion, the kind that settles into your bones after years of the same routine. The same walls, the same faces, the same hollow conversations.

I see my future in her.

"You look like hell," she remarks.

"Feel like it." I lean forwards, elbows on the desk.

Lisa settles onto a nearby desk, mug cradled between her hands, steam rising up from the surface. The scent of cheap instant coffee drifts over.

"What happened?"

I shake my head. "Rough class."

"Rough enough to have half the students walking out like they just saw a public execution?"

I huff a humourless laugh. "It wasn't that bad."

She lifts the mug, taking a slow sip, watching me. "I saw Emma in the hallway."

The knot in my stomach tightens.

"She looked like she was about to cry," Lisa continues.

I exhale through my nose, fingernails cutting against the wooden desk. "She wasn't getting it," I say curtly. "The exam is in two days, and she still doesn't understand how to analyse a damn source. What am I supposed to do? Hold her hand through it?"

"Maybe," she says, calm but firm. "Or maybe just not tear her down when she's already drowning."

My hands clench. The irritation flares up again, but it's weaker this time. Defensive. "I wasn't tearing her down. I was pushing her. She needs to wake up."

"Did it work?"

The question lands like a punch to the gut. I have no answer.

I look at the deep lines on her face, the cardigan draped loosely over her frame, like even her clothes have given up. She's been here too long. Or maybe she's exactly what this place shapes you into.

I drag a hand down my face, exhaling slowly. "She said it was stupid," I mutter, voice lower now. "All of it. The essays. The analysis."

Lisa nods slightly, as if she understands more than I want her to. "And you took that personally."

I let out a hollow laugh. "Yeah. Maybe I did. Maybe I'm sick of feeling like this job doesn't matter. Like I don't matter."

"Andy," she says carefully. "Are you okay?"

The question twists something in my chest.

I force a smile. Shake my head. "I'm fine. Just tired."

She doesn't believe me. I can see it in the way her fingers tighten around the mug. But she doesn't push.

"You should check in with Emma," she says after a moment. "Before the exams. Let her know you're in her corner."

"I'll think about it."

We both know I won't.

Lisa hesitates, then nods. "Take care of yourself, okay?"

She leaves, the door clicking shut behind her.

I stare at the empty space she left, the image burned into my mind.

I see myself in her. Older, worn down, still sitting at this same desk, drinking the same bad coffee. Stuck.

The thought chills me to my core.

I check my phone. *4:23 p.m.*

Some might call it too early for a drink. I call it the perfect time. Mid-afternoon pints have their own kind of logic. Summer or winter, there's always an excuse. In summer, the sun stretches long enough to make drinking feel like a celebration. In winter, the early darkness turns afternoon into night anyway. Either way, the rules blur.

Pop, pop, pop. My brain won't shut up. I need to quiet it. Drown the noise, dull the edge. I shove my hands in my pockets and power-walk away from the school, putting as much distance between me and the suffocating pre-exam stress as I can.

Supercars wizz past like overfed cats, their owners barely sparing a glance at the pavement. Women with designer bags cut through the street with indifference, their eyes glancing over me before dismissing me entirely. The world moves fast here, but it doesn't touch me. Not really.

I spot a pub. Too clean. Too polished. But it'll do.

Inside, I beeline straight for the bar and order a pint. No hesitation. Before the bartender even has a chance to take my payment, I lift the glass and gulp down two mouthfuls. Cold, crisp, numbing. Only then do I tap my card and retreat to a quiet corner, sinking into the seat with my back to the room.

No doubt, word of today's little incident with Emma will spread. Passed from student to student, morphing along the way, until it reaches the headmaster's ears as some exaggerated version of reality. But I can't bring myself to care.

What's the worst that could happen? I get fired? Grace finally decides she's had enough? Fine. Let it happen. Maybe I want it to. Maybe it would be easier to let everything collapse under its own weight than to admit I'm the one holding the sledgehammer.

I sip my pint, letting the thought settle. What if I just walked away? No more exams. No more staff meetings. No more forcing bored, privileged kids to pretend they care about the past. If they can't be bothered to put in the effort, why should I?

No more coming home to a woman who barely looks at me anymore.

I swirl the beer in my glass, watching the amber liquid. The more I think about it, the more tempting it becomes. If everything crashes down, at least I won't have to be the one to set it on fire. Let them push me out. Let them make the decision for me.

And then? Maybe, just maybe, I'll go after what I really wanted all along.

I let the thought languish in the back of my mind, rolling it over like a smooth stone between my fingers. Becoming a historian. Writing about the sites that have fascinated me since I was a kid. Places like Göbekli Tepe, shrouded in mystery, their secrets barely scratched by time. Instead of forcing history onto students who don't give a damn, I could spend my life uncovering it.

I take another sip.

And then there's Ralph's.

Ralph's has taught me freedom. Taught me indulgence. I don't need to be tied to one woman, especially not one who treats me like shit and sneaks around behind my back.

The sting of that realisation has dulled. Hell, it's almost liberating.

I lean back, running a thumb through the condensation on my glass. The clinking of glasses, the low buzz of the city just outside, it all fades. For a moment, the world stops.

I raise my glass to my lips. Already empty.

I chuckle under my breath, amused at the pace I've set. With a shrug, I return to the bar. The bartender clocks me. He lifts an eyebrow but doesn't say a word. Just pours another pint, sets it down. Knows better than to ask questions.

I settle back into my corner, nursing the lager, but I can already feel it. The itch. The restless pull in my chest.

Grace won't be happy when I stumble through the door later. I can feel it coming. She's close to snapping, close to confronting me head-on.

What she doesn't realise is that I already know.

I wonder how it'll all play out.

Tom can have her.

If that's the price I have to pay to keep indulging in Ralph's, Red, Columbina, and whoever else the night brings, so be it. It's a price I'll gladly pay.

The itch deepens. I grab my pint, or what's left of it, and step outside.

The pub sits neatly between high-end boutiques, in an area where everyone seems to have somewhere important to be. I don't.

I light a cigarette.

First drag. Smoke wraps around me, sinking into my bloodstream and mixing with the alcohol.

For the first time today, I feel something close to peace.

A pair of guys in suits step out of the pub, lighting cigarettes beside me.

I watch them for a moment, then nod in their direction. "What's up?"

One of them snaps his lighter shut, barely glancing at me. "You alright, mate?"

"Yeah, all good," I reply automatically, already regretting it. This is nothing. Just another dead-end exchange. I take a slow drag of my cigarette, letting the smoke rise and twist into the city air.

The suits are still talking. Work shit. Deals, meetings, some big shot they need to impress. Same script, different day. They'll have this conversation again tomorrow, next week, swapping out one name for another.

But maybe I can steer it. Try the Brazen thing. No names, no small talk, just confidence. Command the space. It worked on me, so why not on them?

I shift my stance, leaning against the wall, inhaling deep before exhaling. Relaxed. Controlled. "Funny thing about conversations like these," I say, flicking ash from my cigarette.

The taller one eyes me, brow twitching up. "What's that?"

"They're always about work. About people who don't matter, deadlines that won't mean anything a year from now." I gesture lazily with my cigarette. "Why not talk about something real instead?"

The shorter guy smirks, side-eyeing his friend. "Something real?" he repeats, amusement creeping into his tone.

"Yeah," I say, ignoring their shift in posture. Push forwards. Own the moment. "No names, no job titles, just ideas. A proper conversation."

They exchange a glance. The taller one smirks. "Alright, mate. What kind of *real* conversation are you after?"

I take another slow drag, holding their attention. "Tell me what you'd do if you weren't tied to this life. No job. No obligations. Nothing holding you back. What's the one thing you'd chase?"

For a moment, I almost have them. The taller one locks in, like he's considering it. But the shorter one lets out a dismissive laugh. The spell shatters.

"Mate, are you serious?" He shakes his head, snorting.

"Proper philosopher over here," the taller one adds, flicking his cigarette. "You sure you're in the right place? This isn't some uni debate club."

I force a chuckle, trying to play it off, but the sting hits harder than I'd like to admit.

The taller one nudges his mate. "Come on, we should head back in. This bloke's looking for something we're not selling."

They grind their cigarettes underfoot, muttering something I don't catch as they slip back inside. The door swings shut behind them, muffling the noise of the pub, leaving me alone with nothing but the faint, lingering taste of rejection.

I take another drag, but the cigarette's almost gone. A dying ember, barely holding on.

I flick it to the pavement and watch as the last of the ash scatters.

So much for that.

I lean back against the wall, turning my head up. The city doesn't care. It moves around me, alive and indifferent.

I exhale through my nose, the bite of beer and nicotine still coating my throat.

I'm no Brazen.

Whatever magnetism he has, whatever invisible strings he pulls to make people gravitate towards him, it's not something I can fake.

The thought should bother me, but it doesn't.

I finish the last gulp of my pint, letting the bitterness linger, then push open the door and head back inside.

18

Tonight, the host has arranged something different. A grand finale, they're calling it. The crowd buzzes, speculating what the night has in store for us. In the meantime, smaller games unravel across the hall. Innocent, by Ralph's standards. Drinking contests, stolen kisses exchanged under darkened alcoves, a mini dance-off near the bar that ended with the victors vanishing behind a red curtain.

The night rolls in waves. Monsieurs and Madames stumble, laugh, lose themselves in the current. The usual groups mill about. The Pierrots. Columbina and her entourage. Brazen, draped in women, drink in hand. A man in a Venetian mask spills half his cocktail attempting a toast, only to pass the remainder to the nearest girl, who downs it without hesitation.

And then there's Red.

She's been at my side all night, her presence the one thing keeping me from slipping entirely into the madness. We drink together, trading flirtatious glances. Every shot threads us closer together. She's my only stability in this place, even though neither of us is steady.

"Another?" she asks, smirking.

I lean in, close enough to feel the warmth radiating from her. "Why stop now?"

She laughs, and we toss back another round of shots. The burn licks down my throat, spreading fire through my limbs. Her arm drapes around my shoulder, and her fingers skim the back of my neck. Just a touch, but it's electric.

Then, with a flick, she reaches for a small metal tin on the coffee table and opens it. Inside, a neat row of tiny, colourful pills gleam under the dim light, nestled in their case like candy.

She plucks out two, rolling them between her fingers before holding one out to me, her smile playful, daring. "Feel like taking things up a notch?"

I don't hesitate.

She pops hers first, swallowing it with a swig of champagne. I follow. The pill dissolving on my tongue before I chase it down with my drink. The sweetness masks the bitter, chalky taste.

Red leans back, watching me with a glint of amusement, her golden hair catching the glow of the chandeliers. I can't look away.

"Here's to the best night yet," she toasts, raising her glass.

"To the best night," I echo, clinking mine against hers.

We drink as the room continues to unfold around us.

Red turns to me, propping her chin in her palm. "You ever think you'd end up in a place like this, Hannya?" She says my name like it means something. Like it's real.

I shake my head. "Not in a million years."

"Me neither," she admits. "But I don't think I could be anywhere else."

For a second, the world narrows to just us. Her fingers brush against mine, sending a jolt through me.

And then it begins.

It starts as a hum beneath my skin, a warmth in my chest that slowly spreads, working its way through my veins like ink in water. Every sound gets pulled into focus. The clink of glasses, the conversations.

I glance at Red. She's glowing. Not *literally*, but the light clings to her, the golden strands of her hair, the curve of her mouth, all of it hypnotic. She leans in slightly, the whole room moving with her, and I can't help but grin.

"Feeling it yet?" she asks.

I let out a slow breath. "Maybe."

Her smirk widens. "Give it a few minutes. You'll see."

The heat surges, flooding my limbs, wrapping round my ribs. A quiet euphoria rises, and suddenly I'm lighter. More aware. Every brush of fabric against my skin thrums, hyperreal. The thought makes me snort, and Red watches, mouth crooked like she's already ten steps ahead.

And she is.

I see it now.

Everything's shifting.

I lean back, knuckles grazing hers. She doesn't pull away, fingers threading through mine, casual as anything.

"Need water," I mumble, throat parched out of nowhere.

"First rule of the night," says Red. "Stay hydrated."

She flags down a waiter, and a pint glass appears in my hand. I gulp it down, the cold hitting like a lifeline. How's water *this* good?

Red watches me, resting her chin on her hand, her smile softer now. "Better?"

"Much better," I say, setting the glass down.

For a while, we just exist in this moment. Talking, laughing, letting the Molly settle deeper into our veins. The sounds of the party drift around us, but they feel distant, blurred at the edges like a dream we aren't fully part of. Red's fingers trace idle patterns on my arm, and I lose myself in the way her lips move when she speaks, the way her laughter cuts through the noise like a spark in the dark.

Around us, Ralph's continues its descent into madness. Dancing bodies, wandering hands, glasses clinking, whispers exchanged under velvet shadows. But here, in this small corner of the room, it's just us.

I notice *everything*. The way her golden hair catches the dim light, the way the champagne in her glass leaves faint kisses of moisture on her lower lip, the way her mask frames her eyes like it was made for her alone.

"I think," she says, "there's something unique about this place. The masks, the rules, the way we're all here for reasons we're not supposed to talk about. It's freeing. A year ago, I'd have sworn I'd never end up somewhere like this. But now... it feels like I was always meant to find it."

I nod, barely able to look away. "Same. I don't think I could leave this behind now."

Her hand brushes against mine again, sticking around this time, and everything is heightened. The texture of her skin, the warmth of her touch, the way every nerve in my body seems tuned to the space between us.

Neither of us speaks. I reach out, brushing a strand of hair away from her face, tucking it behind her ear. Her skin is impossibly soft.

"You're impossible to figure out," I say, leaning closer. "And I don't think I'd want it any other way."

"Maybe that's the point," she whispers. "Some things, some people... They aren't meant to be figured out."

She shifts closer, shoulder nudging mine. My heart lurches.

A breath escapes her, almost lost under the thrum of the crowd. "Do you ever fantasise about just... vanishing?"

The question wraps around me. I don't even hesitate. "Every bloody day."

She turns, studying me. Her grip tightens, just a fraction. "Maybe we're both fading."

I cradle her hand between both of mine. "Then let's go under together."

Something unclenches in her posture. Perhaps a sense of relief. Her head settles against my shoulder, hair tickling my neck. I breathe out, letting the stillness root itself.

For the first time in ages, I don't feel like I'm floating aimlessly.

She's here. And that's enough to tether me.

The rest of the room fades, leaving only the quiet rhythm of our breathing. We sit like this for what feels like hours, lost in a silence neither of us feels the need to break.

Then, finally, she looks up, her eyes catching mine.

"If you ever feel yourself slipping," she says, "promise you'll come find me."

"Of course I will."

Her fingers remain laced with mine, but her free hand worries the rim of her glass, tracing circles.

"You okay?" I ask, watching her closely.

She offers me a small smile, one that doesn't quite reach her eyes. "Yeah. Just thinking."

"Dangerous habit," I say lightly, hoping to pull her back from wherever her mind has wandered.

She chuckles, but the sound is subdued. "Maybe. But sometimes it's hard to stop."

I watch the way her fingers tap idly against her glass. Something's shifted. The moment before felt open, unguarded. Now there's a flicker of restraint, hesitation, a door closing just before I can step through it.

"Anything worth sharing?" I ask carefully.

She stares into my eyes. "You ever feel like the only person you can depend on is yourself?"

The question catches me off guard. I consider lying, giving her something easy, but the moment calls for honesty.

"More often than I'd like to admit," I answer.

She exhales softly, setting her glass down. "It's not always a bad thing, I suppose. Teaches you to stand on your own two feet. But it can be... lonely."

That last word is soft, unintentional. Like she wasn't meant to say it out loud.

I want to tell her something reassuring, but I can't bring myself to do it. "Being lonely can be hard," I say. "It stays with you, even when you're surrounded by people."

Her fingers tighten slightly around mine. A small, instinctual movement. Like she's testing if I'm still here.

I don't let go.

"Yeah," she says, almost to herself. "That's exactly it. Sometimes I think places like this are the only way to escape."

"Maybe that's why we're all here. To find some kind of freedom from life."

"The pressure to be perfect is never ending," she says, her voice quieter now. "One mistake and it's over."

She says it like a fact. Not personal, not confessional. But I can hear what she's not saying.

I don't push. Instead, I pivot.

"It reminds me of Nikola Tesla," I say, stretching an arm across the back of the sofa. "Brilliant, one of the greatest minds in history. But deeply alone. Obsessed with his work. Lived in his own head. People thought he was eccentric, but really, he was just...isolated."

"And yet, everyone remembers him."

"Exactly. He created something bigger than himself. Even if loneliness tried to define him, it didn't succeed."

A slow, thoughtful smile flickers across her lips. "I wonder if he thought it was worth it in the end."

I lean in, my shoulder brushing hers. "I like to think he did."

She stares past my ear, voice thinning. "It's funny, isn't it? How we can have knowledge, power, even each other, and still feel like something's missing."

"Yeah," I say. "I guess we all want more."

Her hair brushes against my cheek as she leans into me. "Maybe that's why places like this exist," she murmurs. "To tease us with what we're missing."

***

Before long, I notice hulking circular hay targets being wheeled into place at the far end of the room.

Archery. Not what I expected.

I sit up, watching as the servants weave through the hall, clearing space. Not a game I've ever played, but it piques my interest.

That's when I catch it, a flicker out of the corner of my eye.

A shadow gliding across the walls. I turn sharply, but there's nothing there. Just the usual swell of guests, masks shifting under the golden light.

Then it happens again. A darting shape in the corner of my vision. My pulse kicks up as I scrub a hand over my face.

Before I can dwell on it, the host steps forwards, arms spread wide in theatrical delight.

"For tonight's pièce de résistance," he announces, "we have something special. A sport cherished by both mortals and gods alike." His grin is almost too wide, too eager. "Think you're worthy? Now's your chance. We need eight volunteers."

The room erupts in giddy whispers.

A rush courses through me, telling me to *dive in*.

Red's elbow jabs my ribs. "Go on, Hannya!"

Her grin's infectious.

I raise a hand. Others follow, eight of us clustered near the targets.

"The rules are simple," the host calls out. "Three arrows each. Closest to the bullseye wins."

Attendants step forward, distributing bows and leather quivers.

I shoulder the quiver, testing the bow's weight. The grip feels alien yet familiar, like holding a childhood cricket bat.

Movement to my left. Columbina stands there, gaze locked on mine with a proper competitive glint.

Then there's the man in the monkey mask, all jittery, windmilling his arms like he's gearing up for a pub brawl. Comical, that one.

I've barely assessed the competition when the host barks:

"Take aim."

I steady myself and pluck an arrow from the quiver. Nock it, raise the bow. The second I draw, I clock my mistake.

The tension bites, shoulders burning, grip slick with sweat. The bowstring digs into my fingers.

Then, the flicker returns.

That shadow.

Just at the edge of my vision, like a film reel skipping frames.

It's the drugs, I tell myself. *The molly doing its thing.*

I blink hard and try to refocus. My arms are shaky now, the bow's weight knackering. Breathe in. Hold.

Release.

The string snaps.

For a split second, everything slows, the world narrowing to a single moment.

A hollow thud.

Miss.

Laughter ripples through the crowd, soft at first, then growing, crawling under my skin like an itch I can't scratch.

I lower the bow, fingers stiff against the grip. My body is thrumming, the molly turning every sensation electric, but the humiliation cuts through. Why's this getting to me?

I glance back at Red, expecting a smirk, some kind of teasing jab, but she just raises her glass. Not mocking, not pitying. Just watching. It steadies me, pulling me back into myself.

Columbina, on the other hand, moves like she's already won. She draws back her bow with ease, and releases without any hesitation.

Thwack. Bullseye.

The crowd loses it, clapping like she just performed a goddamn miracle. I half-expect her to bow, to bask in the attention.

I glance back to Red again. She's still lounging, relaxed, but now Panta and Lóne are beside her, a little too close for my liking.

A slow, bitter heat rises in me.

It's not jealousy. Not exactly.

"Adorable, Hannya," Columbina pokes fun behind me, too sweet, too knowing.

Her fingers trail over my shoulders, barely touching, but I feel every single brush like a static charge against my skin.

"What are you on about?" I mutter, shaking her off.

She slips around me, pressing in.

"You're so tense," she says, voice laced with amusement. "You should relax, have fun."

She nods towards Red, who is now waving off Panta and Lóne with a sharp flick of her hand.

I exhale, stepping away from Columbina. Red is watching.

"It's my turn," I say, just as Brazen takes his shot. The arrow sinks just outside the bullseye. Eight out of ten.

He steps back, rolling his shoulders. "Good luck, kid."

I take my place again, wrapping my fingers around the bow.

I need this.

Not the win, not the competition itself, just the validation. To matter and be noticed.

I breathe in, steadying my stance. The molly is deep in my bloodstream now, turning everything sharp and stretched.

I exhale. Release.

Thwack. Nine.

An inch shy of the bullseye. Good enough.

Around me, the remaining contestants start to crack. Shoulders slumping, muttered curses, bitter glances at their missed shots. It fuels me.

Final round now. One arrow left.

I'm determined to hit the bullseye this time. I lift the bow, trying to tune out the static under my skin.

The shot flies wide.

Miss. Damn.

The others take their last shots. One gets a ten, another scrapes a seven. The rest don't come close.

Third place. Not bad.

19

The host moves forward. He sweeps a glance over the targets, then at us.

"Good effort," he says smoothly, voice carrying through the room. His gaze lands on me, just for a second. "And now, for our three medallists, a finale awaits!"

A ripple moves through the crowd.

Excitement. Curiosity.

I feel something else.

A slow knot tightening in my stomach.

A finale?

I glance at Red. She's still watching me.

When I turn to Columbina, her lips quirk, just slightly. Like she knows something I don't.

The host raises a hand. The doors creak open.

And everything changes.

The bow slips from my fingers, clattering to the floor.

My breath stalls, trapped under my ribs too tight.

Three figures enter.

Maskless.

FRAGMENTED

No. That's not how this works.

No one comes in without a mask.

The first man stumbles, barely upright, his limbs jerking like they don't belong to him. He has his head bowed, breath sawing through clenched teeth.

Another staggers in. Then a third. All bare-faced.

Their skin is pale, gaunt, streaked with grime. Eyes hollowed out.

A cold blade drags up my spine.

This isn't like the other games. This isn't entertainment.

Wrong. Wrong. Wrong.

My jaw locks, muscles tighten, but the molly twists it all. It's anxiety morphing into rotten curiosity.

I glance at Red again. She's sitting visibly stiff.

The crowd has fallen silent.

No laughter, no cheering. Just waiting.

The trio keep moving forward.

Not walking.

Not leading.

Herded.

I glance around at the others, hoping to see confusion, unease, anything to mirror my own emotions. But all I see are masked faces, leaning forward in glee. Laughter bubbles up from the crowd, low and cruel. Some guests practically squirm in their seats, excitement sparkling in their eyes like predators who've spotted dinner.

The three figures stagger to a halt by the archery range. A staffer snaps, "Strip."

Two of them—a man and a woman—obey instantly, peeling off their tattered clothes, baring their pale, fragile bodies. No hesitation. No shame. Just vacant surrender. *Actors?* I cling to the hope, but their trembling is too raw.

The third man backpedals, voice fraying. "You said there wouldn't be no funny business, mate," he stammers. "I aint doin' this—"

A steward steps in, fist sinking into his gut. The man folds, retching bile onto the parquet.

My lungs seize. My buzz turns jagged, pulse throbbing in my temples.

Another staffer hauls him upright, dragging him towards the hay targets. The other two trail, bare feet scuffing the floor. I keep waiting for the host to crack a joke, reveal the punchline—*See? All part of the show!*—but it never comes.

They're lashed to the targets, ropes biting into wrists. A feeble struggle earns the woman a backhanded blow. Her head snaps sideways, blood blooming at her lip. They're not people anymore. Props. Meat.

Do something.

My muscles twitch.

Say something.

But the crowd's hunger is a living thing. They soak in every second of this, revel in the helplessness of the figures bound before them. I want to tell myself this is another game, another layer of Ralph's twisted fun. But my gut twists violently, and my body knows what my mind doesn't want to accept.

I shouldn't be here.

The pressure in my chest grows heavier, every breath harder to swallow. I scan the audience. All I see are unblinking masks. How can they just sit there?

A darker thought slithers into my mind.

How can I?

The three prisoners sag against the hay, naked and trembling, sweat beading on their skin. Their eyes dart through the room, pleading, but find only masks and champagne flutes raised in toast. No mercy here. No exits. Just an audience waiting for the next thrill.

A line has been crossed, but no one cares.

The host strides slowly forward. The crowd stills, their feverish excitement narrowing into focus. He lifts his arms, his voice more joyous than ever, winding around every syllable like he's conducting an orchestra.

"Madames. Monsieurs. We now enter tonight's final act."

The words strike like a hammer, shattering any last hope that this is a trick, a performance.

I glance at the victims, at the terror carved into their faces. Then at the crowd, bodies thrumming like greyhounds in the traps.

The host turns, sweeping his masked, predatory eyes across us before settling on his chosen names.

"Hannya, Columbina, and Raven," he announces, dragging out the moment. "Step forward."

Raven steps up, black mask gleaming. Columbina follows, chin high, like she's been queueing for this her whole life.

Then, all eyes are on me.

I don't recall moving, but suddenly I'm beside them. A bow's thrust into my hands. Heavier now. Not a toy.

The host speaks again, almost sweetly. "One shot. Aim for a clean, swift kill. Anything less... and they will suffer."

Suffer.

My hands start to shake.

What the hell have I become a part of?

Columbina moves with cold grace, pulling an arrow from her quiver as though she's done it a thousand times before. No hesitation, no second-guessing. Her target, a woman with tears streaming down her face, whimpers softly, her body trembling. I want to scream, to stop her, to ask her what the fuck she thinks she's doing, but I can only stand frozen, helpless, allowing the night to spiral deeper into madness.

The arrow flies.

The shot is so fast and precise that the impact feels anticlimactic. A muffled thump as it pierces the woman's chest. She lets out only a faint whimper before her body goes still. Blood trickles down her skin, and the crowd erupts into applause, as if they've witnessed a flawless performance. It's surreal, horrifying, and they're loving it.

Columbina offers a bow, gracious as a duchess. But her eyes? They're cold and detached. She's accepted this place, this cruelty, whereas I feel the walls closing in, suffocating me. *Not what I signed up for.*

Raven steps forward next, posture wolfish, moving with an eager urgency I can't comprehend. His male mark trembles uncontrollably, eyes wide and pleading. But Raven doesn't hesitate. He draws and releases in one fluid motion.

The arrow strikes the man's throat with a sick, wet sound.

Blood spurts from the wound, splattering across the floor. The applause swells into a sick roar of approval as the man convulses, choking on his own blood.

But he doesn't die. Not right away. He writhes against the ropes, gasping for air, his body twisting in a grotesque dance of agony. I want to look away, but I can't. My feet are glued to the floor while my mind screams at me to do something.

Is this what Ralph's truly is? Perhaps it's always been this way and, blinded by my desperate need for escape, I couldn't see it.

The man's blood coats the floor, his eyes still begging for help. But no one will help him. The crowd watches, enraptured by the spectacle of his suffering, like vultures circling a carcass. They're hungry for more. And I can't stop watching as life drains from him with excruciating slowness.

I should speak up. I should scream. Instead, I remain paralyzed, the words stuck, trapped deep inside me. I wanted to belong here, to be part of Ralph's.

But now?

I don't know who I am anymore.

The man finally flops, motionless. The host claps, and the crowd erupts once more in wild, jubilant cheers, celebrating Raven's ruthlessness like it's admirable.

I glance down at my bow, still heavy in my hands, a weight I'll never escape. I can't do this. I won't. But when the host's gaze lands on me, the sickening realisation hits me like a brick wall.

I'm in too deep.

And I have no choice.

A light nudge at my elbow pulls me back from the edge of panic. "It's your turn. Play along." Brazen's voice is low but firm, his presence both grounding and suffocating. His grip on my arm tightens just enough to remind me—there's no getting out of this.

"I... I can't," I stammer, the bow slipping in my grip. My hands are shaking, my heart racing. I'm trying to hold myself together and act like I belong, but I can feel myself unravelling with every breath.

"You can't show weakness here," Brazen says. "This is your moment. Remember what you told me? What was it?"

I swallow hard, my mouth dry, my voice only a whisper. "I wanted to leave my old life behind, just for a night." The words feel foreign now, like a lie I've told myself for so long that I forgot what it really meant.

Brazen's voice hardens. "Exactly. And you got what you wanted. Now, play the part."

"This isn't what I wanted," I protest, my voice breaking. The words seem weak, like I'm arguing with myself more than with him.

"Beggars can't be choosers, Hannya." Brazen's words slice through me, ice-cold and final. "Now go up there and show them."

He turns away without another glance, leaving me frozen, my thoughts spinning like a broken compass.

What did I expect?

A hand licks my back. I glance sideways and find Columbina's eyes locked on mine, a mocking smirk playing on her lips, like she's enjoying watching me squirm.

"Go get 'em, tiger," she whispers.

I try to step forward, but each step is a monumental struggle. The room's collective gaze suffocates me. My hands tremble as I pull an arrow from the quiver, the bowstring vibrating in my grip like it's about to snap.

I'm no longer in control. My body acts on autopilot, disconnected from my mind.

The man strapped to the target stares back at me, his chest heaving with panicked breaths.

He's not supposed to be here.

I'm not supposed to be here.

We've both crossed into a nightmare where the rules have changed.

I try to steady my hand, but it's no use. My fingers tremble violently, and the bowstring shakes as I pull it back. My vision narrows, tunnelling until all I can see is him, this man's life hanging on the thinnest thread, his existence balanced between agony and whatever twisted version of mercy I can offer.

But mercy doesn't belong here. Not in Ralph's.

Release.

The arrow cuts through the air, striking the man's upper thigh with a sickening thud. A gasp ripples through the crowd, followed by laughter. Detached, cold, gleeful. Then, the delayed scream. It rips through the hall, raw and animalistic, the sound of pure suffering. Blood gushes from the wound, and he thrashes against the restraints, his cries clawing at something deep inside me, a place I didn't even know was fragile.

The host steps forward, shaking his head in exaggerated disappointment. "Oh dear, Hannya," he says, his voice condescending. "What a shame. You could have at least nicked an artery. His wound won't be fatal."

FRAGMENTED

I can't speak. Sweat clings to my skin, and my hands won't stop shaking. My breath comes too fast, too shallow, like I'm suffocating under their expectations.

I've failed.

The man's ragged screams keep coming, but suddenly, I hear more. Faint at first, just a whisper in the back of my mind. Then louder. Louder. An orchestra of agony. Layered, overlapping voices, endless, inescapable. Screams of the dying, of people I've never met, never seen, yet they're here, inside me, twisting my thoughts into something unrecognisable.

I glance at the crowd, desperate to see if anyone else hears it. But they don't. It's all in my head.

I grit my teeth, willing the voices to stop, but the room is spinning, warping, the laughter and cheers smearing together into something grotesque.

Then the staff move.

A group of them swarm the screaming man, their heavy boots striking the marble in perfect rhythm, snapping the host's attention away from me. One pulls out a gleaming knife, its blade catching the candlelight, while another unfurls a whip, cracking it against the floor. The man sobs, his terror reaching an unbearable pitch as they close in.

Columbina leans in, her breath cold against my ear. "I love it," she whispers, her voice gentle, almost affectionate. "Now he'll suffer far worse."

I don't respond. I can't.

I stand there, helpless, while they begin their work.

The knife sinks deep into his skin. A clean, precise cut at first. Then it drags. The blade tears through him, peeling away layers of flesh like burnt paper curling at the edges. His exposed muscle twitches violently underneath, raw and pulsating, fresh meat laid bare on a butcher's block.

The scent hits me next. Coppery. Thick. Sweet in a way that turns my stomach.

His screams shift. They're different now. Lower. Hoarser. Like he's not even trying to fight anymore. Like his body has already accepted that it belongs to them now.

I should speak up. I should stop this.

But I don't.

More figures step forward, masks gleaming, hands reaching. The guests want their turn. The staff pass their tools freely—flaying knives, whips, razors—into the eager hands of the crowd. And then it's a frenzy.

More than a dozen masked figures descend on him, tearing into his body with mindless, ecstatic hunger. Whips crack through the air, slicing his ruined flesh. Knives hack at him in quick, erratic movements, carelessly leaving nothing but a mess of gore and bone.

His body jerks and spasms under their hands, his own muscles betraying him as they twitch against the exposed bone of his flayed arm.

The wet sound of butchery fills the room.

I can't look away.

Tears sting at the edges of my vision, but I force them back. I swallow the lump in my throat, swallow everything. Because this is my fault.

The minutes stretch endlessly. His cries dwindle, slipping into ragged gasps, then silence.

The host's voice cuts through the quiet. "A fine performance," he declares, triumphant, as though this was a play, and the final act has drawn to a close.

Applause. Laughter. Cheers. Masks nodding in approval.

Columbina pulls me away, guiding me through the shifting bodies. The room spins, faces warping, eyes glinting like reflections in a dark lake.

I'm not here. I can't be here. I jerk away from her, not wanting any part of this twisted theatre.

There's only one place I can go. *Red.*

I reach her table, barely holding myself together, my body collapsing onto the sofa like a puppet with its strings cut. The laughter, the applause, all of it washes over me like filth. I feel sick. The world around me is moving on, celebrating, indulging, like none of it mattered.

Red watches me carefully from the other side of the sofa, then reaches for me.

I flinch.

Her face doesn't change, doesn't betray anything, and maybe that's the worst part. She just settles back into her seat, unfazed.

"You did so well," she says gently. "I'm proud of you."

Her voice is soft, but the words slip right off me. The image of the man's tortured face latches onto my thoughts like a parasite, digging deeper the more I try to shake it off. My breath shudders, uneven, and my hands won't stop shaking.

"I know how hard it must have been for you," she continues. "It usually is the first time."

I feel a tremor start in my chest. "I—" My throat tightens before I can say anything else.

She moves closer. "It's okay," she whispers. "It's okay."

It's not. It never will be.

She reaches for my hand again, and this time, I don't pull away. Her fingers wrap around mine as if to hold me together.

"I don't want to get used to this," I choke out, voice breaking. The words aren't meant to be said out loud, but they spill out anyway. I drop my head into my free hand, the weight of it all bearing down too fast, too hard.

Red shifts closer. "You won't."

Before I can stop myself, a sob rips from my throat. It's not quiet, not restrained, but raw and ugly, tearing from somewhere deep inside me.

She slides an arm around me, pulling me in, her warmth pressing against my side. Her other hand finds the back of my head, fingers threading through my hair, gentle, soothing. "Shh," she breathes, holding me as I shake apart.

The room blurs, and I don't care. Let them watch. Let them sneer at my weakness. I bury my face into the crook of her neck, her natural scent anchoring me.

She presses a kiss to my temple. "I've got you," she whispers.

The applause fades into the background. Laughter rises, glasses clink, conversations swirl together, but none of it reaches me. Just Red. Just her heartbeat against my cheek, steady and strong.

Movement catches my attention.

A male guest shoves past one of the stationed staff, his shoulder colliding hard enough to send the concierge off balance. He slams open the heavy double doors at the far end of the hall and rushes through, his movements frantic.

I sit up, wiping at my face, watching as he barrels down the carpeted hallway before vanishing from sight.

Beside me, Red follows my eyes with mild curiosity. "What is it?" she asks.

"That guy." I nod towards the doors. "Guests don't leave during the night, do they?"

She studies me for a moment, her fingers still resting lightly on my thigh. "Maybe he had a wardrobe malfunction." Her tone is light, as though the idea of panic at Ralph's is laughable.

I glance at her, my stomach twisting. "That's it?"

Red shrugs, settling back against the sofa, but she doesn't let go of me. Her fingertips draw slow circles against my skin, like she's trying to keep me here, with her. "What else would it be? People don't leave Ralph's before the night ends unless they're supposed to, and he certainly wasn't supposed to." She raises her glass, taking a long, slow sip as if that settles the matter.

Her nonchalance grates, but her hand is still on me, grounding me, keeping me from slipping too far under.

I should let it go. She's been coming here far longer. She knows the rules. If she says it's nothing, maybe it is. Maybe he really did have an outfit problem that required immediate attention.

Maybe I imagined the panic in his eyes.

I glance at the doors again, half-expecting someone to follow him, but no one does. The staff member he shoved past doesn't react. Just smooths his lapels, adjusts his mask, and resumes his post like nothing happened.

The whole thing lasts seconds, but it leaves a dent in my thoughts.

Why did no one stop him? Why is no one following?

Red exhales, her patience thinning. "Forget about it," she murmurs, giving my knee a gentle squeeze. "You've already been through enough tonight. Don't let some random ruin the moment."

I force a nod, but the unease won't let go.

Ralph's is meticulously controlled. Every moment, every movement, orchestrated. No chaos. No mistakes. A guest storming out in a frenzy doesn't fit. It's a crack in the perfect illusion.

And yet, no one cares.

Except me.

I glance at the doors one last time, but they remain closed. The man is gone.

I want to follow him out, to escape, to never return.

But I can't. Not because the rules dictate it, but because Red and the pull of this place are the only thing keeping my life worth living.

20

Flashes from last week's party at Ralph's replay in my head like scenes from a nightmare, looping, dragging me back into that dark, seductive world. Wouldn't any sane person go to the authorities, spill every twisted detail, bring justice to the poor souls who had to die there? But I'm not the same person I was a few months ago. Day by day, a piece of Andy chips away and is replaced with a piece of Hannya. Dark, reckless, and hungry for more. The lines have blurred so much that I barely recognise the face staring back at me in the mirror.

I've stopped debating what's right or moral, instead letting my mind idle while my body does as it pleases. There's a sick sort of peace in it, a relief in relinquishing all the rules and limits I used to obey. I haven't seen my so-called real friends in months. No drinks, no weekend runs, no casual catch ups over coffee. Their texts and calls were annoying at first, like mosquito bites, relentless in their need to pull me back to that old life. But their attempts soon faded, as if they sensed I was already gone. Hannya doesn't need them. They have nothing to offer that even remotely touches the thirst inside me now.

The summer stretches on, unbearably slow, each day bleeding into the next. Without work to keep me busy, all I do is count down the days until the next celebration, where I can sink back into the chaos and lose myself.

When Grace is at work, or wherever she goes these days, I drift in and out of fantasies. Red, her body pressed close, whispering provocations in my ear. Columbina, teasing and aloof, wild elegance and barely contained lust. The Pierrots with their masks and daring grins, swirling around us like characters in some forbidden theatre production. All of us tangled up across some plush, heavy rug, drinking and laughing and indulging every secret urge. There, everything is real and unreal at once, a mirage where nothing matters but desire.

I plan my next visit. The drugs I'll try, the risks I'll take.

Occasionally, like some boring and unwelcome dinner guest, Andy barges in to disrupt everything. He kicks up the mess, dredging up memories I'd rather leave buried, forcing the taste of blood and the scent of sweat and fear to the forefront of my mind. He haunts me with images of the bodies, the sick laughter, the thrill that coursed through me as the game unfolded. Nausea claws at my throat, and I nearly double over, ready to retch all over the living room floor.

Andy knows it's wrong, twisted, evil. He knows there's something rotten at the core, and that I should have left the night of the archery game, like the man who scurried out the doors.

But before Andy can take hold of me, Hannya surges up, stronger, colder, whispering that it's a small price to pay for freedom. To live without consequence and revel in true, unrestrained pleasure requires sacrifice. Maybe the only thing I'm really sacrificing is Andy—the old, timid, tethered Andy, whose life was little more than a prison dressed up as safety.

Let him fade. Wave him goodbye.

I didn't really notice how distant Grace has become. I don't remember the last time we exchanged more than a handful of words. We exist alongside each other, occupying the same space, but that's about it. Two strangers under the same roof, barely brushing against each other's lives. For the past four nights I've been going out drinking alone, to make myself feel something, but tonight, I want to stay in, cook a decent meal for once. Maybe make an extra portion. Just in case.

I scour the fridge. It's fully stocked. Grace must've done a proper shop recently. I pull out a pack of wholegrain pasta, fresh basil pesto, and organic chicken fillets. Simple ingredients, but knowing Grace, she probably went to that overpriced local store, where everything costs triple what Tesco charges. Not that I can complain about the quality, it's good, but a bitterness bites at me. It's evidence of her freedom to spend without a second thought, while I'm barely scraping by.

I fill a pan with water and place it on the stove. She's living this comfortable life, but here I am, grinding away, teaching spoiled teenage girls history they couldn't care less about. My fists clench. I should get paid more than her. I'm shaping the future, helping these kids grow into adults, while Grace helps make the rich even richer, padding her own fortune while I'm stuck in career stasis. This world isn't fair.

I grab a knife and start dicing the chicken. Each plunge of the knife into the flesh triggers an echo from Ralph's. The bloodshed. The last hunt. My arrow piercing skin. The raw, horrifying scream that followed.

Yet, none of it is enough to stop me from going back. I won't leave. Not without risking everything. And if I tried? Would they kill me?

Honestly, I don't even want to leave.

Not just because of the thrill, but because of Red. She's my anchor, my escape from the boredom weighing me down here. Protecting her, protecting our world, is my real reason for staying. But there's another reason too, one I haven't fully admitted to myself until now.

I'm falling for her.

Ralph's offers me a place where I can shed Andy, even if only for a night. And deep down, I know that if I lose that,

I'll lose myself completely. Hannya has seeped into every part of me, creeping into the cracks, pulling me further from reality. A part of me wants to bridge the gap between the two worlds. To drag Grace into it somehow. Shake things up. Breathe life into whatever we're barely holding onto. There was a time when she had a rebellious streak, a spark that set her apart from the dull, rigid world we built together. If I can just reach her, maybe she'll follow. Maybe she'll let loose, tap into something raw and real.

After nights of primal sex at Ralph's, my body aches with hunger. I've unleashed something I can't cage. Even rubbing one out every day doesn't keep these urges at bay. It's not just the release I need, it's the connection, the skin-on-skin, the wild energy I found in that other world.

So, I've got a plan.

Surprise Grace with dinner. A bottle of wine, maybe two. See where the night takes us.

I'm not blind. I know how far we've drifted, lost in parallel routines, orbiting around each other like strangers. Despite everything—the dissatisfaction, the emptiness—part of me still needs her. Ralph's is my escape, but my real life is here. And without Grace, I'd have nothing solid to hold onto.

So I tell myself I'll forgive her. I'll even forgive Tom.

None of it matters. I don't even care about her in the same way I used to. I just want to bring back a sliver of the thrill, the hedonistic release Ralph's has stirred in me.

Enough to cut through the suffocating silence at home. Enough to feel alive again.

Grace opens the front door as I'm plating the food. She looks tired, her face drawn, but there's a flicker of surprise when she notices the table—two plates, a bottle of wine uncorked, candles flickering in the dim kitchen light. I don't even remember lighting them, but there they are.

"Hey, love," I say, my voice warm, almost hopeful.

She pauses mid-step, leans against the wall, pulls off one boot, then the other. When she straightens, her eyes land on me, narrowing slightly.

"Andy, you look awful," she says, blunt but not unkind. "You've got huge bags under your eyes. Are you okay?"

I force a laugh, brush it off. "I'm fine. Just a late night, that's all."

She frowns. "Late night doing what? It's the summer break. You don't have work."

The silence stretches too long. I feel the pressure mounting. *Think, quick.*

"Couldn't sleep," I blurt. "It's the heat, maybe. Tossed and turned for hours."

Her expression softens slightly, but I still see the doubt in her eyes. "You should take better care of yourself," she murmurs. "You look like you're running on fumes."

"I'll be fine," I say, the words harsher than I intend. "Anyway, I made dinner. Pesto chicken pasta. There's garlic bread too."

She glances at the table, acknowledges the effort. There's a glimpse of something in her expression. Appreciation, maybe. But it doesn't last.

"That's... nice," she says hesitantly, like she's deciding if this is an olive branch or a trap.

I step closer, lean in to kiss her. She stiffens, her cool lips barely responding before she pulls away.

"Did you use the chicken from the fridge?"

"Yeah, I thought it'd be good for this," I say, watching her carefully. "Why?"

"I was going to make a stew with that." A faint edge creeps into her voice.

"Well, we can always buy more chicken," I snap before I can stop myself. "It's not like this is the last chicken in the world."

Her shoulders tense. She exhales sharply, brushing past me to grab a mug and switch on the kettle. She doesn't even glance at the wine or the meal, dismissing the entire effort like it's nothing.

"Never mind," she mutters, heading towards the stairs.

Frustration builds in my chest. "Grace," I call after her, voice tight.

She doesn't stop. Doesn't turn.

Her pace quickens, and I follow, heavy footed.

Just as I reach out to grab her arm, she slips into the bathroom. The door slams shut.

FRAGMENTED

I stand there, my hand hovering in the air, the sound of the lock clicking louder than it should be. A bitter laugh escapes me as I let my arm fall to my side.

The aroma of the simmering food drifts up from the kitchen, warm and inviting, but all I can feel is the sharp chill of rejection.

***

Any lingering adrenaline from our standoff downstairs fades, leaving a hollow ache in my chest and a storm brewing in my head. I stare at the dinner table in front of me, the bottle of wine two-thirds empty, the candles flickering in the dim kitchen like they're mocking me. The pasta sits untouched, cold, congealed. A tasteless monument to my failure, the perfect metaphor for everything I've tried to salvage tonight.

I shove the plate away, the sharp clatter of ceramic against wood cutting through the suffocating silence.

My hands tremble as I pour another drink, wine sloshing over the rim, streaking red across the table. Four glasses in, and the room spins slightly, reality blurring at the edges. My mind won't shut up. Images of Grace with him. Laughing. Touching. Whispering words to him she hasn't whispered to me in years. Each one sharper than the last, tearing through me like glass.

I check my phone. Nearly ten.

Upstairs, the faint sound of footsteps reaches my ears. Pacing. Back and forth. Back and forth.

My stomach churns. Bile rises.

What the hell is she doing up there?

My jaw tightens, my teeth grinding as the thought claws its way in: *Is it him?*

Did she sneak a call in?

Really, Grace? After everything I did tonight—after I tried to make this right?

My hand tremors as I reach for the wine bottle and finish it off, then slam the empty glass onto the table. A few more gulps won't fix this.

The room tilts slightly as I stumble to the sideboard, yanking open the small drawer where I keep my *supplies*. My fingers fumble with the plastic bag, spilling white powder onto the counter. I grab a credit card from my jeans pocket, flattening the mess into thin, uneven lines. The ritual feels mechanical, practiced. By now, it probably is.

I lean down. The sharp burn rockets through me, jolting like an electric current.

I stand upright, sniff hard. The rush hits instantly. My head spins, my heartbeat stutters, then quickens, erratic. Jittery energy floods my system, heightening everything. The footsteps upstairs are louder now, hammering against my skull, their rhythm matching the blood pounding in my ears.

I grab the back of a dining chair for balance, my knuckles white against the wood. A stranger stares back at me from the darkened window.

Grace was right.

I look like hell.

Wide eyes. Pupils blown. Pale, gaunt skin. A shadow of the man I used to be.

Hannya's voice slithers in, clear now, coaxing, threading through the chaos in my head.

Take control.

Show her who you are.

You don't have to live in her shadow anymore.

This is your house. Your life.

The thought burrows deep, coiling around my anger, my shame, my hunger for something more.

Upstairs, the pacing continues, each step scraping against my nerves, a taunt, an accusation.

What's she doing?

Why is she pacing?

Who the hell is she thinking about?

The last glass of wine on the table beckons, but I ignore it.

My focus sharpens. The stairs.

Shallow breaths, too fast. Hands twitching.

She won't get away with this.

I push away from the table, staggering but determined. Each step feels heavier, like I'm dragging myself uphill. The walls press in, the air thick.

My hand brushes the banister as I climb, each footfall heavier, harder, fueled by adrenaline, cocaine, rage.

At the top, I pause, hand hovering over the bedroom door handle. My chest heaves. My mind races.

Hannya purrs, dark and persuasive.

Take back what's yours.

I grab the handle and twist. Locked.

My heart lurches, heat rushing through me, boiling over. Locked?

It's never locked.

My fist slams against the wood, the sound cracking through the hallway.

"Grace." My voice is strained, barely controlled. "Open the door."

A long pause. Too long. Enough to stoke the fire burning inside me.

Finally, her voice comes through—muffled, clipped. Dismissive.

"I'm busy."

Busy?

The room tilts. My grip tightens on the handle.

"Busy doing what?"

My voice rises, cracking at the edges. I knock harder.

"Open the damn door, Grace."

Silence.

Then, the sound of the lock turning.

When she opens the door just enough to face me, her expression is hard. Defiant.

Eyes narrowed, jaw set. Contempt flickering just beneath the surface.

And that's all it takes to set me off.

"What the hell are you doing?" she hisses, voice low, sharp.

The thin thread holding me together snaps.

I shove the door open, stepping inside with too much force, shoving her backwards. She stumbles, the back of her knees hitting the edge of the bed. Her arms flail briefly before she steadies herself, and her wide eyes lock onto mine. For a fleeting moment, I see something that cuts deeper than words ever could.

Fear.

Her hand twitches towards the bedside table. Her phone? A weapon? I don't care. I'm faster. I grab her wrists and pin them down against the mattress before she can move. My grip is firm, unrelenting, fueled by the storm surging through me.

She freezes beneath me. Her breath is quick, shallow, her body trembling just slightly. I can feel it through my hands, and that small, involuntary reaction feeds the fire.

"Why, Grace?" I growl, my voice vibrating with barely contained rage. "Why are you shutting me out?"

Her lips part, but no sound comes. Her gaze darts to the side, like she's searching for an escape. The wheels are turning in her head. I can see it. Feel it. But she doesn't answer. She doesn't even try.

That silence is a dagger, twisting deeper with every passing second.

"Is it him?" I spit the words, venom laced through every syllable. "Tom?"

Her jaw tightens. Her head snaps to the side. It's not an answer, not really, but it may as well be. The single movement is enough. The final push.

Every late night, every cold glance, every moment of distance crashes through me, a tidal wave of resentment drowning out any restraint I might have left.

My grip tightens.

"You think I don't know?" My voice drops, sharp and venomous.

I lean in, my breath hot against her skin. "You think I don't see what's going on? Do you really think I'm that fucking stupid?"

Her breath hitches. Her chest rises and falls too fast.

Then, barely above a whisper, her voice slices through the chaos.

"Let me go, Andy."

My name.

The sound of it knocks something loose in my skull, slicing through the boiling haze in my head like a cold gust of air.

For a fleeting second, I see myself the way she must be seeing me. Wild-eyed. Unhinged. A stranger in our home.

But then Hannya speaks.

Don't stop now.
Control is yours.
She needs to see you. To remember.
You are not invisible.

My grip loosens. My hands drop away from her wrists.

She jerks free immediately, sitting up, pulling her knees to her chest, arms wrapping around herself like a shield. She won't look at me.

Her fingers rub at her wrists, red marks blooming where my grip had been too tight.

She shakes her head, her voice low, brittle.

"Get out."

I hesitate, her words pinning me in place. The room is too quiet now. The silence is suffocating. She still won't look at me, her eyes locked onto the floor.

Whatever just happened... we are fractured beyond repair.

But Hannya's voice is back, steady and certain.

This isn't loss. This is power.
You're not invisible. You're not weak.
You're in control.

I hover for a moment, caught between the need to fix this and the bitter satisfaction of knowing I've shattered the silence between us. Then, before the turmoil inside me threatens to pull me under again, I turn and leave without another word.

The door clicks shut behind me.

21

I wake up on the sofa, my neck stiff, my mouth dry, my head pounding like a war drum. The sun streams through the half-closed curtains, slicing into my eyeballs like pins. For a moment, I don't move, my body weighed down by something worse than exhaustion.

Fragments of last night trickle back—Grace's voice trembling, her wrists in my hands, the fear in her eyes.

My stomach twists.

What the hell did I do?

I sit up slowly, the room spinning as I push myself upright. The empty wine bottle sits on the coffee table, a silent witness to my unraveling. Next to it, the remnants of a poorly cleaned line of coke gleam faintly in the morning light.

My chest tightens.

What's wrong with me?

I rub my temples, trying to piece it together, but the memories are fragmented, jagged. I remember pounding on the bedroom door, the lock turning, Grace ordering me to leave. After that, it's a blur. My chest tightens again, a heavy knot forming as shame and dread settle in.

Stumbling to my feet, I make my way to the kitchen, grab a glass, fill it with cold water, and down it in one go. The chill shocks my system, but it doesn't wash away the sick feeling pooling in my gut. I rinse the glass and set it down, the silence of the house pressing in around me.

I head upstairs, each step echoing like a hammer against my skull.

Apologize. You can fix this.

The mantra plays on repeat, but when I reach the bedroom, the door is ajar. The bed is made. The room is too neat, too quiet.

"Grace?"

My heart sinks as I step inside and see it.

A folded piece of paper on the bed. My name scrawled across the front in her familiar handwriting.

I freeze, my pulse pounding in my ears.

No. No, no, no.

I grab the note, my hands shaking as I unfold it.

Andy,

I can't do this anymore. I need space, time to think.

You need to get help.

There's something wrong, and it's not just the drinking or the lies.

You're becoming someone I don't recognise, and it's scaring me.

I've gone away for a while.
Don't look for me.
Please.
—Grace

My knees almost give out as I sit on the edge of the bed, rereading the words until they blur together.

Gone.

She's gone.

My fingers tighten around the paper, crumpling it slightly as a wave of panic rises in my chest. I grab my phone, dialing her number before I can think.

It rings once.

Twice.

Each second an eternity.

Finally, she picks up.

"Andy."

Her voice is steady but cold.

"Why are you calling me?"

My voice cracks. "Where are you? What does this mean? You can't just—"

"I told you I need time, Andy. I can't stay there anymore. Not like this."

Her words hit like a slap.

I grip the phone tighter, the panic in my chest sharpening. "You're just leaving? After everything? You didn't even..." I stop myself, my mind racing. "Is it him? Is it Tom?"

There's a pause, only the sound of her breathing on the line.

"You mean the client I've been working with? That's what this is about?"

"Don't lie to me, Grace. I'm not stupid," I snap, anger bubbling to the surface despite myself. "I've seen the way you've been acting. You've been distant, shutting me out, and now you're running off? Tell me the truth."

"The truth?" Her tone hardens. "The truth is you've become a stranger, Andy. You come home late, drunk, smelling like perfume that's not mine. You're not the man I married. You're barely even present. And now you're accusing me of having an affair? You really think this is about Tom?"

Her words are a hammer, each one driving nails into the fragile foundation I've been clinging to.

"You don't understand," I say, my voice faltering. "You don't know what it's been like—"

"No, Andy. I don't understand. Because you won't talk to me. You just spiral deeper into... into whatever this is. Drinking, lying, coming home late. Do you even hear yourself? You need help. You're falling apart, and I can't be there to watch it anymore."

Her voice cracks slightly, and for a moment I hear the Grace I remember. The one who cared, who fought for us.

"Grace, please," I start, desperation creeping into my voice. "Just come home. We can talk about this, fix it. I'll—"

"No, Andy."

She cuts me off again, her tone firm.

"Not until you get help. I mean it. This isn't about me or Tom or whatever you've convinced yourself of. This is about you. And until you face that... There's nothing to fix."

The line goes quiet, her words sinking in. I want to argue, to tell her she's wrong, that I'm fine, that everything can go back to normal if she just comes home.

But deep down, I know she's right.

The man she's talking about, the man I've become, isn't someone I recognise either.

"Grace..." I say again, softer this time, but the line clicks before I can finish.

She's gone.

I lower the phone slowly, staring at the screen like if I wait long enough, her name will reappear, and I'll get another chance. But there's nothing. Just the cold, empty silence of the flat pressing in around me, the walls too close, the air too thick.

Hannya's voice creeps in, low and insidious. *She's wrong. You're not the one who needs fixing. She's the problem. She doesn't see you. She doesn't deserve you.*

But another voice, quieter, harder to ignore, whispers something else.

Maybe she's right.

ALEX MURA

Adrenaline courses through me as I pace downstairs, my skin slick with sweat. My fists clench and unclench, searching for something solid to grasp, but all I find is the chaos in my head. Grace's trembling yet defiant voice echoes in my mind. The way she wouldn't look at me. The lock on the bedroom door.

Was she lying? Telling the truth? Who the fuck knows anymore?

And then there's him. Tom. The texts flash in my mind. Emojis, the teasing words, the pet names. It cannot be innocent. People don't talk like that unless there's something they're trying to keep hidden. The pieces twist, knotting tighter with every passing second, choking me with my own doubts.

I yank my shirt over my head, the fabric clinging to my damp skin, and stumble into the bathroom. The sharp glare of the overhead light cuts through the suffocating dimness of the flat. My hand finds the shower knob, twisting it hard until freezing water cascades down in an angry torrent.

I step in before it warms, gasping as the cold shocks my skin. It hurts, but I welcome it. Anything to drown out the madness inside me.

The tiles are slick beneath my feet as I press my palms flat against the wall, letting the water beat against my back. My breath rasps through my chest, shallow and uneven, each inhalation pulling against a tightening coil of rage and confusion. I squeeze my eyes shut, but Grace's face swims into view. Distant. Blank. Unreadable.

I hate that face. Hate how it hides everything I want to know.

Why won't she just tell me the goddamned truth?

Red's face flashes into my mind instead, softening the tightness in my chest. Red wouldn't lie. Red wouldn't shut me out. She'd pull me into her arms, whispering the right words to settle the storm inside me.

"You're not crazy. You're not losing it. Everything's going to be okay."

Her laugh would be low and warm, her touch steadying. She'd tell me I matter.

God, I need her right now.

But she's not here.

And Grace? Grace has abandoned me, shutting me out like I'm a stranger. Like I don't deserve answers.

The knot in my chest tightens again, Hannya's voice whispering in my mind, coaxing, cajoling.

Take control. Don't let her win.

I shut the water off abruptly, the silence that follows roaring in my ears. After grabbing a towel, I dry off in quick, jittery motions, barely feeling the coarse fabric against my skin. My nerves buzz like live wires, every muscle tight with the need to reclaim my sense of control.

The flat's claustrophobic air presses down on me. I grab the baggie from the drawer, pouring a thin, crystalline line onto the edge of the counter. The ritual is automatic now. Rolled note, sharp inhale, the burning rush that follows. My nostrils sting, my throat burns, and then the familiar clarity hits, sharp and immediate, carving through the fog in my head.

I glance at the mirror above the sink. My pupils are blown wide, dark and unrecognisable. The bags under my eyes have deepened, etching shadows into my skin. The reflection shows a man falling apart, but the cocaine pushes the thought aside before it can take hold.

Stepping onto the balcony, I light a cigarette, the first drag burning my throat as the smoke settles heavily in my lungs. The city sprawls out below, glittering and alive, indifferent to the chaos churning inside me. I exhale slowly, watching the smoke curl into the darkness before disappearing into nothing.

My phone vibrates in my pocket. I fish it out, thumb swiping across the screen. Notifications blur together. News alerts. Emails. Missed calls I'll never return. My eyes catch on a headline, bright and urgent.

Breaking News: Prominent CEO of London IT Firm Found Dead in River Thames.

The name jolts me. Jonathan Rawlings.

My stomach drops as I absorb the article, but I already know. It's him. The man from Ralph's. The one who stormed out, shoving past the staff, his pale face twisted with rage.

Authorities have not yet determined the cause of death, but sources close to the investigation suggest foul play.

The cigarette trembles between my fingers, ash falling in uneven clumps. My mind feverishly connects dots I don't want to connect.

The rules. The unspoken threats.

The price of breaking them.

They killed him.

They had to.

A cocaine rush collides with realisation, sending my heart into a frantic rhythm. If they can do that to someone like him, what could they do to me? The thought wraps around my chest, squeezing tighter with each breath.

I flick the cigarette over the balcony railing, watching it disappear into the void below.

Stepping back inside, I lock the door behind me and lean heavily against the wall. I wish I had Red's number. She'd understand. She'd tell me what to do.

I pocket the useless phone and stare at my reflection in the balcony glass.

Hannya's eyes stare back. Dark and hollow.

Daring me to make the next move.

22

The towering double doors of Ralph's close behind me with a deep, resonating thud, sealing off the outside world and locking me back into this strange, glittering purgatory. My pulse is already racing, my breath uneven as I step into the crowded grand hall. The laughter, the music, it all feels sharper tonight, cutting through my nerves like razor blades.

My paranoia is growing. The man from last month, the one who stormed out, pushing past the staff, is still etched in my mind. His wild eyes, the desperation in his movements. And then the news. The river. The lifeless body found floating. I shake my head, trying to push the image away, but it lingers, a dark spectre hanging over tonight.

If they could get to him, they could get to anyone.

To me.

To Grace.

The thought of her twists in my gut, making me feel both furious and hollow at once. I can't shake the way she looked at me that night. Her tired, disappointed eyes, the way she hugged herself like she needed to shield herself from me. The memory cuts deep, sending my mind spiralling further. What if she leaves? What if she ends it with no goodbye, no closure, just silence?

Wouldn't that be what I deserve?

But then there's another thought, darker, more urgent.

What if she doesn't leave?

What if she stays, a constant reminder of everything I can't fix, everything I've broken?

I need to drown these thoughts. Silence them before they claw me apart.

The warm weight of medieval aristocrat robes presses against my shoulders. Tonight's dress code is deep burgundy, trimmed in gold, with intricate embroidery along the sleeves. It's ridiculous and theatrical.

Hannya thrives in this setting, but tonight, he is fragile. Barely holding on. Cracking under the burdens I've dragged here with me.

I scan the room for her. Red.

I *need* her.

It doesn't take long. She's leaning against the far wall, red robes pooling around her like liquid fire, her hair tumbling down her back. She's the only constant in this world, the only anchor I have left.

When I approach, she catches my eye, her expression softening. Instead of speaking, I close the distance between us and wrap my arms around her, pulling her close. She briefly stiffens with surprise before relaxing into the hug. Her arms come up slowly, resting against my back, her warmth seeping into me, steadying me, grounding me.

"You're shaking," she murmurs, her voice barely audible over the noise of the hall. Her fingers trace slow, calming patterns on my back.

"Yeah." My voice is hoarse. "Rough few weeks."

She doesn't press for details. She doesn't need to. Red always knows when to push and when to simply be there. Her presence alone is enough to quiet the storm inside me, even if only for a moment.

I pull back just enough to look at her. Her mask conceals most of her features, but her eyes meet mine with unwavering intensity. She's the only one here who sees me. Not just Hannya.

"I was starting to think you wouldn't show," she says.

"I couldn't stay away," I admit, forcing a thin smile. It's the truth, but not the whole truth. I need her. I need this place, even when it terrifies me. Especially when it terrifies me.

"You're here now. Nothing else matters."

Her hand lingers on my arm for a while, before she steps back, giving me room to breathe. "Come on, let's find a drink. You look like you could use one."

She's not wrong.

We weave through the crowd, the sea of masks and opulent costumes parting around us. The air is filled with the scent of perfume and wine, a faint tang of sweat and leather lingering beneath. The room feels more alive than ever, but it's a life that borders on chaos. On madness.

When we reach the bar, Red orders two glasses of something dark and strong. The bartender slides them across the polished wood, and I take mine, downing half in one go.

The burn steadies me. Dulls the edges of my thoughts just enough to make the room's intensity bearable.

"You're quieter than usual," Red observes, her gaze fixed on me.

I swirl the liquid in my glass. "Just got loads on my mind."

Her eyes narrow slightly, but she doesn't push. Instead, she raises her glass in a small toast. "To surviving another week," she says, her voice carrying a hint of irony.

"To surviving," I echo, clinking my glass against hers.

I can't shake the feeling that survival here is a precarious thing, and I'm hanging by a thread. How long can I hold on?

Red sips her drink slowly, watching me with a calm reassurance. The alcohol helps calm me down, but not enough to drown the horrors, the blood, the screams from last time. The guilt.

"It's a shame we can't talk about anything personal here," Red says, leaning closer so only I can hear.

I nod, reaching out to take her hand. She lets me guide her through the crowd to a quieter corner. The noise of the hall fades. I stop in front of a medieval-style bed, its heavy wooden posts draped with velvet curtains, the deep maroon fabric glowing softly in the dim light.

"Here?" Red asks, tilting her head slightly, a teasing smile playing at the corners of her mouth.

I nod again, pulling the curtains closed behind us. The bed creaks softly as we sit, the air around us suddenly intimate, cocooned in shadows. She sets her glass down on the small bedside table and looks at me, her expression shifting from playful to concerned.

"Something bad happen out there?"

For a moment, I don't answer. Instead, I wrap my arms around her, pulling her into a deep embrace. Her body is warm against mine, solid and reassuring, and the tension in my chest loosens slightly. "I'm so glad I have you," I whisper, my voice thick with something I can't fully name.

Red strokes the back of my head, her touch steady and calming. "I'm not going anywhere. You know that."

We sit like that for a while, her presence a balm to the storm raging inside me. Finally, when I pull back to meet her serene eyes, there's no judgment, only patience and understanding. Something inside me cracks open, and before I can stop them, the words tumble out. "Do you want to hear a story? A romantic one. From ancient history."

She smiles, settling tight beside me. "All right, H. Impress me."

I take a deep breath, leaning back against the plush pillows. "There was a king in Mesopotamia," I begin, my voice steadying as I lose myself in the tale. "His name was Sargon. He fell in love with a woman named Ishtar. Well, that's what the poets called her. She wasn't a goddess, though she might as well have been. She was a fierce warrior, and she had no interest in being a queen."

Red listens intently as I continue, my voice softening. "Sargon didn't tame her. He didn't try to make her fit into his world. Instead, he let her be wild, free. And in return, she fought for him, beside him, like an equal. Together, they ruled not through fear, but through respect and love. The poets said their hearts were like twin stars, burning brighter when they were together."

Red smiles wistfully. "Twin stars. That's beautiful."

"It was," I say, my voice growing quieter. "But it didn't last. Sargon died in battle, and Ishtar? She disappeared. Some say she threw herself into the Euphrates, her grief too much to bear. Others say she went into the mountains, lived out the rest of her days as a warrior."

Red's smile fades, her expression turning thoughtful. "And what do you think?"

I hesitate, the words catching in my throat. "I think she loved him so much that she couldn't bear to stay in the world without him. But she couldn't stop being who she was, either. So, even in her grief, she chose freedom."

Red reaches out, brushing her fingers lightly against my cheek.

"You're like him, you know."

"Sargon?" I ask, brow furrowing.

She nods. "You're trying to hold on to two different worlds. The one that makes you feel alive, and the one you think you're supposed to stay in. But it's tearing you apart."

Her words hit me like a blow, the truth of them cutting deeper than I want to admit. I close my eyes, leaning into her touch, and for the first time in what feels like weeks, I let myself be vulnerable.

"I don't know how to stop."

"You don't have to figure it out tonight," she says. "But you don't have to do it alone, either."

Red shifts beside me, her fingers brushing my cheek as she studies me. Before I know it, she's slipping out of her heavy medieval gown, the fabric pooling at her feet in a ripple of crimson silk. Her bare skin is glowing, smooth and inviting, the curve of her back arching as she moves.

She reaches for the small glass vial on the ornate table nearby, unscrewing the lid with delicate fingers before settling onto the sheets. The pinkish powder inside catches the flickering light as she dips her fingers in, scooping out just enough, spreading it across her stomach in slow, circular motions, like she's painting herself with the very essence of temptation.

"Do you know what this does?" she teases, her voice curling around the words like smoke.

Mesmerised, I don't answer. I don't need to. She already knows I'll do whatever she asks.

"Go on," she whispers. "Take it."

I hesitate for only a moment before leaning down, my breath hot against her skin. The world narrows to this. Her body beneath me, the sharp tang of the powder as I inhale. It slams into my system instantly, flooding my veins, sharp and electric, dragging me away from my thoughts.

Red watches me, wiping the remnants from her skin before leaning in, her lips brushing against mine, soft and insistent. Her hands cradle my face, as if she's holding me together, piece by piece.

"Feel better?" she whispers against my lips.

The rush is blurring the edges of my world, and for a moment, I feel untouchable, invincible.

Red settles back against the pillows, her face illuminating as she lights up a cigarette. "You know," she says, "people like us are always chasing something. Freedom, thrill, oblivion. But no matter how fast we run, the truth always catches up."

I don't respond. I can't. Her words hit something unguarded inside me. She exhales slowly, cigarette smoke weaving around her like a ghost.

"You're afraid," she continues, her eyes fixed on me. "Not of what's out there. Of what's in here."

She taps a finger lightly against my chest, just over my heart.

"I'm not afraid."

My voice sounds hollow even to me.

"Then why are you running?"

I don't have an answer. Instead, I lean back, my head sinking into the plush pillows as the ceiling above me spins in lazy circles. The cocaine, and whatever the hell is mixed in with it, surges through me, heightening everything. The feel of her fingers on my skin. The sound of her breathing. The flickering of the candles.

But it also heightens the darkness, guilt and fear I've tried to bury.

"You think Sargon was afraid?" I ask suddenly. "Of losing her? Of losing himself?"

Red considers this for a moment. "Maybe. But I think he knew the risk. He knew the cost, and he chose to burn, anyway."

The words hit me like a gut punch, and for a moment, I can't breathe. I close my eyes, trying to steady myself, but the images flash behind my lids. Blood. Screams. The man's face twisted in agony.

Red's voice cuts through. "You don't have to do this alone, H. But you have to decide. Are you going to keep running, or are you going to face it?"

FRAGMENTED

I open my eyes, meeting hers. She leans in, brushing her lips softly against mine.

For a moment, the world stills.

23

Game after game, shot after shot. It all blurs together. A monotonous rhythm of excess, teetering on the edge of repulsion. The walls of Ralph's feel like they're closing in, suffocating me. The thrill isn't there anymore. Or maybe I've simply grown numb to it. The line between exhilaration and sickness has blurred, and I can no longer tell if I'm still chasing pleasure or just avoiding the abyss beneath my feet.

The host steps forward, his presence commanding the room with a single theatrical gesture. Applause ripples through the crowd, swelling into eager anticipation as staff members wheel a collection of medieval torture devices across the floor. The guests press forward, masks tilted in grotesque fascination, their murmurs thick with excitement.

My eyes drift over the iron and wood instruments. We all know what's coming. I can already picture flesh stretching, sinew tearing as the rack's iron cranks twist tighter. Behind it, an iron maiden lined with jagged spikes, and a spiked chair, its seat bristling with nails. There's no illusion of subtlety here. No pretence of civility. This isn't a game. It's brutality, packaged as spectacle.

Red's fingers lace through mine. She tugs gently, guiding me through the shifting sea of masks and eager faces, keeping me tethered to her as we weave through the crowd. Her touch is firm, as though she senses the pull of my spiralling thoughts. We stop near the front, just meters from the rack, where a male victim gets strapped in place, his limbs stretched. The ropes bite into his skin, his muscles trembling under the tension. A low, drugged moan slips from his lips as the staff turns the crank, his arms extending just a fraction more, the tendons in his shoulders straining like cords about to snap.

Next to him, a woman is ushered towards the iron maiden. She stumbles, her pupils blown wide, her movements sluggish. Whatever they've given her has softened her perception of reality just enough to keep her compliant. The concierge pushes her inside with eerie gentleness, closing the doors with a heavy clang. The crowd collectively holds its breath. I imagine the spikes pressing against her body. Not piercing, not yet, but trapping her, forcing her to remain perfectly still. Any wrong movement, any attempt to resist, and the metal will sink into her skin. A shiver crawls down my spine.

The crowd's satisfaction ripples outwards, a sickening wave of approval.

My stomach twists tighter with every creak of wood, every muffled gasp. But I can't look away. I'm locked in place, transfixed. Red's hand tightens around mine. Her eyes are fixed on the display, lips parted slightly, chest rising and falling in shallow, uneven breaths.

"This is... something," I mutter.

"Quite a show, isn't it?" She says casually, but I can sense her unease.

Another man is forced onto the spiked chair. His body, sick from whatever they've fed him, twitches as the nails bite into his skin. Tiny red beads bloom where the spikes puncture flesh, trickling into thin, winding trails. His lips part in a silent cry, his head tilting back. His eyes—vacant, unfocused—stare into the nothingness above, as though his mind has already started its retreat from the pain.

"The host really went all out this time," Red admits. But her grip on my hand tightens, just slightly. I glance at her, and for the first time tonight, I see it. The doubt creeping in, the way her breath has shallowed.

She knows this is wrong. She knows this isn't normal. And yet, like me, she doesn't move. Doesn't look away.

Red leans in, her voice dropping to a whisper meant only for me. "Hannya... Sometimes, I wonder if... if we've gone too far."

Her carefully constructed facade cracks. I want to respond, to tell her I feel the same. That this place is devouring me piece by piece. But the words stick in my throat, swallowed by the noise, the spectacle, the host's watchful eyes.

We stand side by side, complicit as the next victim is strapped down, their screams rattling what's left of my soul. Red's hand never leaves mine, her grip a silent tether as the darkness of Ralph's threatens to pull us both under.

Before I realise it, the host is next to me, his voice speaking over the chaos. "Enjoy the show." There's a satisfaction in his tone. His presence sends a slow, crawling chill through me, and his words repeat themselves in my head like poison.

I take a step back, the world around me warping into a sickening blur of masks, laughter, and the tortured cries of the evening's entertainment. My stomach twists violently, the vivid image of the flayed man flashing through my mind like a grotesque slideshow. My chest tightens, bile rising in my throat, hot and acidic.

The nausea swells too fast to fight. Without warning, I lurch forward.

A sickly green fluid spews from my mouth, splattering across the floor, soaking into the thick, elegant rug beneath my feet. The stench hits immediately, mingling with the ever-present metallic tang of blood in the air. I gag again, the aftertaste clinging bitterly to my tongue, my body convulsing with the force of it.

Around me, guests step back, not in alarm, but in mild annoyance, their masked faces tilting in casual disdain.

No one rushes to help. No one even speaks. They barely acknowledge me. Just a brief interruption to their night of indulgence. And then, just as quickly, their attention shifts back to the dying man on the rack. His suffering is far more captivating than my pathetic display.

A wave of humiliation washes over me, burning hotter than the shame curdling in my gut. I feel myself shrinking under their stares, drowning in the silent judgment of a room that has long since abandoned empathy. But Red stays. She doesn't flinch. She doesn't retreat. Her grip on my hand remains firm, steady, the only real thing anchoring me.

Through the haze of nausea and mortification, my eyes find Brazen in the crowd. He's watching me, brows furrowed, concern flickering in his expression. Before I can spiral further, a familiar voice cuts through the ringing in my ears.

"Oh dear, are you alright?"

I turn to see Jumadi standing beside Red, her lion mask staring right through me. Unlike the others, she doesn't look away.

"You've had quite the night, haven't you?"

I open my mouth, but my throat is raw, my words catching before they can form. I gesture weakly at the mess on the floor instead. "I'm sorry."

"Nonsense," Jumadi snaps, waving off my apology as if it's beneath her. "This happens more often than you'd think. You're still adjusting... to how things are at Ralph's. You'll adapt, or you won't."

Red squeezes my hand gently. "Maybe you need air." Her voice is softer now, a balm against the chaos in my head.

I shake my head, eyes dropping to the vomit-streaked floor. "I need to clean up."

Jumadi snaps her fingers at a nearby waiter. "Clean this up. Now." Her tone brooks no argument, and the staff move quickly to obey, their efficiency only emphasizing how insignificant my breakdown is to them.

Red brushes against my arm. "Don't let them see you like this. Take a minute, breathe. I'll be here."

There it is. That fragile thread of reassurance. I grip onto it tightly, giving her a subtle nod before slipping away, moving fast, keeping my head down as I make for the men's room.

It's a sanctuary of sorts, the sound of running water muffling the distant roar of laughter and screams. I brace against the sink, scrubbing my mouth furiously, the sting in my gums a welcome distraction from the chaos in my head. My hands tremble as I grip the porcelain, my mask growing damp with each uneven breath.

The mirror offers back a distorted image of Hannya. Wild-eyed. Crumbling. For a moment, I imagine ripping off the mask, exposing the wreckage beneath. But the rules bind me. The threat of what happens when you break them holds me in place.

The door creaks open.

I flinch, my stomach lurching like I've been caught doing something I shouldn't. But it's only Brazen, strolling in with that usual air of indifference, his posture too composed. I tense, waiting for a reprimand.

"Brazen," I blurt before he can speak. "I can't stand this anymore. They're torturing people. How is this entertainment?" The words spill out, unsteady, barely restrained.

He exhales sharply, rubbing the back of his head like he's dealing with a kid throwing a tantrum. "H, please don't land yourself in deep shit," he mutters, voice tight with something close to exhaustion.

"What are you talking about?" My voice cracks, panic clawing its way up my throat. I clench my fists to stop my hands from shaking. "They're committing murder! They need to go to jail!"

Brazen's face darkens, his easy-going mask slipping. "You committed murder yourself already."

The words cut through the air, clean and precise, leaving no room for argument.

I open my mouth, but nothing comes out. He's right. I pulled the bowstring. I aimed. I shot. The memory of the man's scream is embedded in me, a splinter lodged so deep I can't dig it out.

Brazen watches me, his voice dropping lower. "You think this is some anomaly? This is part of the experience. You don't have to like it, but you've got to accept it. Don't do anything stupid, mate."

The walls press in. My head spins, the bile rising again. "And if I don't? What then?"

Brazen steps closer. "You know what happened to the last person who broke the rules?"

My mind lurches to the news. The river. The bloated corpse.

"It was him, wasn't it?" The words are barely audible. "That CEO."

Brazen nods once. "They made an example of him. And trust me, they'll do worse if you try pulling any shit. It's not just you they'll come after. They'll come for me, too."

I blink, thrown by that last part. He waits just long enough for it to sink in before adding, "I vouched for you, remember? If you go down, so do I."

I feel the air being sucked out of me. My legs are unsteady, my pulse thudding in my ears. The fluorescent light overhead casts Brazen's shadow long against the wall, distorting him, stretching him into something monstrous.

"Why did you invite me here in the first place?" The words slip out raw, barely controlled, scraping against the tightness in my throat.

Brazen shrugs, too casual, and it infuriates me. "It's what you wanted. When we first met, you told me you needed a break from the monotony, from your old life. A spot opened up, and I thought, why not? Didn't think you'd get picked, but our host must've seen the same things I saw in you when they did their due diligence."

"I want to leave." The words are hollow the moment they leave my mouth, trembling with fear rather than conviction.

Brazen exhales, shaking his head with something close to pity. "That's not an option. You've tasted it now, Andy. You've seen what *true* freedom feels like. Could you really go back to your old life, knowing what's out there? Besides, leaving isn't allowed. You know the consequences."

His voice is calm, matter-of-fact, but it settles around my neck like a noose.

"How many people have you done this to?" I snap, needing to throw the blame somewhere, needing to find a crack in this nightmare.

"Just you," he replies without hesitation, looking me dead in the eye. "Club rules. One guest per lifetime. That's it."

The admission stuns me. "Then why me?" My voice is barely above a whisper now, the fight draining from my limbs. "What exactly did you see in me?"

There's a pause. Brief, but enough to make my stomach twist. Then he sighs. "That hunger, that restlessness. You're like me. You just needed someone to show you the door. Call it curiosity."

My breath hitches as he steps closer, resting a hand on my shoulder. His grip is steady, firm. An anchor or a shackle, I can't tell. "I care about you, mate. Truth is, I never wanted kids of my own, too much hassle, but I've grown to care for you. So, I'll say it again. Don't do anything stupid. This place can give you everything you've ever wanted, but only if you play by the rules."

His voice softens slightly, but the darkness in his eyes doesn't fade. "This is just a bad run. Two months in a row. Next time, it'll be calmer. Just parties, drinks, maybe harmless games like before. The rough stuff, it's rare, but necessary. Reminds us of what we have, and what others don't."

"And what's that?"

"Freedom," he says simply, his hand still pressing into my shoulder. "The kind of freedom most people can't even imagine."

I think of Red. Her smile, her touch, the way she makes everything else fade. The idea of a life without her, without the rush of Ralph's, is unthinkable. The thought alone feels suffocating.

Brazen's grip tightens, as if sensing my hesitation. "I know it's a lot," he says, his tone almost fatherly now. "But trust me. Give it time. You'll see. This isn't a prison. It's liberation. You just need to let go of what's holding you back."

I don't answer. I can't. My mind churns, torn between the nightmare of staying and the impossibility of leaving.

Brazen steps back towards the door, his tone slipping back into something light, easy, like we just had a casual chat over drinks. "Come on," he says almost cheerfully. "Let's get back out there. Have a drink, relax. We're not monsters, Andy. We're just living the way we were meant to."

He pats my shoulder and heads for the exit, leaving me rooted to the floor, his words looping over and over in my head. I don't know if he's telling the truth, or if I just want to believe him.

24

I brace myself as I step back into the hall, expecting a dozen pairs of eyes to snap toward me, ready to pounce on my weakness like predators scenting blood, but no one even glances in my direction. The room is a kaleidoscope of hedonism. Bodies entwined, moving to a rhythm only they can hear, pupils blown wide from whatever cocktails of drugs they've taken. My moment of vulnerability is invisible in this chaos. Vomiting seems to be the least of anyone's concerns.

Brazen's already gone, swallowed by the sea of masks and indulgence.

Aimless, I wander towards the edge of the hall, where the lights are dimmer and the shadows stretch longer. The gilded mirrors lining the walls catch my eye. Ornate frames winding like vines, their polished surfaces luring me in.

I stop in front of one, staring at the reflection. The Hannya mask stares back.

The longer I look, the more detached I feel from the figure in the glass. Something is wrong. The way it holds itself too still, too composed, like it's waiting for me to act first.

The sounds of the party grow muffled, the world outside falling away.

Just me and the mirror.

Or so I think.

Out of the corner of my eye, I catch movement. Another guest, his mask nearly identical to mine, his tunic the same deep burgundy. He stands just a few feet away, too still, too focused. The words slip out before I can stop them, low and unsteady.

"You're him, aren't you?"

The man tilts his head, his eyes glinting behind the mask. "I could ask you the same thing," he says, a mocking lilt curling around the words. He takes a slow step forward. "Do you even know who you are anymore?"

A knot tightens in my stomach. I glance at the mirror, and something changes. The reflection looking back isn't quite right. The mask is the same, but the eyes... The eyes don't belong to me. They are hollow, black wells, empty.

A shiver crawls up my spine. The reflection moves its head. Not in sync with me, but independently, as if watching from the other side of the glass.

The man moves closer. "Of course you don't know," he continues. "That's why you come here, isn't it? To forget. To strip yourself down until there's nothing left of the man you were."

The reflection distorts, the mask warping, its horns stretching longer. The eye sockets darken, swallowing the light. My chest tightens, cold sweat prickling at my skin. I blink rapidly, trying to clear the image, trying to convince myself it's just the alcohol, just the drugs, but it doesn't stop. The face in the mirror shifts, its edges fraying, its features unravelling into something grotesque.

The man's voice cuts through my unravelling thoughts.

"You don't want to be Andy Giles, the history teacher. The husband. The nobody. You want to be Hannya. You want to be more."

"No," I whisper, shaking my head. But there's no conviction behind it. Because he's right. Every word of it.

"Look at you." He steps to my side, his voice a low hiss. "You're nothing but a shadow. A hollow shell playing pretend. How long before you disappear entirely? How long before the mask isn't something you wear, but something you are?"

I try to turn away, to look anywhere but the mirror, but I can't. The reflection twists further, the mask cracking, splitting down the centre.

Something beneath it stirs.

I see my own face. Or what's left of it.

The features are sunken, hollowed, as if the flesh is caving inward. The eyes, lifeless, black voids, stare back with quiet contempt.

"Stop," I breathe, my voice barely audible, my throat dry and raw. "This isn't real."

The man chuckles, a low, guttural sound that curdles my stomach. "Oh, it's real," he says, leaning in, his breath cold against my neck. "This is who you are now. You're not Andy anymore. You're Hannya. And there's no going back."

My trembling hands press against the mirror's surface, desperate to ground myself, to find something real. But the glass ripples beneath my touch, distorting like liquid silver.

And then, for a brief moment, I see myself.

My real face. My own eyes staring back.

And then it's gone.

The room rushes back all at once. The laughter, the music. My chest heaves as I stagger back from the mirror, hands still shaking, my mind reeling.

I turn, pushing through the crowd, running from whatever I just saw, from the voice still whispering inside my skull.

I need to get back.

Back to her.

My eyes find Red, perched regally on the edge of a velvet chaise, her legs crossed. In each hand, she cradles a tall glass, the liquid inside glinting like molten gold. The world shakes slightly as I reach her.

"Darling, you're back." She leaps up to greet me, her excitement causing half the drink to spill over her fingers, onto the table. "Are you alright?"

"All good. Must've been something I ate," I lie, my voice steadier than I feel.

Red doesn't press. She never does. Instead, her expression softens, and she reaches out, brushing her fingers against the cheek of my mask. "No worries, love," she says, her tone gentle, as if she knows I can't bear to explain. "Everyone's already moved on. You should too."

She presses a cocktail to my lips, convincing me to drink. The liquid slides down my throat, sweet enough to remind me I'm still here, still part of this world.

"Good boy," she purrs, draining her own glass with a satisfied sigh before waving down a waiter for another. Her laughter ripples through the air, light, easy, as if the horrors surrounding us are nothing more than a passing inconvenience. But I know better. It's a mask, just like mine.

A tortured scream tears through the hall, dragging my attention away.

The man on the rack writhes, his limbs stretched beyond their limits, the grotesque symphony of snapping joints echoing beneath the chandeliers. His screams, ragged, primal, cut through the distortion of drugs and alcohol, burrowing into my skull, impossible to ignore. My stomach churns, my body tensing as the executioners twist the crank again, forcing his joints to pop, one by one.

But before I can fully process the horror, Red pulls me back.

"Don't look at that," she whispers, her breath soft against my ear. "Look at me and just listen."

Her fingers weave through mine. Her other hand cups my jaw, tilting my face towards hers, forcing my sight away from the spectacle. The screams dull, the edges blurring as she hums a soft melody. It wraps around me like a cocoon.

"Forget them," she whispers, her lips grazing mine, her voice melting into the song. "Just focus on me."

I exhale shakily. The tune burrows into my chest, drowning out the distant moans of agony. My heartbeat slows, the tension loosening, just enough to breathe.

"See?" Red says. "You're safe here. With me."

And for the first time in hours, I almost believe her. The screams recede, lost beneath the hypnotic lull of her voice, her presence. The madness of Ralph's fades into something distant, insignificant. In this moment, there is only her, soft and warm.

The room settles. The audience shifts its focus. The game resets.

Red grins, slipping another drink into my hand. Three more cocktails line the table beside her, waiting for their turn. Beyond them, untouched drugs shimmer, begging for attention.

"On three," she laughs, her tone light, teasing, daring. "One, two—"

I don't wait. I down the drink in one go, the fruity taste masking the bite of whatever's lurking beneath. The euphoria kicks in almost instantly, smoothing over the jagged edges, smothering the nausea, the guilt, the fear.

Red collapses into me, her warmth consuming me like a second skin. We slip into idle gossip, meaningless conversation, a carefully constructed illusion of normalcy. But then her fingers tighten around my arm, pulling me back in.

"It'll be alright," she hums. "Don't worry. Look. Columbina's really going all out on that Pierrot."

I force my eyes to follow hers, landing on the scene across the room. Columbina stands over a Pierrot. Panta and Lóne have the girl pinned, their faces twisted with laughter, holding her down as if this is all part of some grand joke.

Columbina circles her prey, teasing. Her fingers skim across the Pierrot's bare chest before planting slow, deliberate kisses along her skin. The girl squirms beneath her, anticipation and fear warring in her wide eyes.

Columbina reaches for a leather whip. She grips it loosely at first, running the tip along the Pierrot's stomach, dragging it over her ribs, her thighs. The girl flinches at the touch, her body tensing, but it's only the prelude.

Then, with a sudden flick of her wrist, the whip cracks through the air. A crimson welt blooms instantly across the Pierrot's pale flesh.

She gasps, her body jerking, but no one moves to help.

I should look away. I should do something. But I can't.

The cocktail. The coke. Red's hand still resting on my arm. They all work together, dulling the edges, turning the horror into something distant, something manageable.

Because here at Ralph's, even the grotesque becomes background noise.

The Pierrot's soft whimpers blend into the music, barely audible beneath the main event. At first, she seems to respond, her body shivering under Columbina's touch. But then the spark fades from her eyes, her movements turning uncertain, hesitant, like she's unsure if resistance is even allowed.

Her quiet pleas only seem to excite Columbina. Each strike of the whip lands harder, angrier, leaving raised welts on the girl's pale skin. The crowd watches, some exuding approval, others watching with glassy-eyed indifference.

And then it hits me. What I've known all along but refused to acknowledge.

The girls in the Pierrot masks aren't here by choice.

They're trafficked, paraded around to satisfy the club's darker appetites.

"They seem to be having fun," I say, testing Red's reaction, forcing my voice to sound casual.

"Everyone but the Pierrot." She swirls her drink, her tone dipping. "Poor girl."

"How much do they get paid for the night?"

"Not a penny."

"Then what are they? Sex slaves?"

She shrugs, unbothered. "Yeah, in a way. Whores," she says dismissively. "They ship them in from Eastern Europe every month. Once we're done, they're shipped out again. But don't tell anyone. It's a secret."

"So... human trafficking?"

Red doesn't answer. Instead, she nudges me playfully. "Come on, you're a slow drinker tonight."

I hesitate, still trying to process what she's just said. "Sorry."

"You're apologising a lot today. Very unlike you. Come on, drink up. I don't like being sober."

I summon a weak smile and grab a fresh cocktail, raising it high. "Cheers."

"Salut!" she chimes, all enthusiasm, all façade.

As always, we down them like shots, the alcohol running its way through my system but doing little to dull the growing unease. Red moves quickly, preparing another line of coke with practiced ease. I follow suit, the ritual mechanical now, necessary.

The powder stings. The room shakes, then steadies, the tension bleeding away in waves. The torture, the music, the lights, the scene of Columbina and her Pierrot.

It all becomes distant, drowned beneath the chemical numbness.

Red exhales slowly, the high settling into her bones. "Y'know..." she says, voice slurred just slightly, "a part of me does feel sorry for them. But you can't let those thoughts wrap around you. If you start feeling bad about every little thing, our whole world will fall apart."

Her words land like ice beneath my skin.

Before I can respond, a fresh scream rips through the air, tearing through my head.

I turn, heart hammering.

The iron maiden.

Its heavy doors are shut, locked tight around the poor fucker inside. My stomach twists as my mind supplies the grisly details. I know exactly how this thing works. I've read about them, studied their history, their supposed brutality.

The victim is forced to stand motionless, encased in a spiked coffin. The moment they shift, even slightly, the spikes press into their flesh, puncturing skin, drawing blood. It's a perfect trap. No room to move. No way to escape. Only pain, creeping in slowly, inexorably, until the body gives up entirely.

I stare at the closed casket, my voice flat, brittle. "You know... there's no evidence iron maidens existed before the 19th century."

Red turns her head, her crimson lips parting in faint curiosity. "Huh?"

I force a laugh, trying to find humour in the grotesque reality before me. The iron maiden, the supposed medieval torture device, was never actually used. It's a myth, a fabrication to make the past seem more barbaric than it was. No records, no proof, just propaganda spun into history books.

And yet, here it is. No longer a myth. No longer just an idea.

"I guess it's not a myth anymore," I mutter to myself.

Red rests a hand lightly on my arm and whispers softly, "just breathe, baby."

Red always knows what to say. She's a glimpse of sanity in a place that erodes it. The only thing stopping me from willingly stepping over the edge.

I stare at the iron maiden, listening to the muffled cries that mirror the ones clawing at the inside of my skull.

Red grips my arm suddenly, yanking me away, her pace brisk. Like she's physically dragging me from the abyss. "Let's forget about that shit," she says, her voice laced with drunken resolve. "We need more booze. Lots more."

We stumble towards the bar, where shelves lined with glistening bottles stretch high, a display of excess. Red waves her arm dramatically at the bartender. "Give us something strong. No, give us everything strong."

The bartender hesitates, then obliges, pouring a row of deep-coloured liquors into crystal shot glasses. I grab one and down it in one motion. It scorches its way down my throat, momentarily clearing my head. Red follows suit, slamming her glass onto the counter, throwing her head back with laughter.

"Another!" she commands, and we keep going, shot after shot, until the tension in my chest loosens, until the screams blur into the background.

"Look at them," Red says, her words slurring as she gestures towards the centre of the hall.

A mess of tangled bodies writhes in a chaotic orgy, limbs intertwined. A nearby group plays some twisted drinking game, their raucous laughter carrying across the room. Another cluster of guests has turned their entertainment into a judging contest, rating contestants on absurd, made-up sex positions like it's a sporting event.

And then there's Columbina.

She stands atop a table now, her whip discarded, the Pierrot kneeling before her. She's aching her body in slow, teasing movements as she commands the girl below.

"Meow," Red teases, curling her fingers like claws before breaking into laughter, the sound grating against my nerves. "Why don't you go have fun with them?"

"With who?" I ask, my voice distant, like I'm speaking through water.

"That one," she says, tilting her head towards Columbina, who's now draped across the table, offering herself like a goddess demanding worship.

I shake my head, rubbing my nose absently as the cocaine tingles through me. "Nah," I mutter. "I like someone else."

The alcohol must be kicking in because, for the first time, I let my hand drift onto Red's thigh. My fingers slide up, slow, deliberate. Testing. I've imagined this moment too many times to count, but I've never acted on it. Until now.

At the top of her leg, I hesitate, holding my breath. Waiting. Wondering.

Will she pull away? Reject me?

She doesn't.

Her eyes meet mine, lips slightly parted.

Taking her silence as permission, I let my hand drift further. She exhales sharply, a soft gasp slipping past her lips as she falls back onto the sofa. Her drink slips from her grasp, the glass shattering on the floor, but neither of us reacts. The sound is meaningless, just another noise in a room full of them.

Red's breath is warm against my skin as she sprawls beneath me, fingers tugging at the fabric of her dress, pulling it higher. "Do whatever you please," she purrs.

The words send a sharp jolt through me, the kind that ignites something deep in my bones. I can feel myself hardening, the ache of it almost unbearable. Every man in this room wants her, but right now, she's mine.

"Do you like me?" she asks suddenly, her voice cutting through the haze of lust.

The question catches me off guard, but I don't hesitate.

"I love you," I answer, my voice rough with desire.

"How much?"

I don't answer with words. Instead, I lift her dress, exposing her fully to me. Without breaking eye contact, I lower my head, my tongue tracing a slow, deliberate path that makes her shudder.

She moans softly, arching beneath me.

The past two months have been foreplay enough.

"I love you too," she whispers.

Her nails dig into my skin, pain and pleasure bleeding into one another.

Red spreads her legs wider, then, suddenly, snaps them closed, locking me between her thighs. I groan against her, the friction intoxicating, maddening.

"I want you inside me," she breathes, her voice trembling, pleading.

I drag her towards me, rougher than I should be, but she only gasps, her body tightening around me.

And then, nothing else matters.

25

The fog of lust recedes, dragging us back to reality. Blood stains her once-pristine white dress, seeping into the fabric like a cruel reminder of how far we've gone. The sofa beneath us looks like a crime scene.

Red pulls her legs together, trying to hide the mess.

"Hannya," she whispers. "Be a darling and ask the staff if they have a spare dress, please?"

"Of course," I say.

She manages a tight smile. "Thanks. I'll clean up in the ladies' room." She hurries off, almost stumbling.

I turn towards the nearest waiter. The embarrassment must be written all over my face.

"Yes, Monsieur?" the waiter inquires, polite but detached in that unsettling way they all are.

I explain the situation vaguely, careful not to reveal how I lost control. He nods, then signals to another staff member, who disappears without question to fetch a replacement dress. It's disturbingly routine, handled with the same efficiency as topping up a glass of champagne.

As I wait, I glance down at my own tunic, streaked with smears of red, and a laugh bubbles up before I can stop it. Carrie. The image flashes through my mind. Red's dress soaked through, just like the infamous prom scene. How absurd it all feels. How childish.

The waiter returns, holding out the dress. His eyes flick over me, over the blood, the mess I must look like, and then he asks, "Are you alright, Monsieur?"

I clap him on the back. Too hard. He stiffens.

"I'm fine," I mutter, and I hear the edge of madness in my own voice. "Take it to the ladies' room."

He forces a polite smile before turning away. But I can feel it. The silent judgment. The way he sees me unravelling at the seams.

I return to the table, reaching for a drink, something to steady me, but as soon as my fingers brush the glass, the memory slams into me. The arrow, the man's leg, the scream.

It's unbearable.

I push back from the table. If I stay still, the thoughts will catch me. The screams will swallow me whole. I pace, circling the room, my feet pounding against the marble as if movement alone will keep me sane. I feel myself floating, untethered, meters above it all. The adrenaline spikes, pushing me higher, but beneath it, the panic waits, a predator in the dark.

FRAGMENTED

Laughter cuts through the haze, high and wild. I glance up just as Panta and Lóne bound towards me, their movements exaggerated, almost childlike. There's something unnerving about how carefree they are, but it's infectious. Despite everything, I feel my lips twitch into a grin.

I don't like them—or at least, I tell myself I don't—but in this moment, their energy is a welcome distraction. Before I know it, we're laughing together, hopping in a clumsy circle, our bodies colliding with each bounce. The absurdity of it all pushes the darkness further back, loosening its grip.

"Looks like someone's been sniffing a bit too much of the good stuff," Lóne teases, elbowing me lightly. The touch lingers a fraction too long.

"Got a smoke?" I ask, my voice distant, detached.

Without a word, Panta spins dramatically, skipping back towards their table. His exaggerated movement sets off another round of laughter, and the world spins with us, everything blurred at the edges.

"He's off to his rabbit hole," Lóne chuckles, throwing an arm around me in a rough, brotherly hug. "Anyway, congrats, mate. You did it. Banged Red."

I nod, but my mind is stuck on the memory. The warmth of her body, the way she trembled beneath me, the way she whispered my name. It feels too raw, too personal to reduce to something so shallow.

Lóne doesn't notice my hesitation. "Blood, huh? Must've been going at it hard."

The comment jolts me, but I keep my face neutral. "Maybe I should get a new tunic," I joke, forcing the words out.

"Nah, mate, no point. Night's almost done. Just take it off."

Lóne reaches for the hem of my tunic, his fingers brushing the fabric.

Instinct kicks in.

I bat his hand away, harder than I mean to.

For a split second, Lóne's face changes. A glimpse of something vulnerable, something unguarded. But he masks it quickly, flashing his usual smirk.

Panta returns, tossing a pack of cigarettes and a lighter onto the table. "Here, mate," he says, his gaze flicking between Lóne and me. There's something knowing in his eyes, like he's reading between the lines.

I fish out a cigarette, lighting it with shaking fingers. The burn of the first drag grounds me, pulling me back from wherever my mind was spiralling.

Panta watches, then raises an eyebrow. "What's with you two? You've gone all quiet."

His words barely register.

I take another drag, focusing on the inhale, the exhale, the way the smoke works its way up the dim light. My nerves settle. Lóne's touch, it was nothing. Just a moment. Just surprise.

A long silence comes over us. At least it's not particularly awkward. The night is winding down.

I glance at Lóne, but he's already moved on, scanning the room, our uncomfortable moment erased as if it never happened. Panta, still buzzing with energy, is back to his usual antics, acting like nothing out of the ordinary has occurred.

The cigarette helps, but not enough. "Think my buzz is wearing off," I mutter, more to myself than anyone else.

I wave down a passing waiter with exaggerated flourish. "What does a man have to do to get a drink around here?!"

Panta lets out a hearty laugh, raising his glass. "Damn, Hannya, you've really loosened up! I like this side of you."

The waiter places fresh drinks in our hands.

Panta starts counting down over the noise of the room. "Three... two..."

Just as he reaches one, I catch a flicker of movement in my periphery.

Red.

She's standing there, barely visible in the dim light, hands clasped behind her back, watching us from the shadows.

Panta and Lóne down their drinks, their laughter growing louder, more unhinged. The sound distorts in my ears, warping until it becomes a cacophony, the room spinning, stretching into surreal, soft streaks of colour.

I can see them—Panta and Lóne—laughing, talking, but their words dissolve into static. Their faces flicker like broken images on a TV screen.

I reach for my drink, but my hand doesn't feel like my own. The glass slips from my grasp.

The need to escape claws at me. I leave the table without a word, my heart thudding as I stumble towards Red. The laughter and chaos fade behind me, dull and distant, as I collapse beside her, the plush sofa swallowing me whole.

"You okay?" I ask, my own voice sounding far away, like it's coming from someone else.

"Yeah," she replies softly. "The alcohol's really getting to me now. Let's just sit for a bit."

Relief floods through me. "Yeah. I've been feeling it for a while now."

She offers a small smile.

I'm stuck in a trance, staring at her lips, her golden hair. She's nothing short of a goddess.

She lets out a giggle, pressing a hand to her forehead. "Why are you staring?"

"You're the most wonderful girl in the world." The words escape before I can stop them.

Because it's true.

Because I'm captivated by her in a way that feels dangerous.

Her long hair, the way she moves, the way she sees me—it's all-consuming. It makes it easy to forget this is a game. A fantasy we're both playing out.

Red blushes, reaching for my hand. She brushes her thumb over the back of it, scooting closer. "I think you're wonderful, too." Her voice is soft, intimate. "You always make me feel safe when I'm around you."

Despite all the horror of the night, I smile. She's an angel, and her presence alone makes the worst thoughts seem insignificant.

"I'm so glad you ended up here. Such a coincidence. It must be fate," she says, voice soft. "After that first night, I knew you were different. You didn't rush anything, didn't pressure me. You were fun, polite, kind, and I don't know... I felt like I knew you. Like I've always known you."

She smiles, drawing me in for a tender kiss, like slipping into a dream. When we part, she meets my eyes and murmurs, "You're Mr. Giles, aren't you?"

The name—my name—hits like a knife to the chest.

I feel it physically. A lurch in my stomach, a rush of cold down my spine. The illusion I've wrapped myself in at Ralph's, the anonymity, the freedom, fractures in an instant.

My chest tightens. My vision tunnels. The walls seem closer, like the whole room is shrinking.

No.

I force myself to breathe. Keep my voice even. "How do you know my name?"

She gives me a playful slap on the shoulder. "I thought you'd have figured out who I was by now."

A joke? A test? No, too much certainty in her voice.

Panic claws its way up my throat. I scan her face, desperately trying to place her. I rack my brain for details. Blonde hair, delicate features, but the pieces refuse to click into place.

Then it hits.

The garden party.

My throat locks up. "Amy?"

She beams, gripping my hand, excitement buzzing through her. "Yes! You do remember me!" She squeezes my fingers, bouncing slightly. "What are the odds? Out of everyone here, I end up with you."

But I'm not thrilled. I'm suffocating. She knows about Grace. She knows the life I live outside these walls.

How long has she known? How long has she played along, letting me believe I was someone else?

"I... I don't know what to say," I manage.

"I know it's a little weird," she admits, "But now..." She leans in, whispering, "We can meet outside of Ralph's."

That should be a good thing. It isn't.

The walls of Ralph's contained this, our twisted little secret, the double life I could compartmentalise. But now she's reaching across that divide. Pulling me out.

I shake my head. "Amy, we can't—"

She cuts me off. "Why not? I broke a rule telling you this, you know." A pause. "Because I like you. Because I trust you."

I exhale sharply, running a hand through my hair. "It's not that simple."

"Because of Grace?"

I flinch.

Her fingers tighten around mine. "Andy, I don't want to be just a secret you leave behind in this place. Tell me you haven't thought about it, like really thought about it."

My mouth opens, but nothing comes out. Because I have thought about it. More than I should. And the moment she says it, the thought grows teeth. A fantasy blooms. Reckless, impossible. Us, leaving.

Living out some strange, untethered life together. We'd buy a van, fit it into a mobile home, drive north, spend mornings in the Highlands, watching mist climb over the lochs. Or maybe we'd leave England altogether. The south of France. The quiet streets of a coastal town. A life of indulgence. Freedom. No responsibilities.

She sees it in my eyes, because she smiles, threading her fingers through my hair.

"You're picturing it," she whispers.

I close my eyes for a second, breathing her in.

She shifts closer. "We could, you know. No one's stopping us."

A sharp inhale. My hands tremble where they hold her.

Because I want to believe her.

I cup her face, brushing my thumb along the cheekbone of her mask. She leans into the touch. It feels like we're standing at the edge of something dangerous.

And then, I kiss her.

She melts into me, her arms wrapping around my neck, pressing closer, deepening the kiss. For a second, I let myself believe it's real. That I could wake up tomorrow and be him. The man she sees me as. That I could erase the rest of it.

But I can't.

Because there's still Grace.

And if anyone found out...

The host. What would he do to her?

Her dad. Would I lose my job?

I rip myself back to reality.

"Amy—"

She touches my chest lightly, her voice barely a whisper. "Please say yes."

I exhale heavily, then pull away. "I... I need a second," I rasp.

"It's okay... You don't have to decide now," she whispers, but there's a tightness beneath her softness, like she's afraid I'll vanish if she lets go. "We can figure this out. We can make it work."

I swallow hard, my heart throbbing like a drum. She's not wrong. We could make it work. I could let her consume me completely.

Her fingers slide up to my jaw, coaxing my face toward hers. I don't stop her.

Her lips brush against mine..

And then I break.

I kiss her like I'm drowning, like she's the only thing keeping me afloat. She exhales a soft sound against my mouth—not quite a gasp, not quite a sigh—but it fuels something reckless in me. My hands tangle in her hair, pulling her closer.

She melts into me, clutching at my back, gripping me like she's terrified to let go. Like she needs me to hold on just as much as I do.

And for a moment, I forget everything. Grace. My job. The version of me that exists outside these walls.

All that's left is us.

She lifts her head, resting her forehead against mine, her breath warm against my lips. "Meet me after the party tonight," she murmurs. "Just us. We'll keep the night going."

I don't hesitate. "Okay."

I tighten my grip on her waist, pressing her closer. "Meet me at Green Park station."

Her eyes flick over my face, searching, her fingertips trailing lightly over my leg. "Yeah?" she whispers.

I nod. "Yeah."

A slow smile curves her lips. "And where will we go?"

"Anywhere." I exhale, running my hands along her back. "And next week. You and me. Somewhere nice. Somewhere far from here."

Her breath catches. I feel it more than I hear it.

"Spain," she murmurs. "The coast. Somewhere warm. We could disappear."

"I'd love that." It's a fantasy. But it's ours.

Her fingers trace up my neck. "Meet me," she whispers again, softer this time. "Don't change your mind."

I run a hand down her arm, squeezing gently. "I won't."

She lets out a quiet, satisfied hum, fingertips brushing over my collarbone before she pulls back, adjusting her gown. "Now go," she playfully nudges me, smirking. "Enjoy yourself before the party ends. I don't want to hoard you all to myself."

I hesitate. I don't want to move.

But I obey.

I step back, smoothing my hair, fixing my mask.

She watches me with a lazy smirk, running a finger over her kiss-swollen lips.

I cast one last seductive look before turning and heading towards the bar at the far end of the hall.

26

At the bar, I take a steady breath and order lemon-infused water. Shocking, I know. But I've had my share of booze for the night, and for once, I want to think clearly. The bartender sets down a glass. I grab it, feeling the coolness against my fingers, and down half of it in a couple swift gulps. Refreshing.

I stare into the glass, watching the lemon slice drift, knocking gently against the sides. Then, behind me, Brazen's familiar voice cuts through.

"H!"

He slaps my shoulder like nothing in the world could rattle him. "You're looking too serious for a man who just had a good time." He waves the bartender over. "Didn't take you for the brooding type."

I glance up, offering a faint smile that doesn't quite reach my eyes. "Yeah. Just... a lot on my mind."

"And what the hell is this? Don't tell me you're drinking water!" He takes the stool next to mine and orders an espresso martini.

I want to let out everything I'm harbouring inside of me. If I can tell anyone, it's him.

"Sometimes," I say, choosing my words carefully, "the mask feels heavier than usual."

"Heavier, huh? You must be thinking too much about the world out there," he points out towards the sky. "Remember, here you have no past, no worries about tomorrow. Just the moment."

He pauses as his drink arrives, and takes a long sip. Then he turns back to me, watching, studying. "You look like you could use a reminder."

I stare at Brazen, frustration building beneath my skin. I want to tell him that the mask isn't as freeing as he claims, that it's suffocating me, tearing me in two. Instead, I say, "Yeah, maybe. But I think I'm losing track of who I'm supposed to be."

Brazen raises an eyebrow, leaning in. "The whole point of Ralph's is to lose that 'supposed to be' crap. You think any of us walk around outside these walls as who we are in here?"

His words don't bring the solace I'd hoped for. If anything, they intensify the feeling of slipping further from my real life, from the man I used to be. I want to ask him, beg him, how to reconcile these two selves, but the rules grip my tongue, holding back the confessions I need to spill.

I stare down at the polished bar top, my fingers gripping the glass. "It doesn't feel like freedom, Brazen. It feels like something else. Something I can't control."

Brazen studies me, his eyes narrowing. "You need to snap out of it, H. Doing too much thinking, when you should be enjoying yourself. I've given you something people can only dream of out *there*," he says, pointing into nothingness.

My jaw clenches. His words should reassure me, should remind me why I came here in the first place, but all they do is tighten the noose around my throat.

A question burns at the back of my mind. One I shouldn't ask, but one I can't ignore. I lean in slightly, lowering my voice to hide the urgency trembling in my words. "Say someone broke a rule... Not blatantly, but just a slip-up. What do you think would happen?"

Brazen's smile slips. "Dangerous question, H." He swirls his drink. "Saw what happened to that lad last month. Ralph's cleans up messes quick. Don't tell me you did something stupid... Ralph's doesn't like loose ends."

A chill runs through me. My mind flashes back to Red—Amy—her confession gnawing between us like an open wound. "Wasn't me—"

"Then quit moping!" He barks a laugh. "Move on, what's done is done. No use flogging yourself over spilt milk."

The image of Amy dragged into some backroom—*loose end*—hollows me out. Guilt? Fear? Doesn't matter.

I down the rest of my water. "Thanks, Brazen."

He offers a casual shrug. "Come on, Hannya," he says, voice low and conspiratorial. "Don't let someone else's small slip ruin the night. You're too tense. Have a *real* drink, let go. Forget about life's problems, eh?"

I force a smile. "I think avoiding life's problems is what got me here in the first place."

The irony stings. Brazen forces a laugh, but before I can even process the moment, a shadow falls over us.

I glance up, and there he is.

The host.

His smile is wide, almost inviting, but his eyes... His eyes.

They cut into me, seeing everything I thought I'd kept hidden.

"Ah, Hannya," he says, his voice rich, authoritative. He steps closer, gaze pinning me to my seat. "I've been meaning to speak with you."

Beside me, Brazen doesn't flinch. He stares into the host's eyes, one arm draped lazily over the bar. Then looks at me, his mouth quirking into a sorrowful smile.

The host clears his throat. "I need to borrow Hannya."

A moment passes—too long—before Brazen nods. "Course you do." His tone is light, but his fingers tighten imperceptibly around his glass.

The unease in my gut sharpens. I swallow, schooling my face into neutrality, but my mind races. Since when does the host wait for Brazen's approval?

Brazen claps my shoulder, holding on for a second too long. "Play nice, eh?" His thumb digs into my collarbone.

As I stand, the host dips his chin at Brazen. A nod of... *deference*?

Brazen doesn't react. Just sits there, watching us.

The Host turns, gesturing for me to follow. "Let's go somewhere a little quieter."

I follow, my movements automatic, legs stiff.

As the host moves through the crowd, people part for him like a tide being pulled back, creating a clear path. Some glance our way, but no one really looks. No one ever looks too long at the host.

I follow, my pulse hammering, my thoughts running wild.

I have no idea where he's leading me.

But I know, without a doubt, that I can't refuse.

He leads me to a secluded alcove, shielded by heavy velvet drapes, hidden from the main hall's chaos. His own private space. Two towering men in matte black masks stand rigid at either side of the entryway. Inside, the air is still, almost sterile. A luxurious sofa sits in the centre, like an oasis of control amid the madness.

The host gestures for me to sit. I hesitate for only a fraction of a second before obeying, every instinct screaming at me to stay on guard.

He takes the seat across from me, crossing one leg over the other. He doesn't speak right away. Instead, he studies me, that same faint smile playing at his lips, as if he's savouring something I can't yet see.

"Tell me, Hannya," he finally says. "Are you enjoying yourself here?"

I nod mechanically. "It's... It's been an experience."

He raises an eyebrow, amused. "Oh, I'm sure it has. You've taken to this place naturally, haven't you?"

I hesitate under his stare, which presses into me like he's peeling back layers I don't even know I have. "I guess you could say that."

The corner of his mouth twitches, his amusement deepening. "That's good. Very good. You see, Ralph's isn't for everyone." He leans forward slightly, his eyes gleaming like a predator's. "But for those who truly belong... Well, there's nowhere else in the world like it."

His words slither into my mind, coiling around the conflict already festering there. It's as though he's speaking directly to the part of me that craves this place, the part that wants to stay, that wants to let go.

"You know, Hannya," he continues, his tone almost conspiratorial, "Ralph's is a refuge. A sanctuary for those of us who need an escape from the trivialities of everyday life. It's a place to shed the mundanity, the expectations." He pauses. "But that requires a certain level of commitment, doesn't it?"

I nod slowly, tension winding tighter inside me. "Yes, I... I understand."

He studies me, silent for a beat too long. "Good. Because Ralph's doesn't accept half-measures. It's all or nothing here. The moment you cross through those doors, you leave the outside world behind."

A shadow moves at the edge of my vision. One of his black-masked henchmen materialises, a dark, polished wooden box in his hands. The host gives a slight nod, and the man kneels, lifting the lid as if presenting something sacred.

Inside, a knife.

Thin, razor sharp. Its blade shines under the low light. The handle, intricately carved, dark metal curling into twisting, organic shapes.

The host plucks the knife from the box, turning it in his fingers, watching the way the light dances along its edge. Then, without ceremony, he extends it towards me.

"For you," he murmurs. "A gift. But it's more than that. It's a test."

A cold weight settles in my stomach. My hand closes around the handle, and the chill of the metal seeps into my skin. It's heavier than it looks. Heavier than it should be.

The host's hawk-eyes sharpen. "You see, Red—or Amy, as she revealed to you—broke one of our most sacred rules. In doing so, she's risked the balance that keeps Ralph's alive, keeps it hidden, keeps it safe." He leans in slightly. "Without rules, without commitment, this place crumbles. She knows that."

My fingers tighten around the blade as dread churns in my chest. "Surely you're not telling me to—" The words die in my throat. Saying them aloud would make them real.

The host doesn't blink. "No way around it." His voice is silk over steel. "Our world is fair, but with that comes rules. And I don't tolerate the breaking of them."

My eyes drift across the room, through a narrow slit in the drapes, landing on her. Red—Amy.

She's standing with her back turned, chatting with a small group, unaware. Smiling. A rare, unguarded moment of happiness. The image is a gut punch.

The host moves closer, his breath warm, sickly, against my ear. "She crossed a line, Hannya. Sentiment. You know what that means here. It's fatal."

His words suffocate me.

A trap.

And I've already stepped inside.

The knife in my hand pulses like a second heartbeat. I nod, a mechanical motion devoid of will, as though the blade itself has already chosen me. My eyes dart across the room to Columbina. She's watching. She always is. Her lips curl in that wicked, knowing smile.

"You see," the host continues, "you're either in all the way, or not at all. And being all in means you shed the past. The entirety of it. This is your final commitment. Your ultimate, irreversible step into freedom…"

FRAGMENTED

A sharp, wild anger ignites in my chest. My fingers tighten around the knife, and before I can stop myself, I whip around, the blade flashing as I press it against his jugular, drawing blood. "Commitment? You fucking bastard. I should kill you instead."

The room stills.

He doesn't flinch. Doesn't even blink. Instead, he laughs—a deep, slow chuckle that slithers under my skin, wrapping around my spine. The guards close in, but the host waves them off with a lazy flick of his wrist, as if I'm nothing more than a petulant child. "You must do it, Hannya," he says, amused, undeterred. "That's the only way forward."

My pulse pounds against my skull. "And if I don't?"

His smile fades, his eyes darkening into something vast, bottomless. "No loose ends, Hannya. That's the rule. That's what keeps Ralph's safe. Keeps you safe."

The words drop like stones into the pit of my stomach.

The memory of Red's laughter, the way her touch steadied me through the chaos, flickers through my mind. For a second, I almost let it sway me. Almost.

The host leans close again, his voice now a soft whisper. "She's dead weight, Hannya. A sacrifice for your freedom. You've come too far to let sentiment pull you back into chains. Think of this as taking control, of leaving behind the weak, half-lived life you had before. You want this, don't you?"

I can't speak. My throat locks, my eyes dropping to the knife in my hand. The blade gleams under the dim light, its reflection fractured, distorted, showing only pieces of me. Hannya stares back from the broken image, the face I've worn here, the face I've become.

But beneath the mask, something else resurfaces. Andy Giles, the man I was before. A life I let slip through my fingers.

Red's face flashes through my mind again. Her laughter. Her touch. The way she looked at me, like I was still someone worth saving.

But the host's voice cuts through, drowning out the guilt. *Freedom. Power. Control.*

"She's already gone, Hannya," he says with a finality in his voice. "You're just finishing what she started. A small price to pay for what you've gained."

I lower the knife from his neck, down to my side, my breath coming fast, uneven. This can't be the only way.

A rush of nausea twists my stomach.

I look away, my grip on the knife tightening. Red's face flashes in my mind. Her touch, her voice. Our plans to meet after the party. The thought of me holding her in my arms without the masks.

I could kill the host here, now. But that won't do me any favours. No matter what master plan I conjure up in my head, nothing will get both me and Red out of this predicament.

And yet—how can I do this?

How can I take her life?

The woman who made me feel alive for the first time in years. The woman who pulled me back from the edge when I was drowning in my own self-destruction. The only thing that felt real in all of this.

I squeeze my eyes shut, pressing my fingers hard against the hilt of the knife, like pain will somehow snap me back into clarity.

I could run. I could take her hand and bolt for the doors, consequences be damned. We could disappear, leave London behind, vanish into some nameless town where no one would ever find us. It wouldn't be impossible. I've imagined it before—Red and I, walking along some windswept coast, renting some tiny flat with peeling wallpaper and a broken kettle. Something simple. Something real. She'd curl up beside me at night, and for once, I wouldn't be haunted by the ghost of the man I used to be.

But I know better.

There is no running from Ralph's.

No one gets away.

If we run, they'll find us. They'll kill us both.

And if I refuse, they'll still kill her. Maybe slower. Maybe worse.

The bile rises in my throat.

I picture Red's face, the way she looked at me when she said she wanted more. More than Ralph's. More than a life in the shadows. I promised her that, didn't I? That we could escape. That we could find something better.

But now, that future is an illusion, slipping like water through my fingers.

My hands shake. My chest constricts, panic clawing up my ribs like a living thing.

I can't do this.

But if I don't, I lose everything.

The life I once had. The life I could still rebuild.

I turn back to the host, forcing myself to meet his eyes. My voice is steadier than it has any right to be. "There's one condition."

His brow lifts slightly. "Go on."

I draw in a slow breath, trying to cage the chaos in my head. "I want to leave Ralph's. For good. And I want to do it without... consequences."

His expression remains unchanged, but the air shifts, crackling with tension.

"Without consequence," he repeats, like I've just suggested something absurd. "Hannya. Once you're part of Ralph's, you're part of it forever."

"I understand the rules," I say. "But I'm asking for a reprieve. Just once. I've done everything you asked. I've played the game, followed the rules, lost myself in every sick indulgence you put before me. Let me go, and I'll disappear. You'll never hear from me again."

He studies me now, his sharp eyes searching for cracks. Amusement flickers beneath the surface, but it's laced with something heavier. Calculation.

"Why should I believe you?" he asks at last. "And why would I bend the rules for you?"

I don't hesitate. I let my fingers tighten around the knife at my waist. Let him see the resolve in my face, even as my stomach twists in knots.

"Because I'm willing to kill the woman I love."

The words taste like acid. I force them out anyway. I make them sound real.

"I'll leave Hannya behind for good. Right here. With you. I'll never look back." My throat constricts, but I push forward. "I want my old life back. The one I threw away."

The host tilts his head, watching me closely. "You're willing to leave Red behind?"

It hurts more than it should. And he knows it.

I swallow hard, forcing down the emotion clawing up my throat. "I'll do what I have to." My voice is barely above a whisper. "I've made my choice."

His lips curl slightly at the edges, but the usual amusement is gone. It's approval now.

He nods slowly, the silence stretching like a blade between us.

"I can respect a man who knows when to sacrifice one part of himself for another." His smile returns, sharper than before. "Very well. You have my word. Leave this place, and you'll be free of Ralph's."

I nod, my pulse hammering in my skull.

The knife is cool against my ribs as I slip it beneath my tunic, pressing into my skin.

Kill her, or you die.

27

Each step towards the crowd feels heavier, my legs trembling beneath me, barely able to comprehend what I'm about to do.

Beneath the mask, my breath quickens, hot and stifled. The fabric sticks to my damp skin, suffocating me. And then, without warning, the tears come. Hot, silent, sliding down my cheeks, pooling at the edge of the mask. I swipe at them, but they don't stop. I can't stop them.

Red's face flashes through my mind—her laughter, her voice, the way she looked at me like I was worth saving. She doesn't know. She can't know. If she did, what would she say? Would she fight? Would she run? Would she forgive me?

I stagger towards the bar, desperate for something—anything—to drown the panic closing in on me. The room blurs into a mess of colours and movement, laughter jagged in my ears, a cruel soundtrack to the nightmare unfolding inside me.

I grab the nearest bottle, pour shot after shot, knocking them back in rapid succession. The burn does nothing. The alcohol barely registers. My hands shake. My skin is crawling. The noise is too much.

With my pulse hammering, I slip a small baggie from my pocket and duck into the shadows behind the heavy velvet curtains. My fingers tremble as I tear it open.

The cocaine glitters under the dim light, mocking me.

I'm about to kill someone. And I'm still chasing numbness like it's a cure.

But it's not a choice anymore. It's survival.

I inhale the line in one sharp, burning drag. The rush hits instantly. A violent, electric surge, slamming into my bloodstream, setting my nerves on fire. The world sharpens and fractures all at once. The music, the laughter, the faces, they all snap into focus, too vivid, too real. My heartbeat slams against my ribs.

The knife presses harder into my side, as if it knows what it's meant to do.

My breath stutters, fast and uneven. I grip the curtain, my mind spinning with thoughts I can't control. Red's name pulses through me, pounding, demanding, relentless. I want her. I need her voice. Her touch. She'd know what to say.

She'd tell me I'm not a monster.

Even if it's a lie.

But she's not here. She's waiting somewhere, trusting me. And I'm walking towards her with a blade beneath my clothes.

Hannya's voice slithers through the drug-fueled haze, calm and cold.

You're already dead if you don't do this.
She'd understand. She'd forgive you if she could.
But this isn't about her—it's about you.

I press my back against the wall, my entire body trembling. The music swells, the world tilts. My mask feels too tight, suffocating. My hands shake as I clench them into fists, trying to steady myself.

She doesn't deserve this.

But Ralph's doesn't care what anyone deserves.

I push myself upright, the cocaine and adrenaline buzzing through my veins, numbing everything I don't want to feel. Each step forward is a betrayal. The blade digs into my ribs, reminding me of what I have to do.

Then, through the crowd, I see her.

Columbina.

Her gaze locks onto me like a predator scenting blood.

She moves toward me, weaving through the chaos, her feathered mask a striking contrast against the dark, flickering light. Her movements are too fluid, too deliberate, the air around her bending to her will.

By the time she reaches me, I can already feel the weight of her presence.

Suffocating. Intoxicating.

Columbina's fingers trail up my arm, slow and possessive, her touch cool and calculated. She knows.

"Got something you're hiding, Hannya?" she purrs, amusement curling around each syllable. She leans in, breath warm against my neck, her lips twisting into something dangerously knowing. "What did the host say to you back there?"

A knife of panic lodges in my chest, the memory of my conversation with the host clawing its way back to the surface.

"Nothing you'd be interested in." My voice is too tight, betraying the storm brewing inside me.

Columbina chuckles, a low, sultry sound, her nails digging just enough into my shoulder to sting. "Oh, I doubt that. You're different tonight." She circles me like a vulture, eyes searching for cracks in my mask. "Something's weighing on you. You seem... vulnerable."

The word hits like a slap. I rip my gaze away from hers, but the drink and the coke have done nothing to dull the tangled mess of thoughts spiralling in my head. Grace's locked door. The host's warning. The knife pressing into my ribs.

"Tell me, Hannya," she whispers, her voice a silk-thread caress, nails raking lightly down my arm, pulling me back into the moment. "What could bother you in a place like this? What could you have to hide?"

Her words grind against me, each one scraping at the frayed edges of my control. My fists clench at my sides, knuckles white. She's baiting me. Columbina represents everything about Ralph's that I both crave and despise—the decadence, the escape, the illusion of power. Her touch ignites something base, something dangerous, but it's the last thing I can afford to give into.

"Nothing," I snap, yanking away from her grasp, the words sharper than intended. "Just leave me alone."

Columbina stills. A beat of silence. Then, the faintest flicker of surprise behind her mask, quickly swallowed by something colder. Annoyance. She's not used to being dismissed. The tension between us thickens, the air crackling like a charged wire. Then, slowly, her lips curl into a smirk.

"Interesting," she murmurs, mockery dripping from her tone. "Perhaps I overestimated you, Hannya. Or underestimated what's really eating you alive."

I don't let her finish. I turn on my heel, pushing my way through the crowd, her gaze burning into my back.

The noise swells. Laughter, whispers, the bass of the music, morphing into a pulsing cacophony that beats against my skull. The room feels too tight, too crowded, the walls inching closer.

And then, I reach her. Red.

Head thrown back in laughter, her auburn hair catching the dim light like molten fire. So effortless. So unaware.

But when her eyes meet mine, all the ease drains from her expression. She knows.

A step back. Lips parting. Hannya. A whisper. "You're really going to do this?"

The room falls into silence. Everyone is staring. The host's gaze presses into me, patient and unrelenting. Waiting.

I grip the knife harder, my pulse a hammer against my ribs. Every part of me screams to stop, to turn around, to run, to abandon this nightmare.

But escape isn't an option.

Revolt is.

Heat rushes to my head, my limbs burning, trembling. Move now. Make the right choice.

I spin, knife raised—aimed at the host.

A ripple of shock moves through the crowd. Gasps, murmurs, a single, sharp intake of breath.

The host remains still. His eyes widen slightly, no more than a glimpse of amusement, watching me as if I were a child caught mid-tantrum.

There's no fear in him. No hesitation.

Just that same, cruel, knowing smile.

The knife trembles in my grip. My heart pounds, louder than the muted crowd, louder than my own breathing.

"Make your decision," the host says.

My fingers tighten around the hilt.

Act, act, act.

But what happens next? If I strike him down, I'll be nothing but another victim swallowed by Ralph's. Another body discarded in the Thames.

I'm trapped.

And then I feel her. Close beside me. Watching, unblinking. Not afraid.

I turn the knife towards her.

Red doesn't tremble, doesn't beg. She just watches me, her gaze sharper than the blade in my hand.

"You don't have to do this," she says, voice steady, unwavering. "You think you do, but you don't. You could just stop."

I shake my head, throat tightening. "You don't understand—"

"What could the host have offered you, for you to completely lose yourself like this?"

A murmur moves through the crowd, but Red doesn't flinch. She steps forward, forcing me to see her, forcing me to listen.

"Look at yourself," she continues. "You think this is control? You think this is power? Your life may not be perfect outside these walls, but you're holding a knife to my throat for god's sake. *My* throat. You don't even know who you are anymore."

I flinch, but she doesn't stop.

"This isn't power, Andy. This is obedience. You don't think. You don't act. You just follow. They pull the strings, and everyone in here dances."

My breath comes fast, uneven. "I'm sorry—"

"They carved you up and remade you into something they could use," she snaps. "And you let it. And for what? A mask? A new name? You think you've found freedom here? This isn't freedom. This is a cage."

Her words dig into me, splintering through the fragile framework of every excuse I've ever built for myself.

"Tell me," she presses, glancing over to the host, then back at me. "What could he have promised you, for you to betray yourself like this?"

I feel it—the anger, the shame, the fear—rising in my chest like bile.

I hang my head, staring at the floor as I say it. "Freedom."

Red steps in closer, her head leaning in against mine. "You think you're making a choice *right now*," she says, voice quieter now, almost pitying. "But I think you already made it the moment you let them change you." She slides her hands down my arms. "You know, I really hoped we could have that getaway, run away together. But I should have known it was just a stupid girl's dream."

She doesn't step back. She doesn't cower. Her words slice through me sharper than any blade, because I know that she's right. I am a coward.

If I let her live, both of us die.

If I kill her, I'll have to live with the fact that I've become a monster.

Red locks her eyes with mine, unblinking. She doesn't seem afraid. Not of Ralph's. Not of death. Not even of me.

"You'll never be free," she whispers into my ear, finality in every syllable. "Not really."

Her legs shift. Arms move.

The blade's snatched from my hand. I step back. It flashes through the air.

Red slices across her own throat in one swift, brutal motion.

The world stops.

Blood sprays, hot and thick, splattering across my face, my hands, soaking into my sleeves. Red's eyes widen, shock overtaking terror, her fingers flying to her neck as if she can undo what's been done. A choked, wet gasp rattles from her lips. She claws at her skin, struggling, trembling. But it's too late.

She stumbles, her legs buckling beneath her. Then she crumples.

Her body convulses on the floor, the blood pouring from her in thick crimson waves.

I don't move. I can't move.

My breath stutters, coming in sharp, jagged gasps.

A soft, broken sob escapes her throat. Her hand reaches for me, fingers twitching, grasping at nothing. Desperate. Pleading. Then—limp.

The light in her eyes dims.
The warmth drains from her skin.
She's gone.

A violent wave of nausea overtakes me. I stagger back, a choked cry tearing from my throat as vomit spews through my fingers. The burn mixes with the thick iron tang of blood, coating my tongue. The world spins violently.

Hannya, whoever that was, disappeared with Amy's last breath.

The room stands in suffocating silence. The audience, masked and expressionless, watches. And in the crowd, The Host stands motionless, observing, a glimpse of satisfaction in his eyes.

My knees give out. I drop beside her, hands trembling as I reach for the fading warmth of her skin. The mask she wore slips loose, tumbling from her face, landing in a pool of her own blood.

She looks peaceful. As if she's only sleeping.

Tears burn my eyes, blurring my vision as I trace the face to memory. My fingers brush her cheek, her skin soft but cooling fast. My breath hitches, a sob rising like bile in my throat, breaking free as I look at her—really look at her.

The world vanishes.
It's just me and Red.
And now, she's gone.

The world crashes down, dragging me under, suffocating. I did this. Not Ralph's, not The Host. I held the knife. I made the choice, and Red just executed it for me.

A muffled sob pulls me back to the present.

I lift my head, startled.

Columbina stands nearby, shaking. Her hand is pressed over her mouth, her eyes brimming with silent tears. She's crying. But she doesn't move. She doesn't run. She just watches, as if she's trying not to let the mask slip, but failing miserably.

And for the first time, I see her for what she truly is.

Not a villain.

Not a monster.

Just another broken person playing her role.

Because that's all this is, isn't it? A charade. The games, the rules, the masks, none of it is real.

But we play along.

We *all* play along.

Because what else do we have?

This place is all we know.

The silence is shattered by the slow, calculated footsteps of two staffers. They move towards Red's body, arms outstretched, ready to remove her from the scene, like she's just another prop to be discarded.

Rage ignites inside me, raw and unchecked. I lurch forward, shoving them back with a snarl. "Don't you dare touch her. Don't you lay a single fucking hand on her."

The men hesitate, but they don't look at me. They look to the host, waiting for his word. His silent command.

My arms tighten around her lifeless form.

My tears fall onto her face, mingling with her own.

I brush them away, whispering to her. Praying she can hear me.

"I'm sorry, Amy. I'm so, so sorry."

I look up, blood boiling. "Where do I take her?" I already feel her fading, slipping from this world. "Tell me where to take her."

The host doesn't answer right away. He watches, drinking in the scene like a masterpiece painted in blood. His masterpiece. A slow, dismissive nod follows, his mask gesturing to the far end of the hall. "Through the red doors," he says smoothly. "You'll know where to go."

I don't wait. I turn, moving as though in a dream, one where my limbs aren't my own, where my body is only an instrument for something far crueller. Her head rests against my chest, and for the briefest moment, I let myself believe she'll wake up. That this is just another one of Ralph's illusions, another game. That she'll open her eyes and laugh at how dramatic I'm being.

But the warmth is leaving her. And no game can undo that.

The crowd parts around me. The same masked figures that once cheered for brutality now stare with empty, unreadable faces. No one stops me. No one dares. They simply observe, detached, indifferent.

Not all of them.

Jumadi stands near the edge of the crowd, her body trembling against Brazen's shoulder, her face buried in his chest, wracked with silent sobs. Brazen comforts her, whilst staring daggers at the host. For a moment, I think he might do it. Might break the rules. Might lunge, attack, tear the host apart with his bare hands.

But he doesn't. None of us do.

A few steps away, Panta and Lóne are enraged. Their fingers twitch at their sides, curling and uncurling, as if restraining the urge to rip the room apart. But like Brazen, they don't move. We are all prisoners here, bound by the same unspoken laws, watching one of our own be taken to the grave.

Each step drags heavier than the last, like I'm pulling my own soul across the floor, like it's tethered to her and I'm being ripped apart the farther I go.

The red doors loom ahead.

I push through.

Beyond them, silence swallows the world.

A dim, sterile corridor stretches into shadow, stripped of decadence, of indulgence. A world meant only for endings.

At the end of the hall, a small room waits, stark and cold. An empty bed sits in the center, pristine white sheets glowing under the weak light. It's made for this. Designed for moments like this.

I lower Red onto it, laying her down with the care of a man who refuses to believe she's gone. Her hair fans out over the pillow, her lips parted slightly, as if she might whisper my name. As if she's just asleep.

I pull a blanket over her. Smooth it down with trembling hands. Brush the hair from her face, as if she'll flinch at my touch, bat my hand away, roll her eyes and smirk. But she doesn't.

Her skin's already cold.

And those eyes, the ones that held me together when everything else was falling apart, stay closed.

I sink to my knees beside her, pressing my forehead against the mattress, my breath shuddering.

There is nothing left of me.

Not Andy Giles. Not Hannya.

Just *nothing*.

I press a kiss to her forehead, remaining there as if I can steal back the warmth leaving her body. My fingers trace her cheek, then her lips, ones I've memorised with touch and taste, ones I swore I'd never forget.

"I'll carry you with me," I whisper. A promise she'll never hear.

But I will.

I will carry her ghost in my chest. Every breath I take will be weighted with the memory of her, with the knowledge of what I did.

I don't know how long I sit there.

Long enough for my legs to go numb.

Long enough for the world outside to feel like something I no longer belong to.

But eventually, I rise.

I turn to the door, hesitating, waiting. For her to wake, for her hand to reach for mine, for some last miracle to undo what I've done.

But she remains still.

Unmoved. Untouched by the chaos that still lingers outside these walls.

The door creaks shut behind me. Sealing her away.

The walk back through the corridor is endless. Each step heavier, pulling me further from her, from the life I've shattered, from the part of me that died with her.

I feel like I'm dragging a corpse. My own.

A female staff member waits by the doorway. She says nothing, only gestures towards the changing room. I follow, stepping inside, letting her peel away the layers of my disguise.

The medieval costume.

The gloves stained with her blood.

The mask that is no longer mine to wear.

Piece by piece, Hannya is stripped away, leaving only Andy Giles, standing there in a cheap button-down, wearing a face I no longer recognise.

The staff member looks at me. And for just a moment, there is something human in her expression. Sympathy, maybe. Understanding. But she doesn't speak. She looks away.

And so do I.

I turn, moving through the main hall, towards the exit.

Laughter still echoes. Music still plays. People still drink and dance and fuck as if nothing has happened. Because nothing has.

Not here.

Not to them.

Just as I reach the final corridor, a sudden shattering splits the air. The sound of glass exploding against marble. A chorus of screams follows. It's not fear. It's anger. Or maybe both.

A thread has snapped.

Something inside Ralph's has broken.

I pause. My heart pounds. Morbid curiosity whispers in my ear, begging me to turn, to look, to see what's unravelling behind me.

But I don't.

I can't.

Because I already know.

Instead, I press forward. Step after step, back to Grace.

FRAGMENTED

Back to reality.
Back to a life I no longer belong to.

28

The road stretches endlessly ahead, headlights carving a narrow path through the dark. Cigarette after cigarette burns down to the filter between my fingers, the smoke curling in the stagnant air of the car. I had everything I needed. The thought loops in my mind, gnawing at every raw nerve, taunting me with its bitter irony.

After trading in every piece of myself at Ralph's, after drinking and snorting and fucking away the last scraps of my soul, I'm driving back. Back to reclaim the life I abandoned.

I picture Grace. The curve of her smile on better days, the way she used to laugh without hesitation. When was the last time I even heard it? Months ago? Longer? I should've been there, but I let myself sink into my own misery, let it fester and rot. And Tom. Christ, Tom. I convinced myself she'd already betrayed me. That she'd moved on, that she'd given up. But she hadn't. I was the one who betrayed her.

I flick the cigarette out the window, immediately lighting another. The nicotine does nothing to dull the clawing guilt. I breathe in, lungs stinging, the car thick with smoke and regret.

The memories roll in like a slow tide, each one a fresh wound. The nights I stumbled home late, reeking of booze, smoke, and guilt. The cold silence at the dinner table, stretching between us like an open wound. The way she looked at me, her eyes full of worry, like she could see the cracks spreading, splintering me into something unrecognizable.

I press harder on the gas, as if I can outrun the weight of it all.

The lights of Windsor creep into view, muted against the night. I take the turn onto the winding streets leading to her mother's house, my grip tightening on the wheel with each turn. What the fuck am I expecting? That she'll just open the door and forgive me? That I can stitch together the pieces of my life like none of it ever happened? She deserves more than this. More than me.

But the thought of her walking out of my life rips my fucking guts out.

I pull up outside her mother's house. The place looms in the dark, an imposing old-world structure steeped in wealth and history. I've only been here a handful of times—Christmas, birthdays, anniversaries. It's the kind of house that feels sentient, watching, storing secrets in its walls.

Grace's father passed years ago, leaving her mother alone to rattle around this massive place. More than once, I've had the morbid thought of her mother dying, of us inheriting it. Not that I want her to die—but it would be a safety net. A tangible, sprawling anchor against the uncertainty of everything else. I've never said it aloud, wouldn't dare. But the thought lingers like a bad taste in my mouth.

Through the large, curtainless windows, the warm glow of lamplight spills onto the drive. She's home.

I step out, crushing my cigarette beneath my heel, smoke trailing behind me in the cold night air. My body sways slightly, leftover booze, adrenaline, exhaustion all conspiring against me. I slap my face once. Then again, harder, trying to shake the haze.

My feet feel leaden as I make my way up the path. Every step heavier than the last.

I knock.

Each tap reverberates through my bones.

The door creaks open.

And there she is.

Grace.

She looks... drained. Pale. Dark circles bloom under her eyes, her face drawn with exhaustion. She stares at me, and there's no warmth, no recognition of the man she used to love.

"Andy." Her voice is hollow. Flat.

"Grace... I'm sorry," I blurt out. The words feel pathetic, small, useless.

Her expression doesn't change. "What's left to say?"

"Everything." I step forward, desperation clawing at my throat. "I know I fucked up. I know I hurt you. I lost myself, Grace. I don't even know who I was anymore. But I'm here now. I want to make this right."

She exhales sharply, looking past me like she's scanning for an escape route.

"I gave you enough chances, Andy." Her voice is quiet, but there's finality in it. "I can't do this anymore. You've become someone I don't recognize."

Her words hit like a hammer to the chest. My control unravels, thread by thread, snapping under the weight of it all. She's right—she's always been right. I wasn't there. I let myself disappear into another world, a world where I didn't have to think about what I was losing.

But then Hannya's voice rises, dark and defiant, curling around my thoughts like smoke. *You can't lose her. It's a command, a promise. She's yours. You deserve better than this.*

"Just fucking stop," I snap, my voice rough, raw, fraying at the edges. "You're being ridiculous. I don't know what you think I've been up to, but it's not what you believe."

She flinches—just slightly—but it's enough. Her arms cross over her chest, her expression cooling into something sharp and unforgiving.

"There it is," she says, her tone like broken glass underfoot. "That aggression. That edge. You don't even see it, do you?"

I shove my shaking hands into my pockets, trying to smother the rage curling inside me, but she notices anyway. Her gaze flickers to the clenched fists beneath the fabric before lifting to meet mine. Her expression shifts—less anger now, something closer to pity.

"You've been drinking obsessively," she continues, voice eerily calm, slicing deeper than if she had screamed. "I'd bet anything there are drugs involved too. Am I wrong, Andy?"

The words are venom, burrowing under my skin, exposing every rotten, hidden part of me. The drinking. The drugs. The nights at Ralph's. The mask I wore there, the man I became. I am unrecognizable. But the anger flares again—a knee-jerk reaction to being cornered.

"Don't do this," I grit out, voice strained, unsteady. "Don't make me the bad guy here. You've been distant too. You've been shutting me out just as much as I shut you out. Don't pretend you're fucking innocent."

Grace doesn't flinch. If anything, she seems tired. Frustrated. The faint tremor in her lips betrays the emotion she's barely holding back.

"Innocent?" she repeats, like she's rolling the word around in her mouth, testing its weight. "I'm not pretending to be anything, Andy. I'm not perfect. But I'm not the one who disappeared. I'm not the one sneaking around at all hours, coming home reeking of alcohol, acting like a fucking stranger."

The accusation lands harder than I expect. I feel it in my gut, in my spine, in the way my whole body stiffens like I'm preparing for a fight I know I'll lose. But I can't let her see that. I cross my arms, trying to project strength that isn't there.

"You think I'm sneaking around? You think I'm not dealing with anything? Grace, you have no idea—"

"Then tell me!" she cuts in, her voice rising, cracking at the edges. "Tell me, Andy. What's going on with you? Where do you go? Who are you with?"

Her voice fractures on the last question, and for the first time, her Armor breaks. Vulnerability bleeds through, her eyes searching mine, pleading, desperate for something real.

"You think I haven't noticed? The bags under your eyes? The way you barely sleep? You're changing, and I don't even know who you are anymore."

I can't answer.

The words lodge in my throat, caught between the need to say something, to make her understand, and the reality that I can't. Ralph's has its claws in me. I can't tell her. To even hint at the truth would be a death sentence.

"I can't," I manage, the words barely audible. "I just... I can't."

A bitter laugh escapes her lips, raw and hollow. "That's it? That's all you have to say?" Her head shakes, her tone icing over. "You think that's enough for me, Andy? After everything? 'I can't?'"

I step forward, hands lifting in some useless, helpless gesture. "It's not that simple, Grace. You don't understand—"

"You're damn right I don't understand!" she snaps, her voice sharp enough to cut. I take a step back. "I don't understand how the man I loved turned into... this."

Her chest rises and falls with shallow, uneven breaths.

"Whatever this is, Andy, whatever's going on, there's no future for us unless you tell me the truth."

I want to.

I want to lay it all bare, confess the depths I've sunk to, the blood on my hands, the darkness I've embraced.

But Hannya is there. Whispering. Laughing.

Reminding me of the cost.

I swallow hard, throat closing around the words I can't say.

"I wish I could," I whisper, and it's the most honest thing I've said all night. "But I can't. Please, Grace... just trust me."

She stares at me for a long moment, her eyes searching mine for anything that might give her hope. But I see the exact moment she gives up. The fight drains from her shoulders, her expression hardening into something cold, unreachable.

"I can't do this anymore, Andy," she says softly. "Whatever this is... whatever you're going through, I can't be a part of it. Not when you won't even let me in."

A sharp, hollow ache spreads through my chest. My lungs feel too tight, my ribs caving under the weight of her words.

"You don't mean that," I say, my voice trembling. "We can fix this, Grace. We can—"

"There's no 'we' anymore," she interrupts icily. "You've made that clear. You've chosen whatever it is you're hiding over me. And maybe I should've seen it coming, but I didn't. Now, I'm done."

I open my mouth, but nothing comes out.

"Grace—"

"Before you leave, I guess now's the perfect time to tell you... I'm pregnant."

The world tilts.

"You're what?" The words stumble from my lips, clumsy, slow, like I'm struggling to catch up. I glance down at her stomach. There's no visible bump yet. No proof. But she wouldn't lie about this.

"That's... amazing." The words feel foreign in my mouth. "We're going to have a child."

Maybe this is it. Maybe this is my way back. My lifeline.

But Grace doesn't soften. She doesn't smile. Instead, her voice tightens like a noose around my throat.

"I already said there's no longer any 'we,' Andy."

I shake my head, stepping forward, grasping for something, anything to hold onto. "I know I messed up, Grace. But I love you. I love you, and I want to fix this. Just... just give me one final chance. We're going to have a baby, after all."

She laughs, a sharp, bitter sound that makes my stomach lurch.

"Fix this? You think one conversation can fix months of betrayal?" Her voice trembles with something raw, something barely restrained. "Andy, you've been lying to me. Hiding from me. You think I don't know about the other women?"

The air rushes out of my lungs.

I don't even bother denying it. There's no point. The truth is already between us, festering like an open wound. And little does she know, my infidelity is the least of my sins.

She takes a step back, arms crossing over her chest, closing herself off completely. "I can't do this anymore, Andy. I don't want this. I don't want you."

"Grace—" My voice cracks, her name barely escaping my lips. A whisper, a plea. "Please. Don't do this. I'll change. I'll be better."

She shakes her head, her eyes gleaming with something final. "You had your chance. And you threw it away."

The weight of reality crashes down. I feel it in my bones, in my teeth, in my pulse hammering against my skull.

"But... what about the baby?"

Her gaze doesn't waver. "This child deserves better than the mess we've become, Andy. I'm not bringing a baby into this world with a man who's already halfway out the door."

A cold wave crashes through me.

"What... what do you mean?"

She exhales, steady, controlled, like she's rehearsed this moment a hundred times. "I'm going to terminate the pregnancy. I'm getting an abortion."

The words hit like a sledgehammer.

I stumble back, breath hitching, my vision narrowing. No. She can't. She can't. She's carrying my child, our future. The chance to make things right.

"Grace—"

"If you ever decide to tell me the truth, maybe I'll listen." Her voice is firm, emotionless now, like the decision has already been made. "Until then... I can't do this. You need some time alone to think about what you really want."

We hold each other's gaze for a moment longer. I open my mouth, ready to say something, but there's nothing left to say. No words that could fix this. No way to make her stay.

She steps back.

The door closes.

And just like that, she's gone.

I stand there, staring at the door, her words ringing in my ears. My chest feels tight, breaths shallow and uneven. I can't even process what just happened.

She's gone.

She walked away.

I feel like I should move, but my legs are leaden, my body sinking under the weight of what I've lost. My mind reels, spiralling through the fallout, unable to latch onto anything solid.

What now?

My flat. Her flat. She pays most of the rent. Without her, I'll lose it. With what I earn at the school, a pathetic excuse for a salary, I'll end up in some damp, box-sized shithole. Some miserable little bedsit with a single mattress shoved into a corner, peeling wallpaper, a leaking ceiling, and neighbours who scream at each other through paper-thin walls. The kind of place that stinks of mildew, no matter how many air fresheners you burn. A place that reminds you, every second of every day, that you've failed.

My job. God, my job. The endless, mind-numbing cycle of it. Teaching history to kids who couldn't care less. Watching them text under their desks while I explain the nuances of war. Handing back exams they didn't bother studying for. It's not even a job—it's a sentence. Without Grace, without the fragile illusion of normalcy I built around her, it's all I have left.

A never-ending purgatory of pointless lectures and disciplinary emails.

A life stripped of purpose, of meaning, of her.

And now... the baby. Our baby. A child that will never be born. A future that won't exist.

I should walk away. Get in the car. Drive until my mind goes blank.

But I don't move.

I just stand there, staring at the door that won't open for me again.

A dry, bitter laugh escapes me. "This is it, huh?" I mutter to no one, my own voice sounding foreign, hollow.

I fumble in my pocket for my keys, but my hands won't stop shaking. I need to move. To do something. The car is only a few steps away, but each movement drags, my limbs weighed down by the suffocating gravity of an uncertain future. My vision tunnels, sweat slicking my palms as I finally wrestle the key into the lock. I get in, slam the door shut. The violent thud of it rattles through the silent street.

I grip the steering wheel, my breath fogging the windscreen. Steady. Just steady yourself. But my hands won't stop trembling.

The engine growls to life. I'm driving, not thinking, just letting the road blur beneath me. Streetlights smear across the windshield like ghosts, stretching and bending through the rain-slicked glass. My mind loops, replaying her voice. "You need some time alone."

Alone.

That's all I've ever been.

If Red were here, she'd know exactly what to say. She'd tilt her head, that sly, knowing smile tugging at her lips, and tell me this was just a blip. She'd pull me close, whisper in my ear, her voice low and sultry, urging me to forget everything but her.

I pull into the first pub I see, the tires screeching against the curb. Before I even register the motion, I'm already out of the car, the door slamming shut behind me. The moment I step inside, the thick, stale air clings to me—beer, sweat, a hint of something rotten. It's a dive, barely alive at this hour, but that's what I want.

"Moretti," I mutter to the bartender, my voice raw.

He doesn't ask questions. Just pours.

The first sip barely registers. Cold, bitter, sharp. The second goes down easier. By the third, my head lightens, the spinning slows just enough to let the numbness in.

But it's not enough. Nothing ever is.

I glance around. Shadowed faces, hollow laughter from a corner table, a couple arguing by the jukebox. None of it feels real. Like I'm watching a scene from a play, detached from the actors, from the stage, from everything.

I leave my pint half-finished and head for the toilets. The moment the stall door locks behind me, my fingers are already digging into my pocket, searching. The small baggie is still there, tucked into the lining of my coat—a leftover from Ralph's. A little insurance policy I didn't even realise I'd kept.

FRAGMENTED

I hesitate for only a second.

Then I empty the powder onto the back of my credit card, slicing it into jagged, uneven lines on the toilet tank. My hands tremble, but I lean down anyway. The sting is sharp, immediate. A fire searing through my sinuses, burning away the grief, the guilt, the unbearable weight of knowing.

By the time I step out of the bathroom, my heart is hammering. The pub feels too small, too claustrophobic. The air presses against my skin, sticky and suffocating.

I need out.

I leave the drink, the bar, the lingering eyes of strangers, and rush back to the car. The second I slide into the driver's seat, I roll down the windows, sucking in the crisp night air to stop the walls from closing in. My fingers drum anxiously against my thigh, the jittery rush kicking in. The coke mixes with the alcohol, an unsteady blend that makes my thoughts both razor-sharp and impossibly blurred.

I jam the keys into the ignition, hands slick with sweat. The car hums to life, the radio crackling to fill the silence, but nothing can drown out the chaos in my head.

I back out too fast. The tires skid on the damp pavement.

The road stretches endlessly ahead, headlights carving a narrow path. Cigarette after cigarette burns down to the filter between my fingers. *I had everything I needed.* The thought loops in my mind, gnawing at every raw nerve, taunting me with its bitter irony.

After trading in every piece of myself at Ralph's, after drinking and snorting and fucking away the last scraps of my soul, I'm driving back. Back to reclaim the life I abandoned.

But there's nothing to reclaim.

The motorway is near-empty, the rain starting up in soft, unhurried sheets. The wipers drag sluggishly across the windshield, barely keeping up. Every streetlight stretches unnaturally across the wet glass, bending and smearing in my peripheral vision.

The last thing Grace said keeps circling back.

"I'm going to terminate the pregnancy."

It lodges itself between my ribs. I see her face, the way she wouldn't let herself cry, the way she squared her shoulders like she'd already decided she wouldn't break over me anymore.

A wave of nausea rolls through me. I blink hard, gripping the wheel. The speedometer creeps higher.

I don't know where I'm going.

Not back to Grace. Not back to that empty fucking flat.

The lines on the road blur. My foot eases harder on the gas.

Somewhere, at the edge of my mind, Hannya laughs.

"Go on. Faster."

The rain thickens, a steady drumbeat against the roof. I barely feel the wheel under my hands anymore. My fingers are numb. My chest is a raw, hollow cavity.

Another cigarette. Another sharp inhale. The smoke burns, mixing with the scent of damp upholstery and stale beer.

The radio crackles, a ghost of static before the melody filters in.

Unchained Melody.

I suck in a sharp breath. My vision tunnels.

Grace's voice, singing under her breath that night. Her fingers twined with mine, her warmth pressed close. A memory so distant now it feels like someone else's life.

A sharp gust of wind rattles the car, dragging me back.

The road bends. The lights smear.

I jolt, yanking the wheel too hard.

The tires shriek. Everything tilts.

The headlights catch a glint of wet tarmac, the blur of a road sign, the blackness beyond the barrier.

And the world flips.